Chasing Harmony

by Melanie Bell

Published by
Read Furiously

Read (v): The act of interpreting and understanding the written word.

Furiously (adv): To engage in an activity with passion and excitement.

**Read Often. Read Well.
Read Furiously**

Chapter 1: *Burning*

Age Twenty

Anna takes a lighter to the poster, watches the paper brown. She can still hear the band's last song, that too-sweet guitar riff, the tramp of their boots as they walked out. She can still see the lead guy's smirk. Flames zigzag across his moustache, crisp his cap. She can still hear the clapping.

They were good, those kids, some of them younger than her. They fit right in with the splashy abstract paintings and herb bundles dangling from the rafters. The customers gobbled their burritos and sipped their organic lemonade and loved them. Let their faces crumple up.

A shout from the kitchen: "Jesus, is the food burning?"

She starts, looks down at the half-wrecked poster. No one else has come into the cramped back room yet, but—

She blows out the flame, crushes the poster into a ball as bits of ash flake off. She can't let them catch this.

Another voice: "I swear I didn't burn anything!"

She grabs the stack of old band posters from the file shelf and stuffs them in her bag. No one else working at The Green Staircase cares about these posters. It was Anna's idea to keep them.

"Maybe it's the radiator."

All those bands, her pride and joy. Who was she kidding?

"I think it's coming from over there—"

Quick! Into the alley, garbage bins reeking. What bin should burnt paper go in—recycling? Compost? She tosses and runs wildly down the street. Her shift is over. She's done her job.

Out of habit, she stops at the community center on the corner. It's late Friday evening, still open, no floor hockey games or beading club for underprivileged youth. No one at the pool tables or arcade.

She rushes to the piano.

No one is there to clap as she launches into the band's last number, a tender little piece sung by Moustache Man whose burnt face now graces a compost bin. She hasn't played it before, but that isn't a problem. Her fingers relish the slick feel of keys, the quick acrobatics of motion. She riffs on the melody, improvises, and adds a solo section. For those lyrics she remembers, she sings along, not powerfully but perfectly in key.

> *Down underwater my Laurie stays*
> *Down where anemone and fishes play*
> *Life lies above but our dreams swim below*
> *Down underwater where the sun won't go*

She imagines there's a talent scout to hear her, some smug plump man in a pinstriped jacket or a grizzled old rocker who's devoted his retirement to the recording arts. Someone who would nod and smile and pull out a contract. But she isn't little and cute anymore—she wouldn't sell. Besides, she's just playing someone else's song.

Her choice to stop all that. Exhaustion in her bones,

music turning tinny in her ears. Hands that had worked so hard until the day they wouldn't. Her choice to flee the voices droning "You could, you could, you could…" until no one said that anymore. Just her own mind.

She bangs on the keys, slumps back on the bench. For a splinter of time she wishes the band were there, so she could play with them. Could play with *someone*.

She leafs through the stack of band posters. Almost every group is her own find, chosen through careful listening. All have delivered on their promise. Lily Alvarez, piano soloist, creator of intricate harmonies—calypso hands and minor key bass lines, a bird-like vocal shriek. Pebbles in the Pond, who make their own instruments and have reclaimed the circular harp—long silence, an ethereal plinking, a rustling of leaves, and then the rain.

Then a poster of a globe enclosed by a jewel-bright snake, tail in mouth. Two women's faces superimposed on the continents: a proud one with high cheekbones, almost scornful, and a small sharp one, with glossy curls and eyes that flash defiance. Sound floods Anna's ears: guitar grating against tremulous violin, the lead soprano cutting across like glass. Ice water pours through her.

It isn't enough to burn just one.

She takes her stack of posters into the bathroom, places one carefully in the grubby sink. Next comes the friction of thumb against metal, the emergence of a thin orange flame. Lily Alvarez's goofy grin crackles. There go the lips, the ear. Anna turns the faucet on the ashes, dumps the soggy mess in the paper towel bin. A gawky twenty-year-old watches from the mirror, patches of her pale face obscured by bathroom grime, red silk scarf and black lace dress no real disguise for her gawkiness.

One band, then another, then another. Her reflection almost smiles.

The globe poster is the only one left. She places it in the basin. Frowns as water seeps into a corner, and quickly pulls it out.

Coward.

Footsteps in the entryway. Some teenage boy drawls, "Nothin' to do here anyway." The footsteps pad closer. She folds the poster into quarters, crams it in her purse.

She thinks of colleagues shouting, of the cook's contorted jowls, of pink slips, of police sirens (though what could the police do?). Her feet take off underneath her.

Vancouver's beach is paved with crowds, mostly the young. Couples sit on logs strewn about the thin gray sand, absorbed in conversations she can't hear. A volleyball game weaves among them. Men hawk hot dogs from white-painted stands. She tries not to think of the beaches she grew up around on Prince Edward Island, those placid red spaces with shallow tides and sand bars she'd dig in for clams before moving right across Canada. She could catch hermit crabs, write her name in the sand with sticks, and pop the bubbles on seaweed without meeting a single soul. "You could, you could, you could…" Here bikers whizz past her, laughing.

The sky is tinting cantaloupe and pink above the hazy blue mountains. The sea air balloons her lungs. She tears away from the beach-goers, bustles past into green, runs in her fancy sandals until she reaches Stanley Park. The trees engulf her.

Chapter 2: Box

Ages Three and Six

Anna Stern's mother swept across the living room to the door—one pace, two paces, a slight rhythmic sway to her walk. Anna, watching from the carpet, moved her plastic animals back and forth and thought that her mother looked almost like a ship, at least from what she'd seen of ships on TV. She kept her clothes as clean as the house.

The door opened on a puff of black and purple. "Caroline! Good to see you!"

"Ginny, come in, come in," Mom motioned. "I shall have to get you some tea!"

The neighbor lady had already stuffed her coat in the closet, plopped her shoes on the rack, and made her way into the living room.

"You people from away! 'I shall have to get you some tea.' Can't you talk regular for once?"

Anna set down a plastic zebra, stopped pretending to play, and listened to the grown-ups.

"I'm from here as much as you are. Hank's an islander, we bought the house ourselves and—"

"Once from away, always from away, dear."

"And you know I'm not serious when I talk like that. It happens every time I start wishing I was in an opera instead of, you know, here."

"What did I tell ya? You people from away always want to be back there. Here's not good enough—"

Ginny's voice dissolved into steamy noise as they meandered into the kitchen. Anna was left alone with the view. She leaned against the streaky velvet couch and surveyed the room that looked like her mother. A Japanese fan with two goldfish passing each other, red embroidered curtains, paintings in silver frames.

She heard Ginny again. "Where is Anna?"

She felt the warmth of attention soak through her, invisible behind the couch.

"Anna!" her mother called. She looked at her neat row of animals, then ran into the kitchen.

"There you are!" Anna looked up at Ginny's hair, which curled in yellow puffs. "You've gotten taller, haven't you?"

"Come have tea with us," said her mother, and steered Anna into a chair. "Sit up straight."

Anna had never had tea before, and wasn't prepared for the way it scraped her throat. She wondered why grown-ups drank this stuff. She saw her mother pressing buttons at the tape recorder, and suddenly music cut into the air. A rich hollow thrum of strings, then a voice sang out sweeping words in a language she didn't know.

"Da-dum da-dum, da-dum da-dum . . ." Ginny's voice, sour over the music. She didn't know the words either, and seemed to be pretending with made-up ones. Anna wished she'd stop. Mom's voice came in then, higher than the singer's, warmed honey in a wordless ah. She felt it braiding, threads of its texture spanning the space around her as clearly as sight.

The door creaked open and thudded shut. Heavy boots

stomped in. "Carol! I got the wood all chopped."

The tape and her singing cut off at the same time. "Oh?"

"You'll have to help me put it in the basement." Her dad tracked from the mudroom to the kitchen, trailing the smell of sawdust.

"Not if you don't take off your boots, I don't," Mom let out a loud breath. Anna couldn't see her, but knew her face looked stormy.

"I've been chopping wood for hours. Maybe Anna can help too. D'you think she's big enough?"

"Hank, you're out of your mind!"

"Don't you think she can carry the little pieces?"

"The boots. Take. Off. The boots."

Ginny's voice: "She's not even four yet. Give the poor girl a break."

Dad's round face bobbed down in front of her. "Hey, Anna, would you like to help carry wood after supper? It'd be an adventure!"

She nodded. She loved the smell of wood, and her dad was right: she knew she could at least carry the little pieces. Probably some bigger ones, too.

"See, Carol? She wants to."

⁊

They were listening to a tape that Anna had picked out— "the Box one, the one with the flute on it."

"Bach," Mom had corrected.

The kitchen was filled with a clear fluid sound that Anna knew and liked. The piano sounded almost like a fountain, only the notes were much too fast.

"Turn off that music," Dad clomp-clomped into the room. "Time to get to work."

They went out to the backyard where hunks of wood sat all over the grass, under the maple tree, even beside the trash cage.

"Couldn't you have put them in piles, Hank? And Anna, are you sure you want to do this?"

"Yeah!"

"What's the point of piles when they're gonna get unpiled and moved anyway?" Mom asked.

Instead of answering, Dad went into the basement, where a window to the outside of the house hid behind a board. Anna watched as the board swung in and her father's hands appeared, then set the board on the grass.

"You can carry over the little chunks," said Mom.

Anna scanned the yard and walked over to the biggest log. She put her hand on the rough bark and thought that if she wanted to, she could scrape her hand against it hard enough to bleed. She put her nose to it and smelled its heavy wild scent. Her arms wouldn't fit around the log. She grabbed the bark and tugged, but it wouldn't move and only made her arms sore, so she found a little white piece of wood and carried it to the basement window easily. It was a game, her collecting the smallest scraps—pirate treasure—and bringing them safe to the window cave. The basement had shadows and cobwebs, a mud floor and jars of things on shelves, a big-bellied stove and pallets to stack the wood on. Sometimes little animals crawled from under them. She never went into the basement unless she had to.

The small chunks were finished quickly and Anna fit her arms around a bigger one—too heavy. Her grip slipped and she fell onto the lawn.

"Anna, are you OK?" Her mother stared down.

She collected her breath. "Yeah."

"I think you've worked enough. Want to go inside now?"

Anna looked around. She was tired and the yard, more than half empty. Little red lines striped her palms, marks on her skin from dragging. She was glad to be done with the wood.

Inside the house, she looked for something to do. She started lining up her plastic animals but that was boring, too much like carrying the wood. The house felt like a cave now, big and empty without people, without sound. She couldn't reach the tape recorder and she couldn't read what the tapes said anyway.

She looked around the living room and saw the piano. It was old, her great-grandmother's, with birds carved into the wood on the sides, and it was her mom's thing. She kept it dusted, and once a month a man with a blue hat would come tune it. She'd play it at holidays with Anna on her lap and sing Christmas carols. Anna never sang with her because she couldn't remember the words.

She'd never touched the keys herself.

Why hadn't she?

She looked at the piano again. The keys were covered by wood with shadows cutting across and a knob that her mother or the hat man would push back. The bench was tall, and she wasn't sure if she could reach it on her own. She pictured the white keys and the jagged black ones.

She'd just had tea and helped stack wood. Maybe she could try.

What would Mom say? She'd find her, daring to make noise, and she'd stare like a snake about to hiss.

Anna inched forward, stopped, then forward again. She tried to jump onto the bench. Tried until she was finally sitting on it. She couldn't reach the keys, so she got down, pushed in one side of the bench, the other, jumped back on, and stood up. The piano loomed in front of her, bulky and forbidding.

She reached for the knob and pulled. The first flap on the wooden case came up and she held it. Underneath were the keys laid out like teeth, half hidden in darkness. She quickly pushed the casing back.

She pressed her finger on the key in the middle and listened to the molasses tone until the sound had all drained. Another. Two at a time. She put her whole hands down. She made quiet noises and huge clashing loud ones. She made her fingers climb around. She felt the power in her fingers to make clouds and fairies come alive in the living room. It wasn't like the tambourine or play drum in the toy chest, things you shook or banged on that only made a few kinds of sounds.

It was like on the tapes! Maybe she could play the Bach song. The piano sounded heavier than the flute but the keys made the same noises. Her fingers searched until they landed on the first note. She tried for the second until she found it. Second-first again. Second-first-third. That wasn't quite right. The first note was held for a lot longer, and the others sped up. She searched, played back what she'd figured out, adding a new note or two each time, holding them the way she remembered from the tape. She tried playing very fast, and laughed. It felt like racing, and took the breath from her chest. Back to finding notes. It wasn't hard. There were no extra notes to muddle the sound of the song.

She heard boots. "Anna, what are you doing at the piano?"

"Shhh." Her mom was there too.

She pretended she hadn't heard them. She kept untangling the notes from each other, playing them in the right order until the song was done. It was like a smell. Even after they were gone, the notes hung there flavoring the air. She listened until there was no noise, though a thin shiver still stirred her body. It was time to start again. This time she sped up and played the middle louder. She only hit one wrong note. Her hands were horses carrying themselves with measured hoof-stamps, then quieting to a stop.

"Anna!"

She'd forgotten her mother was there.

"How the hell did you figure out how to play that?" Her dad yelled or almost-yelled. It hurt her ears.

"Honey, your language."

"Look at her. She just played one of them symphonies, the whole damn thing!"

"Sonata. Bach's Flute Sonata in E, I believe." Mom's voice had gotten too quiet . Her face looked almost hungry, like the monsters in stories that ate you in the dark.

Anna looked down at her fingers on the keys and tried to taste the music back into the air.

"Anna," said her mother, "would you like to take piano lessons?"

♩

The classrooms smelled like old polished furniture. That was the first thing Anna noticed. Kids scuffled like mice in all directions, making the floorboards squeak. Anna wished they wouldn't see her, and they didn't seem to. A pair of boys in blue shirts were talking already. Did they go together or was it only the shirts? There were four kids in the front row, so she went to the back corner—the wooden chair was heavy—and sat in it. Was she supposed to? Well, that's what people were doing, all out of order. One girl in the middle with a pink ribboned dress—why couldn't she be wearing a pink ribboned dress?—was munching. It was a snake or something, no, it was a fruit roll-up. She kept her blue sneakers, a present for her sixth birthday, as still as possible.

A teacher stood tall in front of the room, her hair in two brown braids, a string around her neck that looked like colored coins. There was nothing soft in her high face, and also nothing mean.

"Welcome to Pine Grove Music School." Her mouth formed a moving line. "My name is Mrs. Benjamin." She wrote it on the chalkboard in loopy letters. "Everyone sit down, please."

Anna watched as the last kids shuffled into seats. A short Black boy, twin Asian girls with pigtails, a boy with yellow hair, a big redheaded girl drumming on the desk. And the smallest girl of all sat in front of her, with copper-colored skin and glossy black tangles of hair. She had on just jeans and a red sweater. Her head bent low.

The frog-faced boy beside her whispered something rude, but Anna didn't want to listen to him. Mrs. Benjamin was more interesting, like a talking piece of furniture.

The smallest girl sat bundled on the swing set. Her red sweater was too big for her. Anna walked by, trying not to look, and heard whimpering. She looked. The girl was rubbing and rubbing at tears.

"What's wrong?" asked Anna.

The small girl started to talk. All the words ran together.

"My dog, I miss my dog, I want to go home and they won't let me call my mother. I told the teacher she'd growl at her for it. My mother said if I phoned she'd be up here right away." She didn't really look, she just kept rubbing. There were raccoon patches under her eyes. But now her face was dry and she tilted her head up to stare straight at Anna. A bright, pointed stare. Not a raccoon, then. A fox. Anna shrunk to mouse size.

"What instruments do you play?" A tear-string rolled across her cheek and she scrubbed it away with angry fingers. On to the next thing.

"The piano," Anna answered.

"Oh, is that all? I learned piano at age three, well I'm still learning, but my mother made me start violin at age five. I want to learn the viola someday, don't you?"

She had a sharp sad face. Anna could almost see the bones.

"I said, don't you?"

"Yeah." The viola, that was like a big violin, right, or was that the cello? Anna felt like she was lying at first. She'd never thought of playing one. But if this wild-looking person, this fox girl, learned to hold and make sound come from that case of wood, suddenly she wanted to do the same. She wanted her hands to be that thin and to cling to the swing chains like they owned them.

"Did your mom send you here, too?" the girl asked.

Anna thought of the examiner, a man shaped like a teapot, who'd listened to her play a shiny black piano. Her mom had said that if she didn't get into music school, she'd go to French school. Her dad had said they both had playgrounds. The teapot man had said lots of things about talent and attention, or was it potential? Some kinds of big words.

"I think I sent me here," said Anna.

The smaller girl shrugged, suddenly bored. "What's your name anyway?"

"Anna Caroline Stern." She liked the serious sound of it.

"That sounds like an old person's name. I'm Liss. My birth mother called me Felicity but no one says it, it's too long, and plus I hate it anyway."

"I like Felicity."

"Don't you ever call me that, you hear? It's Liss." She stared hard. "Do you know how to do the spider?"

"No." Was that something like the viola, part of an adult code she'd never been taught?

"Well, come on, then. Get on the swing."

Anna obeyed. Fear and excitement tangled in her belly.

"What you do to play Spider, you go on your stomach and spin 'til there's as many knots as you can get." Liss had gone belly-down while talking and was spinning around. Anna felt dizzy watching her. Then she stopped and sat under an impressive ladder of knots, her feet barely scraping the ground. "Then you pull your feet up and unspin."

Anna got on her stomach and spun around. Her feet scraped against the sand until the chain knotted down to her back and there was no more to twist.

"There," said Liss. "That's how you do it. Now take your feet up."

Anna's stomach twisted. "You first."

"Chicken! Bokbokbokchicken!"

Anna didn't want to be a bokbokchicken. She raised her feet. The schoolyard spun around her in a greengraybrown blur. Her feet kicked, she was going to fall.

She stopped in the middle of the air. Swaying, dizzy, but still on her swing. Liss laughed.

"You're holding on so tight you'd think you were scared or something!"

"I wasn't scared," Anna lied.

Liss kicked the rocks beneath her feet as Anna got off her swing, then sat on it right side up. Liss kept looking at her. Opened her mouth.

"Do you know if you're the kid your parents were supposed to have?"

Chapter 3: *Check and Mate*

Age Sixteen

"Fuck jumping the octave," Anna told the "Do Not Enter" sign on the wall. She wouldn't swear so casually around her parents, but alone, the biting words fell flat. She set her clarinet on the bed for a minute. Her elbows ached from leaning against the window.

Sixteen was supposed to be young, a time to be the Dancing Queen Almost Seventeen, to dye your hair and stay up too late and blow off homework and sneak alcohol, a time to feel excitement rush through blood. Some days Anna felt old already. Mastering the clarinet was much slower than mastering piano. Her fingers got in each other's way when she tried cadenzas. It helped that piano notes were one finger each, if often simultaneous.

The window overlooked the woods, bleached branches almost bare between dark needles. Road signs covered the walls, some genuine and some from the dollar store. Caution. Beware Falling Objects. Go Slow: School Zone. Enter at Your Own Risk. A hammock from the ceiling held stuffed animals: a giant crocodile, squashed red and pink teddies, a duck with the head of a bear. The fluffy gray kitten, a long-ago present from Liss, she kept on her pillow. Her CD rack stretched almost to the ceiling, the worst ones on top.

Her door was shut. That was the advantage to a wind

instrument: it could be practiced in private. All others could know outside the door was whatever the sounds betrayed.

She played a long C, noticed it was off, and unscrewed the mouthpiece slightly. Tuning was fickle. Long tones. Scales. Arpeggios. Then back to her solo, newly composed by her clarinet teacher Michael O'Hara (never Mike). The sound was never as clear as she wanted, a pool whose reflective powers were mucked up by the least clot on the surface.

When the lunch bell rang, the girls took off to Dusty's Fried Chicken in Sarah's car. Horrible food, Dad always said, all deep-fried and so many hormones in those birds, although he ate it well enough when they were short on money and sometimes brought the Family Meal Deal home. Michelle smiled at the guy behind the counter—he had messy hair and a few pimples, but a nice build—and ordered "The tender chicken sandwich and a hot fudge sundae, please."

"Just the salad, please," said Chen behind her.

"I'll take the spicy burger combo with crispy fries," said Anna.

"You never worry about your weight, do you?" Irena scowled.

They took their food to a table and ignored the flecks of salt and pepper on top. Dusty's had been renovated that summer, a rotating bucket of chicken installed by the sign and the inside stripped of its flowered wallpaper, repainted mustard yellow with ketchup-colored trim. Anna sat on the bench between Chen and Michelle, a twin on either side.

Across from them, Sarah leaned on the table and unwrapped the yellow paper from her burger. "I can't believe they want us to practice before school starts."

"Yeah, Mr. McAvoy's crazy," said Irena.

"Kinda cute, though."

"No way!"

"Did you guys all get your essays done?" asked Chen, fingering her cap of straight hair.

"Stop changing the subject," said Michelle. "We're talking about men here."

"Yeah," Sarah added. "Any love interests lately?"

"Um, not really," said Chen.

"Not really. Not really." Michelle went to reach across Anna to heckle her sister, but Anna blocked her. "You have to take an interest someday in *someone* who's not an anime character."

Michelle had something of an anime look herself, thought Anna. Her delicacy was not simply physical but stylized. She wore tiny cardigans, jean skirts with patches, a headband with a tiny satin rose, and kept her hair long and glossy for the full princess effect. Chen was just as small with the same pronounced cheekbones, but if she had a style, it was sparseness. A hummingbird who chomped through life and a barn owl who wavered. Irena was a blonde swan, Sarah a tanned and curly-haired grackle—

"You still nursing hopes of Ed, Anna?" It was Sarah, of course, grinning.

"Come on, that was years ago." She pushed some curly fries around their container with a fork.

"Any other guys?" Sarah winked.

"Or girls," said Chen.

Sarah shuffled awkwardly. Anna wished her friend hadn't

brought that up.

She wished the girls would talk about running away, sometimes. About going to Alaska or studying Spanish in Argentina or moving to the mainland and opening a chain mail jewelry store.

"Come on, Anna," Irena cut in. "Who's your secret crush?"

"I guess the guy at the counter's cute," she mumbled.

"That doesn't count. You're as boring as my sister," said Michelle.

Chen elbowed her, grinning.

Was she like Chen? She hoped not. She'd scarcely seen a spark of passion on Chen's face in all the years they'd known each other, while she herself had felt so much her body seemed, increasingly, brittle glass. But maybe it was there in both cases, just invisible. She touched her wrist nervously, checked for a pulse.

⁊

"New guy alert." Irena nudged her in the clarinet section.

The guy in question wore a neck strap and knelt on the floor, fitting the reed for an alto saxophone.

"I thought new people weren't allowed to start after the first week," Anna whispered back.

"Maybe he was sick. Or maybe he's good enough that they bent the rules." Irena seemed pleased by either possibility. Anna looked again. He did seem well built, although all she could see was his back and a fluff of rusty hair. Maybe he snuck in, Anna would once have suggested with equal relish. Maybe he's an impostor, maybe he bribed somebody to get in (Who, Laine? Highly unlikely), maybe he slept with someone, maybe he's a prodigy who had to move to P.E.I. from Juilliard. A dashing intruder in the midst of concert band sectionals. But she was too old for that.

He turned around. His face was slim and chiseled (genetically gifted, she thought), though she could hardly tell the specifics since he went to sit down quickly and everyone around them started tuning. Adjust the reed, adjust the barrel. She and Irena angled their clarinets towards each other and checked if their tones blended.

Mr. Haslam waddled to the podium and raised his baton. Shorter than Anna, he looked and moved like a penguin. They tuned with the sleek black device in his hand. *Sharp*, thought Anna, *we're all sharp!* But he seemed satisfied, and wouldn't have believed or listened to her.

The new march reminded her less of soldiers than of circus music, parading performers on stilts, or the bouncy up-down, up-down of a Whack-a-Mole game. She counted rests while the saxophones hit the notes with an imaginary mallet, and watched Irena's head bob to the rhythm.

After packing up their instruments, Irena nudged Anna to signal they should stay. "Oh, please," Anna whispered, but already Irena had begun a few brisk strides towards the corner where the new guy and Paul, the baritone sax player, were chatting. Anna followed.

"Hi! Welcome to Pine Grove." Irena held out a hand, smoothly. Just as smoothly, he shook it. "I'm Irena Nikanova."

"Pleased to meet you. Darien Ross."

He held himself stiffly. A musician uncomfortable with overtures. Ironic, Anna thought, and Irena took her smile to be directed at Darien.

"This is Anna, our resident piano prodigy," Irena introduced her before she could speak.

"Irena composes stuff," said Anna hastily. Stuff. How unattractive-sounding. She should have kept her mouth shut.

"Sounds talented," said Darien.

"Yeah, she's getting some pieces picked up in teaching books soon." Maybe if Anna could write anything half interesting, she'd be getting published too. Maybe if she could do something other than replay what everyone else came up with . . .

"A talented talker too," said Paul. Irena shot him A Look.

"Surprising for a clarinetist," said Darien. "I've noticed people usually match their instruments. The quiet ones will play clarinet or flute, and the loudmouths will be in the trumpet section."

"The blowhards," said Paul. They chuckled.

"And the bari sax is the worst of all," said Irena, her neck high.

"Seriously, if we were going by your logic," said Paul, "all pianists would have a penis. And that's obviously not true."

"No," said Irena, "luckily."

Anna pretended to laugh.

"You should hear Irena's compositions sometime," she said. "Darien."

"Sure. That would be great."

"You doing anything for lunch tomorrow?" asked Irena.

A smile, so much subtler than Michelle's, her head remaining untilted.

"Besides eating, I have no plans."

"Want to go to Jenny's Cafe with us?"

He hesitated for a second. "Why not?"

Irena beamed at Anna as they left the music room. Conquest! Soon she would be taken, the Swan Princess's every curve inclined towards her leggy freckled Swan Prince. Anna rolled her eyes.

She caught a ride home with Chen and Michelle, who lived even further from the school than she did. Chen wanted to put on some Philip Glass tracks, but Michelle searched her iPod until she found Surrender and turned the volume up.

"Hot guys who can actually make music," she yelled over it. "That's a work of genius if you ask me."

I'll be standing here when the sun collides with Earth
I'll be standing here when the Judgment Day shows up
I'll be standing here when the ground gives meteors birth
I'll be standing here when the waters all rise up

And I promise, this I promise, I will never
Never move since I'll be standing here forever

Anna wished the traffic would move faster. A potato truck ambled past on the other side of the road, humped up with cargo, leaving a few rolling after it. She wondered why no one honked at these things. They drove past the stuffy Catholic church where, she was grateful, she no longer set foot. A sign marked its name, and below it JESUS SAVES! POTLUCK SATURDAY. In the dentist's yard, dozens of ducks and chickens squalled.

"Did you hear about the new guy?" Anna asked.

"What?" Michelle grinned suddenly.

"There's a new guy in woodwind sectionals who just transferred to our school. Damien or something. Irena seems to like him."

"If Irena wants him, Irena will have him," said Michelle. Anna couldn't see everything from the back seat, but she thought she heard a kick.

"Well, unless you want him, Chen. Good luck with that."

"Guys," said Anna, "you haven't even met him. And that's my driveway. Slow down."

7

"Here, birdie-birdie-birdie!" Mom would be at work for another little while, and the parakeet had to be fed. Anna shook some pellets into Callas' bowl. He turned his head so she could only see the side, the pale eye haughtily watching, the Elvis-tuft of yellow feathers above it spoiling the effect. "Silly bird," she said. "Eat your food." She closed the cage, walked off, and looked back. Callas looked up from his bowl to stare. "Yes, you were eating, good birdie. You know you were. I saw ya."

She set a pot of water on the stovetop to boil and took out a box of macaroni and cheese, glad that her father wasn't living there anymore. Enough time to go out while the water boiled. She used to hate how her music couldn't follow her outside, but now Anna had not only her old Walkman but a new MP3 player. She carried it out in her jacket pocket and stood on the old gray prayer rock and clasped the dogwood branch above her out of habit. She searched the little device until *Ride of the Valkyries* came searing through the forest, unheard by anything but her.

Ay-a, Ay-a, stars in my body... Stop it, she thought. The chant was old and silly. Heck, she'd made it up in first grade. She couldn't remember if she'd actually seen something she thought was her goddess above that rock, or just imagined her there. Ay-a had a body as slim as a tree, she'd decided, one that bent just as easily. Silly. Humans had many more joints than trees did. Why not a flower? Flowers were short and stubby, even the regal ones, compared to the woods. Ay-a's eyes were whatever color the sky was that day, whether it be blue or almost black or dingy yellow-gray.

There were good things about the chant. It adapted to any tune. Anna let her arms unclench and her eyes be drawn upwards in this tiny clearing fortressed with trees. The light here was leaf-sieved, mixed with the scent of sap and pine needles. She let go of the dogwood branch. The Valkyries filled her veins, flung her arms out.

Her hand knocked against the branch and she felt silly. Turned the music off, switched to a dirge, and walked inside. The water had boiled over.

Mom came in swinging her briefcase. "I made us dinner," said Anna. "I fed the bird."

"Good," said her mother. "Have you had time to practice for your solo for the orchestra?"

"No, I just got home!"

"Well, what are we having for dinner?"

"It's on the stove."

Mom went to look. "One of us should make a salad. It's good that we're finishing up the macaroni, though. We need to get that stuff out of the house before my mother comes."

From the living room, Callas cheeped loudly.

"Sometimes I wonder how much English he understands," said Mom.

"He's a bird. I doubt it's much."

"When did you get so cynical on me? You wouldn't have said that last year."

"Yeah, I would. It's a bird, for god's sake." Would she have?

Mom was already pulling vegetables from the crisper. "Anna, I have something to tell you that you're not going to like."

"What?"

"Well. You know. Well." She took out a bowl, a chopping board, a cleaver, and started washing the lettuce. What was it? What was it? Why the secrecy, from her?

"Well, you know how your father's been gone for a little while."

She tried to ignore the churning in her stomach.

"Well, I met someone at work." Anna jolted. Watched her closely. Could see the side of her mother's face, edging upwards in a silly smile.

"When was that, Mom?"

"Oh, well, weeks ago. I mean I knew him for a couple years, but we only started dating recently. It wouldn't have been right to do anything earlier."

"Tom?" said Anna, startled.

"How did you know?" Mom kept her back to Anna as she chopped lettuce furiously.

"He's the only male colleague you've talked about much." One of those colleagues she'd never even met. Nice guy. Tom said he liked my blouse today. Tom's daughter's away at McGill. You might want to go there, Anna, it has a good music program. Tom brought in muffins for the office. Tom's so good at his job. Tom and Mom. Mom and Tom. Mommy and Tommy up a tree ...Grow up, Anna! Stupid Tom. No. Let Mom be happy. Gods know she needs it.

She hoped he wasn't gorgeous like the new kid. She hoped he had plumber pants that showed his butt crack or something.

"You're a perceptive one, Anna." Her mother hacked at lettuce shreds that had already been chopped. If she kept going at this rate, they'd soon need to eat with spoons to get all the bits. Salad with a spoon. Ridiculous. Stupid Tom.

"That's great, Mom."

"You really think so?"

"Yeah. Of course I do."

"You're not traumatized by my running wild?"

"Shut up and let me grate the carrots."

"That would be lovely." She grinned, Anna thought, like a teenager who'd gotten away with something.

"What's Grandma gonna say about this Tom guy?"

"Don't say a word. That's one reason I told you before she could find out. Could you help me hide it, if it comes to that?"

"I don't see how Grandma of all people could find out who you're dating! For heaven's sake." She peeled the carrot faster, wishing she could listen to her music without looking disrespectful. "It's not like she'll stalk you at work or anything."

"You're right, you're right, I'm worrying again."

They finished the salad and ate with lit candles on the table. Mom's idea. It would only take a small push to shove one into the napkin holder.

"You're awfully quiet tonight."

Anna didn't do it.

Mom forgot about her silence and started talking. "I'm so glad I told you. Oh, I'm so glad you're not upset. He's really a sweet guy. I think you'd get along well. He loves Beethoven. That's your favorite, right?" She didn't say: No, Mom, I like Chopin better now. "He's so quick with French, probably the best translator the bureau's got. I wish you'd learned. Do you want to try lessons again, maybe?"

"I don't have time."

"Well, you are pretty busy. But I could teach you on my own time, *si ça te convient*."

"See-saw? What?"

"Oh. If it works for you."

"We'll see."

The macaroni and cheese tasted like paper with a liberal dose of mayonnaise and the salad dressing was too watery, but Mom beamed the whole way through. Don't remind her of Grandma. Don't.

A god in the kitchen watched over the goings-on of the house. A goddess in the garden ensured that sprouting things continued to grow. A god in the driveway ensured clear passage in all of life. Over the years, they'd crept into every corner Anna went. She spilled her hands over the piano keys and forgot to think of Tom somewhere in Chopin's Nocturne in C Sharp, Opus 27. The gods of music, invisible as atoms, soaked through her. Many tiny gods bent her spine to the rhythm.

❦

Anna skipped lunch with Irena and Darien by hiding for the first half hour in the music room before getting her sandwich. Last thing she needed, lunch with someone else's Tom. Irena could tell her later what was going on with this mysterious boy. Irena could claim him for her own—she always did.

"You stupid girl!" said Sarah. Michelle had gone off with Sean, her "I-like-him-but-am-not-committing-at-this-stage," and Chen was probably in a practice room, trombone in hand. She didn't fit the people-match-their-instruments rule.

"So stupid," said Anna, "to do what I want to during break. Last I heard, it's a free country. And I'm sick of lovebirds. Even my mom's dating someone now."

"Really? Details, girl!"

"Well, I haven't met him. All I know is that he's some translator colleague named Tom."

"Ooh, workplace romances are the best," said Sarah with relish. "I bet they have so much in common! I bet they leave secret notes for each other in their cubicles."

"Actually, they're mostly working on-site."

"I bet they take those goofy ear phones during breaks and

use them to say romantic messages to each other."

"I don't think ear phones even work like that."

"So, is your mom bouncing off the walls?"

"Yeah, pretty much."

"A sure sign of roooo-mance!" Sarah sang that last part, an alto scale that drew stares even in music school. Singing wasn't done in the cafeteria. Anna wondered if she was blushing; Sarah wasn't.

House vacuumed, mopped, and dusted: check. Groceries bought: check. Items purchased to look good, like fresh strawberries and salmon pâté and five kinds of crackers. Tablecloth: check. White lace that looked crocheted—the box that betrayed its factory origins had long been used as stove fuel. Flowers on the table: check. Mom had bought the cliché dozen red roses because Anna hadn't been with her. Pull-out bed made in the living room: check. So the sheets weren't satin. Grandma would just have to deal.

"Anything we forgot?" Mom called out, zooming around the house with a list.

"Doubt it."

"You should do something with your hair. It looks messy."

Anna grabbed the black elastic from her wrist and pulled it into a ponytail which, she thought, looked just as messy.

"She'll only be here a couple weeks, I think," said Mom. "We'll be fine. You'll have to play her your clarinet solo. God, I hope she goes to bed early."

Anna quietly decided to spend a weekend at her dad's place. He wasn't far, and his apartment in town was much closer to Pine Grove than the house. Aunt Bet and Uncle

Theo might come over. There wasn't a piano there, but there was one in the community center just a walk away that had decent sound quality and was only a little flat. On the other hand, it would be a great excuse to take a couple days off practicing.

"Hop in the car! Hop to it already!" Mom tended to say silly things when she got rattled.

"Can I drive?" Anna tried.

"Not this time. I'm too nervous and you'd run into everything on the road."

"You being nervous makes me run into things?"

"We can practice again when she's gone."

Two whole weeks. Well, Dad had a car, and Uncle Theo and Aunt Bet's family had three between them all, plus the pickup truck…Did Darien drive? Would he chauffeur Irena around? Would he play her songs and tell her stories about the big city or wherever else he came from?

She had to talk to him again.

The car ground from gravel to asphalt, and they set off down the road.

Chapter 4: *Grass Forts*

Age Six

"Do you know if you're the kid your parents were supposed to have?" asked Liss.

"Do I what?"

"My parents were supposed to have another kid but she died," said Liss, suspended beneath her knotted swing chain. "That's why they adopted me. Are you adopted? I bet you got real parents."

Anna had never wondered that. Suddenly her throat knotted like the chains. "I think I do."

"They never told you, then. Maybe you're not their kid."

The throat knot burrowed a little deeper. "Of course I am."

"Well, maybe they'd wanted another kid but they got you. There are tons of us, you know. Kids who are replacements for someone else. If we all got together in the same place, we could make a whole country. Maybe even a continent."

Anna tried to picture a map of Canada with people standing all across it, people who hadn't been wanted in the first place. She had a hard time thinking there were enough of them to fill P.E.I. But maybe there were lots of people who were secretly replacements, so secretly they didn't know it themselves. Maybe she was one of them.

"Let's make a fort," said Liss. "Let's make our own

country."

"How can we make a fort when there's no snow?"

"Haven't you heard of a grass fort, stupid?"

Anna hadn't. She felt suddenly too young for school. There were too many things that everyone knew and no one had bothered to tell her.

"Well, come on then." Liss grabbed Anna, a claw around her wrist, and headed to the fence that bordered the schoolyard. The grass was long around it, with clover and goldenrod and asters growing. Miniature spruce sprung evenly along it like green traffic cones. Some older kids sat a few feet away, ripping up grass. Liss began to do the same thing.

"Look, you've got to get a bunch of grass to make the walls. That's why it's a grass fort, of course."

Anna started pulling, glancing between handfuls to see if any teachers came around. Her mother had told her not to pick grass or flowers in public places. What would the teachers say if they caught her picking all the school's own grass, how would they stare at her, what noises would swell up from their throats? What would they make her do? She'd heard the word detention, but only knew it was what happened when you did Something Bad. Would they send her home from music school forever, to the tape recorder and French Immersion, send her home when she hadn't even started learning?

She saw a tall shape moving briskly towards them and moved to hide behind Liss. Her breath came short. Should she drop the grass? Liss held hers balled in her fist as she picked more. She seemed not to notice.

The teacher moved closer, walking like a heron on stilt-legs, wearing a black suit.

"Hello," she said.

"Hello," said Liss.

The teacher's gaze was no less intent than Liss's —her eyes a darting hazel. She looked behind Liss, to where Anna was trying to hide. "Hey, you. Come out. Did you think I was going to eat you?" She chuckled, a French Horn sound. Anna edged slowly from behind Liss, holding the grass crumpled in her palm so it wouldn't be seen.

"I think I know who you both are." The teacher scratched her chin. "You're Felicity, and you must be Anna."

"My regular name's Liss," said Liss. Anna wondered how she could stay so unafraid, her head so straight it was almost thrown back. Her own head felt too heavy to stay up.

"And you are Anna, right?" Anna had to look. Eye contact. Don't be dis-ris-pect-ful.

"Yeah—yes."

"My name's Laine Winters, but please just call me Laine."

"I knew that," said Liss.

The French Horn, again. Liss's shoulders drooped.

Anna wondered. This was the first time a grown-up had asked her to call them by their first name. She'd been scolded when she called her mother's-side grandma Mary on the phone, after hearing her father call her that. It Wasn't Very Polite. Did first names mean they were in trouble? Was that a nice laugh or the laugh of a wicked queen in front of her mirror, polishing an apple?

"Well," said Laine, "I just wanted to say hi. I'm the principal here, which means I'm the one people get mad at if anything goes wrong. Oh, and you might have me for piano." She pushed a strand of hair behind an ear with a squirrelish movement.

Anna thought of her old piano teacher, Mrs. Hobbes, with her nervous face. Their lessons had stopped that week. She'd said that Anna played about as well as her now, and let her pet the old snoring cat goodbye. She wondered if Laine had a cat, but that was probably a stupid thing to ask. If she did, it wouldn't come to school.

"I'll see you at the assembly," Laine said. "I'm going to be talking to the whole school this afternoon. Not my favorite thing to do, but I won't go on for too long." She waved and turned and walked away.

"Bye!" called Liss.

Anna found it easier to breathe again. She remembered the grass in her palm, squished and sweaty, and started picking more.

"Let's make the foundation," said Liss. She patted down a square of grass behind a traffic-cone tree, picking some for material. Anna joined her. Pat-pick-pick, pat-pick-pick, until the square was flat. Liss sat down in it and started arranging grass around the border. Anna did the same. "We need more grass," said Liss once the square was completed. "Can you guard it?"

"OK." Anna wondered what the dangers were. Pirates, poachers, bears?

"Don't let the other kids wreck it. My cousins said they do that sometimes."

Liss walked off. Anna sat in this picture frame of grass, her back against the tree. Its bristles only hurt a little where her arms were bare, and the prickliness was interesting. It wasn't a very big fort. Just big enough for the two of them to sit in comfortably. She watched a caterpillar crawl across a goldenrod stalk, black and yellow with fur. Its many feet went slow (one-two-three-four), and its body bent in the middle to walk.

Liss came back, her arms full of grass. They set to work stacking the walls higher until the fort was above their ankles. Liss sat down cross-legged inside and Anna followed, feeling the grass squish under her. "Let's have this fort be our country," Liss said.

"Yeah, let's." Anna thought about the possibilities. They could have a flag, make holidays, laws, their own language, adopt a caterpillar as their castle guard . . .

"It'll be the country of music," said Liss.

As the class lined up for the assembly, Anna watched the buttons on Mrs. Benjamin's necklace swim back and forth. They were brought into the same auditorium where Anna had gone to the Christmas concert for the past three years. They waited while more people rustled in—all the new students, Mrs. Benjamin said, in different grades.

"Hello." (Ello-lo.) Laine Winters walked out onto the empty stage with her baton. There was no one to conduct, so she rolled it from one hand to the other. "I'm sure you're sick of hearing this, but welcome to Pine Grove Music School. There used to be pines here, but people chopped them all down years ago. Sometimes I hate people."

Anna looked to Liss but her hawk eyes were watching Laine's. Some students in the audience half-laughed. A couple teachers whole-laughed.

"Some of you may think you got in because you have

talent." Laine spun the baton. "Well, I have news for you. There is no such thing as talent."

The shuffling in the audience dropped off.

"Talent is what happens when you work hard. How much you achieve is determined by the effort you put into it. Every one of you is able to put in effort. That's why you are here." She tapped the baton against her hand. "The other reason you are here is because you're lucky. You had parents or teachers who were willing to put a lot of effort into helping you. All those times they made you practice, you were getting better. Think about it."

A chorus rose in Anna's ears. Ginny and Aunt Bet and Uncle Theo and Uncle Jeffrey and Aunt Carrie and Aunt Sue and Mrs. Hobbes and Grandma Mary on her mom's side and Grammy and Grampy on her dad's side. "Listen to her!" "My God, you can play that thing." "Amazing." "She got her talent from her mother, that's for sure!" (But she wasn't her mother.) "Anna, that was ...remarkable." "Opera in her blood." (But she didn't sing opera. Her voice was thin and quiet.) "Perfect pitch." "Natural sense of rhythm." "Can pick things out by ear." "Did it occur to you that she's got incredible talent?" (But there was no such thing.)

Something sharp against her arm. Liss's elbow. "Ow! Stop it!"

"Anna, she's done talking. Get in line before the teacher thinks you're stupid."

Instrument lessons happened twice a week, Mrs. Benjamin explained. Half the class had them while the other had choir, so there were two choir classes and everyone had to be in one. Mrs. Benjamin called out names for the first choir class. Carl Arsenault, Brandon Betts ...Anna tapped the Waltz of the Flowers rhythm against her desk, waiting to hear Stern. Sloan... Travers.

The line was made, and she and Liss weren't in it. Liss turned and whispered to Anna in the back row. "I had to bring my violin, but I don't suppose you have to bring a piano."

"Do you like to sing?" asked Anna with insects in her throat. She would have to go to choir tomorrow.

"Of course, don't you?"

She couldn't sing like her mother, and the next day Liss would find out. Maybe she could hide—but maybe Liss would find her. Her bottom lip shook.

"What, are you scared of that too or something?"

"Do your mom and dad sing?" asked Anna quickly.

"Not really. But my little sisters do. My mom and dad just work all the time."

Anna had to meet Laine Winters in a room downstairs. She repeated the number in her head—122, 122—as she walked across the pebble-patterned floor past the fish tank, down the big staircase, past doors full of colored pictures, all with numbers. 122 was a closed white door. Insects scuttled in her throat. She knocked.

Laine opened it. "Oh, hi. Come on in." She was more than twice as tall as Anna, who followed her uncertainly. There were two pianos in the room, side by side against the right wall. A small wooden one, brown and polished, and a grand piano, black and polished. Words on their sides in gold looping letters. The room echoed. Anna knew because the hollow tromp-tromp of Laine's polished black pointy shoes and the usually dull scuff-shuff of her Zellers-new, town-bought blue sneakers - were magnified to dignity.

Laine sat down at the grand piano's bench, leaving Anna to sit at the little one. She scooted the bench in and was tall enough to reach the pedals without a pillow. That had happened about a month ago. "So, you're Anna," said Laine. Anna said nothing, wondering if a yes was expected. Her father's voice in her head: An-na, An-na, in her blue pa-jam-as. No, she wouldn't tap the rhythm.

"So. Can you play something for me?"

The salamanders in her brain were all saying different things. Für Elise. The Bach So-Na-Ta. Something from the Nutcracker Suite. Mozart. Handel.

"You nervous?"

"No." She bit her lip.

"How about we talk?" Anna waited for her to say something else while the clock kept time like a metronome. "So, what does your family do?"

"They, they—" the insects choked her off. They'd built nests in her throat, from sand and paper. She turned and her fingers hit the keyboard. The Four Seasons came spilling out, the piece she'd practiced most lately. She loved how the song wasn't anything else, just leaves and birds and snow and branches hurrying to happen. There was air in her throat again, Vivaldi's springtime in her lungs.

"Thank you," said Laine. "Now play it for me slower."

Anna's arms felt heavy, but she did. Laine stopped her halfway through Spring. "Let's hear you play those last two bars again. Pay attention to the order the notes come in. Don't let them get ahead of each other or muddy each other up."

But it's Spring, Anna thought of saying, and Spring is all mud! Of course, she didn't say that. She was old enough to know that wasn't what Laine meant, and that this particular song wasn't about mud. Probably driveways weren't full of red muck in the Spring where Vivaldi had lived. Probably cars did not get stuck in them.

She played the bars, carefully, handling a glass ball between her fingers. This time, not a single note was mud. "Better," said Laine. "Now let's hear you try with the energy back in it."

She couldn't do any of this right. Laine got her to practice bar after bar, fix this, fix that. "You have a strong grasp of this piece but you need to pay more attention to technical details." The little things in fingers and throat that scritch and scratch and grab you. Laine sent her out the door with a list of things to practice.

Anna didn't take the bus home like Liss did. Mom came to pick her up. The school was in Summerside, 45 minutes away from Creighton—three drives there make a Christmas concert—and there weren't enough students from the country to have a bus. Creighton was only Creighton for fifteen houses spread out between potato and hay fields and cow pastures and barns and strips of trees. Then it became Salmon Falls on one side and Yorkville on the other and after that something else and something else, spelled out on blue signs.

"How was your first day of school?" asked her mother, pressing down her hair.

Anna said nothing. She watched the swing set and the traffic-cone trees by her grass fort shrink to the size of candy corn.

"Was it OK, I hope?"

"Yeah."

"Good. I made a carrot cake for when you get home."

She watched the big houses in town with flower planters and curly trim, the one with a stained-glass window, the one with turrets. She watched the Tim Horton's and the Burger King and the shopping mall with the kite logo and the signs she couldn't read but would learn to.

"Do you have any homework?"

"Just music stuff."

She couldn't ask the question. She didn't know which question to ask, if one of them would dissolve the lead ball in her stomach, if one of them would have an answer that would make things make sense. Even if it was the worst answer, moving on salamander feet. It was only once they were driving past fields again that Anna tried to straighten her words and ask.

"Was I the kid you wanted to have?"

"Of course you are! Why would you even ask that?"

It was alright then. Wasn't it?

But at home she had another question before she could let herself be hungry. "How do I know I'm your real kid?"

"Darling, just look at yourself in the mirror!"

Mom led Anna towards the mirror on the bathroom door. It wasn't interesting, just the same thing she saw every time she passed.

"See the shape of your face? It's round like your father's, but you've got my smaller chin. See your nose? Look at my nose. It's just the same. Our hair is the same kind of brown."

It wasn't straight like Mom's but had some of her father's

waves, not enough to be curly. She was built like her mother, thinly, so her body didn't quite go with her face. Anna the Scarecrow with a pumpkin head and a missing tooth. Her skin was white like the grubs you find under logs. Or maybe not quite as white as that, but almost. Not coppery like Liss's. Her eyes were a weird color. Mom's were coffee like her hair, Dad's were the gray-green of dusty moss, but hers were like puddles in fall with golden-orange reflecting through the brown.

"You look too much like your father and me to be someone else's kid," said her mother.

Anna pushed her bangs from her face to see if she'd look more like Mom. She didn't. Maybe more like Dad. She didn't like that, and pulled them back in place.

Her mother had to be right.

"Can we have the cake for dinner and the roast beef for dessert?" asked Anna.

Dad laughed. Mom didn't. "You wouldn't eat any meat if we did that," she said.

They had the roast beef from Uncle Jeffrey's cows and green beans and potatoes from Dad's garden. They almost always had potatoes, which could last the winter in cold barrels in the basement. "All local," said Dad. "No pesticides. If only that was the mandate for crops here, by God, I'd love doin' my inspections."

"The standards are horrible, we know," said Mom. "Just make sure to keep your job."

Even after carrot cake, Anna dragged. While Mom washed dishes, she took out her theory book and played the new chromatic scale over and over, but her fingers didn't move as fast as usual. Slow was good, Laine had said so. Then Spring, with attention to the notes and bars. *"Let's hear you try with the energy back in it."* But the flower petals wilted.

A deep voice cut through the noise, the fading flowers. "Take a break," said Dad.

Anna's hands tightened. She had to get this right. "No."

"Stop it. You're exhausting yourself." She couldn't tell which Dad he was—the gentle one who understood the things she didn't know how to say, or the scary one who yelled and stormed, mostly at her mother.

She pressed a hand to the keys, but his eyes were hard arrows, the green in them spiking out. Standing over her, low on the bench, he was twice as big as Laine. At least.

"Stop bangin' on that piano. We're going to the park."

He took her by the arm and they walked to the car, insects still scratching her throat. "Have fun," called Mom as the door closed. Did she see the two Dads too?

They drove to the playground circled by trees and trails and a river that led to the ocean, a walk from the Marina where Mom sometimes brought her in the summer to do nature crafts with kids who talked and laughed and yelled a lot, broke the crayons and spilled the paint and split wafer cookies in half to share. The radio played one of Dad's favorite songs: *"If you drink don't drive, do the watermelon crawl."* It didn't make any sense to Anna, but he sang along. His voice was much better than the singer's, which seemed to be off key on purpose. A tenor, Mom called him, more chocolate than watermelon or twanging guitar.

They got out and Anna ran to the swing set. She did the Spider, twirlingveryfast, again and again until it wasn't scary and the high-pitched jolt in her stomach felt like excitement. She'd show Liss! She looked backwards and saw her father on a bench, watching. She kicked up and swung, tilting her head back, letting her hair swish with the motion, Spring in her lungs if not in her fingers, fall starting with a very few yellow leaves in the trees she faced, her feet reaching higher than their tips. If only there was a swing set at home, if only, if only—

A seagull squawked as her feet scraped the gravel to land. She jumped off. "Want to play on the see-saw?" her father called, happy. "Or how 'bout I spin you on the merry-go-round?" She let him spin her until she was dizzy and her screams tore out and it wasn't fun anymore. They went up and down on the see-saw and he kept her in the air for almost too long. She hated that she couldn't keep him up too. She ran to the slide. Covered in metal, it burned bare legs in the summer but now it was too cold to hurt her hands. She slid down on her back and on her belly.

"We should go fishing here sometime," said Dad, pointing to the river that ran under the road and between the park's trees. "I can't believe I've never taken you fishing here."

Anna could remember fishing maybe three times, with worms that squiggled horribly. She wouldn't put them on the hooks. Last time she'd caught some flounder with both white eyes on one side next to each other. She'd watched them die in the bucket at home, their flat mouths gasping.

They walked the river path between trees and ferns turning brown, stepping on needles and springy moss and already a few leaves. Anna looked down often so the roots wouldn't trip her flat. "There used to be a mill here but it went out of business," said her father. Anna heard the gurgle of the river and, growing ever louder, the swooshing of the sea. Forest gave way to marram grass, pine path to boardwalk and sand. They followed the boardwalk past dunes of piled-up seaweed, blackgreenpurple curlybubblystrings, and out onto the dock. It was a short beach, and the water quickly became a deep basin Anna couldn't stand in. Sea gulls and cormorants flew around making hungry sounds. Two gulls held part of the same fish in their beaks and pulled at it.

"Look in the water," said Dad.

Anna followed his finger and there was something pink! A jellyfish drifting, the soft glass of its body displaying the streaky dial of its insides. There was another one, clear white and small enough to fit between Anna's thumb and pointer finger. "What are they doing there in the fall?" asked her father.

Animals that weren't supposed to be there. Anna ran to the other side to see if there were more. Then to the end of the dock. She didn't see any others, but the water was full of seaweed with fat bubbles, seaweed like strips of slimy grass and mats of curled red hair. Through layers of water, a crab followed its mechanical sideways path between rocks.

The jellyfish breathed their bodies in and their tentacles out. Sea flowers suspended, in no hurry. Maybe they lived in a different time signature from people, a dirge to their presto. There was no railing, and their stinging closeness thrilled her. Standing on the edge of the dock, she held her arms out.

"Don't jump!" yelled Dad.

Anna hadn't realized she'd been about to. She pulled her heavy crouching body back, slowly. Looked at her father whose face was thunder, who held up fists, and looked away prestissimo. She wanted to go further, to touch those things in the water that were more beautiful than anything else. Her head streamed wind-tossed tentacles.

Her father's voice was harsh and soft at the same time. "Whatever you do, don't jump."

Chapter 5: *Love Shack*

Age Sixteen

Anna's first sight of Mary Clemens was a black speck bobbing amid the crowd. As it got closer, she saw the speck wearing a hat. Closer still, a tall woman in a black pea coat with a bob of stark white hair. A grandmother from a makeover movie.

"Carrie!" Grandma pulled Mom towards her and held on. Anna edged behind and tried to read her mother's expression, but she was squished against Grandma. Anna knew her mother hated that nickname; she'd told her that, but possibly not her own mother.

One Mississippi, two Mississippi, three Mississippi... at six, Grandma pulled away. Anna watched her eyes rove up and down. "You haven't lost much of your beauty, Carrie dear, but be careful not to let your hands get too dry. You've always had finely shaped hands."

"I brought Anna with me, Mom," said Anna's mother stiffly, indicating her.

Grandma looked around, handed her luggage brusquely to Mom, walked over, and investigated Anna like an object. "This is Anna? I hardly recognize you. You've rather filled out." She grabbed Anna's shoulders with bony hands and held her at arm's length. Like Mom, she was taller, though not by much more than an inch. "Though that isn't quite true, I suppose. You're just tall. Fairly flat-figured, but you're thin. Definite potential for elegance." Potential, Anna supposed, was what you had when you were too gawky for cute but couldn't quite be said to have beauty.

The opening bars from Beethoven's Fifth ran through her ears. *Da-da-da-DUMMMM!* She wasn't sure whether to giggle or cringe.

"Where am I sleeping?" came Grandma's cheese-grater voice.

"We have a bed for you in the living room," said Mom. "I hope that's alright." It sounded tentative, not the *it had better be alright* version she'd use with Anna.

"That's fine, Carrie." Grandma began a march towards the exit, leaving daughter and granddaughter to grab her suitcases and trail her out. She acted as if she knew where the car was, though the old one had broken down a year ago and she hadn't seen the new one yet. Mom led the way to their parking place, but Grandma somehow managed to look in charge.

"You hungry, Mom?" asked Mom while Anna tried to look at the car-sparse gray expanse of parking lot instead of at her grandmother.

"I suppose I will be in a few hours."

"We have some things almost ready for dinner—salmon, Waldorf salad, fresh fruit. They'll only take a minute. And I bought a nice new vase for the living room. Online shopping is so convenient. You have to be careful if you're buying art to make sure it's genuine and reliable, of course, but it's a great place to find new artists. And it's so wonderful for Christmas presents, just wonderful. I don't know how we managed without it for all these years." She was babbling again, all the way home. "Here's the new Superstore, I don't know if you've seen it. Not that you'd be impressed coming from Westmount. They have a vegetarian section in there, so that's definitely progress. They still don't have one in our Price Saver, but I saw someone with sprouts in their cart today, and people are starting to know what frozen yogurt is."

"Progress indeed," Grandma scoffed. "Does your coffee shack make espresso yet?"

"It's a donut place, but they do now."

"Well, whatever they call it."

"Anna had a job there one summer. She can make coffee for you when you want some."

Anna didn't relish the thought of attempting an espresso for Grandma, who would demand extra foam or a more pungent brew or something. And coffee shack? Tim Horton's was no shack. It was not only the community's main hangout (Dusty's coffee sucked) but as commercial a place as any other fast food joint, using the same mass-produced recipes as they did in Montreal. Not somewhere her parents were keen for her to work, but how many money-making options were there for teenagers in West Prince? Her piano playing at Kelly's Family Restaurant could only go so far. Besides, she got free donuts. Such a slim young woman wasting her stomach on greasy food: Grandma wouldn't approve of any of it.

Mom followed an agenda once in the house: neat arrangement of suitcases, Maria Callas CD, *Anna how about you talk to your grandma at the table while I get dinner ready, maybe play dominoes* (conveniently set out). Grandma, hovering, had her mind on other things. "A bird in your living room?" she gawped.

"He's very sweet, Mom. His name's Callas, just like your favorite singer." Mom answered with her back to them, chopping celery.

"Don't tell me that thing can sing."

She sounds like me, thought Anna, for a moment surprised.

"In his own way, yes. If you want to hear music, Anna's gotten quite good at both her instruments."

"She's always been good," said Grandma dryly. "What does that bird eat?"

"Mostly his feed mix. Some leftover vegetables. Sometimes millet if he's good."

"Good for garbage disposal, I suppose. And how are things with you, Carrie-bird? Are you singing again?"

No one should call me Carrie-bird and live to tell about it, Mom had once said. Anna stifled a giggle.

"I've been in the choir for fourteen years, Mom."

"I meant *opera* singing, not that creaky amateur praise-the-Lord stuff."

"It's good practice. And I still sing my arias. There should be an opera company here soon." She worried the salmon pâté into whorls on multigrain crackers and topped them with parsley, to make up for her lying.

"Well, I don't see why you stick around when there's no culture in this place. No good men either, if that last one's any indication."

Callas cheeped while she spoke. "It sure does make an

awful sound," said Grandma, hands folded primly.

꙳

Anna arrived at her locker to find Irena leaning against it. "Where were you for lunch with Darien? I could have used some moral support!"

"Let me get my books," said Anna, scanning Irena's face. A gloat edged its way through the pouting mask.

"Not before you tell me where you were." Irena crossed her arms. In her platforms she was definitely taller than Anna, her blouse and jeans fitted, hair braided, eyebrows plucked thin and arching sternly. Anna considered shoving her.

"Just in a practice room."

"Why didn't you want to go out with us?"

"You guys needed some special time alone!" A Sarah-like smirk crossed her face. "So move, then tell me how it went."

Irena complied and Anna bent to collect her books. Irena didn't speak until she looked up.

"He's so nice, strangely polite and everything. He kept asking about my friends and school and the town. He has the cutest—do you mind if I gush a little?"

"Go ahead," Anna laughed.

"Anyway, he has the cutest smile, and he insisted on paying for everything. What a gentleman, right? I wonder if that means he likes me. He kept asking about my compositions, and my family moving here from Russia. He wanted to hear everything! OK, forget I said a little. Shut me up. He's so cute. No, beyond cute. Don't you think he's gorgeous?"

"I guess so."

"We're going to practice together today and try each other's instruments. He's never played a clarinet before. He's asked some other people to come too, so you should come with us."

"Sure." She hated the thought of watching Irena and a new love interest coo at each other, but this was her chance to corner the guy, find out if he was actually interesting. What else would she do anyway, listen to Sarah plan another fantasy date or go outside to sulk?

She slung on her backpack and started towards class.

Laine was late, which wasn't like her. Anna sat at the smaller piano and waited. Normally, she didn't practice before a tutorial. Like writing an exam, she liked to have her head clear before she started. But sitting on the bench in the utter quiet of a soundproof music room provoked too many voices: *That isn't quite true, you're just tall. Does your coffee shack make lattes yet? We only started dating recently.* Get started on this and the path of order would unravel. She slammed into the Presto movement from Ravel's Piano Concerto. The concert piece was a speeding train, a manic swinging bridge, the only way to banish—others' words? Dust.

"Your playing has energy today." Laine's lanky figure stood above her, hair askew. *She moves like a cat*, Sarah had said once, and they'd had fun theorizing ways the awkward woman could have learned her stealth. Anna imagined that Laine's brusque demeanour must block the bile of others' lives from her mind. The thought was likely false but comforted her anyway. "Though I'm pretty sure it's called Presto for a reason, and not Prestissimo."

Anna was an emotional pianist the way some people were emotional eaters, and Laine knew that by now. Anna simply grinned at the accusation. "Just warming up."

"If you don't slow down, I'll have to bring out the metronome." Laine swung herself into place at the grand piano bench. "Are you nervous?"

"Not really. Well, not about the concert," she amended. "It's not like this is my first."

"True, but I was nervous at least the first twenty times I did it." So casual, like dropping a pebble into a lake, stirring the waters. "Do you want to go over the program again, tell me if it's OK?"

I don't see how we could change it at this point, Anna would have said to her mother. But not to Laine. She nodded. Laine rummaged through her briefcase and pulled out a typed sheet.

Fall Program with Pianist Anna Stern
Accompanying Pianist Laine Winters
Island Symphony Orchestra

Anna scanned the program. Start off with Beethoven for a dramatic entrance, then Chopin, Ravel, and Saint-Saens, ending on *The Carnival of the Animals*. Anna had suggested that because she knew Laine would laugh. She liked how the composer's "animals" included things like fossils, pianists, and a jab at music critics—"people with long ears."

"What do you want me to play now?" asked Anna, setting down the program.

"Everything's OK?"

"Yeah."

Laine paused. "Let me hear you play that Presto a little bit slower. Try not to muck up any notes this time."

It was hard to get the zest back. Anna's fingers felt too measured for the swinging-bridge rhythm. "I'm sorry," she muttered as she finished, pressing her hands together to avoid banging them on the keys. She began again. Faster but not much better.

"Let's take a break from that," said Laine. "Play something you want to play."

She plunged into a piano version of Wagner's *Ride of the Valkyries*. Ay-a, Ay-a. Don't think of that, just move your hands into a thunderous crescendo.

"You like that song," said Laine. "Want me to add it to your repertoire?"

Adrenaline. A splintering sound. "No!"

"A song for just yourself. I understand."

That wasn't it, and Anna didn't want to clarify. It was nice of Laine not to ask questions.

"Feel up to practicing another concert piece?"

"Maybe *Marche Funèbre*."

"Go ahead."

The Chopin funeral march was detached, hollow, with bars of measured grief periodically interrupted by bars of furious jollity. Weight gone delicate. Anger in a happy mask.

"Let's hear the first few bars again."

For the rest of the lesson they went through the Chopin, phrase by phrase, polishing. Anna didn't notice the time until the bell rang.

"As soon as you're able," said Laine as Anna shrugged

into her backpack, "I'd like you to work on Ravel's Presto again."

Anna looked up at her. From that angle, the sun through the music room blinds threw a stripe across her face, and Anna felt a brief pang of attraction. She looked down at Laine's long knotted hands and saw the same fingers that corrected her piano playing every week. She willed the pang away.

Anna disliked Math class even more than she'd disliked Chorus in the years it was mandatory. She sat by herself, doodling while Michelle and Sean helped each other with equations or wrote each other notes (she couldn't tell which) at the desks in front of her. Anna's Masterpiece #1: The Lopsided Espresso Cup! Anna's Masterpiece #2: The Grand Piano with Scowly Face! (Come to think of it, that face looked a little like her grandmother's.)

"To find the circumference of a circle, you . . ."

Masterpiece #3: The Bored Chipmunk. Masterpiece #4: The Evil Cooking Pot. Masterpiece #5: Cartoon Anna, Onstage in Sleek Dress. Her face was too thin (if only!) and her eyelashes were too long. The piano didn't have a scowly face. She drew the silhouette of a swan behind her. That wasn't a swan, that was an awkward-looking duck. She was glad when the bell interrupted her failed attempts to fix its bill.

She grabbed her clarinet from her locker and headed for practice room 102, their usual spot. Chen and her trombone were already there. "Hey. Are Irena and Darien coming to this one?" she asked.

"I don't know. Probably. What do you want to play?"

"How about the German hymns?"

"Sure." They searched their folders for the medley they were practicing for concert band.

They heard laughter before the door swung open. Irena had a hand on Darien's shoulder. Anna was relieved that his wasn't on hers.

"Irena was just telling me a joke," said Darien. He turned to her. "You should tell it to your friends."

"Oh, they've heard it before."

"I've got another one," said Darien. "An Irishman, a Scotsman, and a Frenchman walk into a bar. What an excellent example of cross-cultural integration!"

"They're missing the non-Europeans," said Chen over Irena's laughter.

"So they are. We need a search warrant!"

Irena scowled. "Should we practice?" she said, opening her clarinet case. Darien opened his alto sax case and secured his neck strap.

"You know, you really shouldn't have brought that in here with us," said Anna.

"Why?"

"Men aren't allowed to have sax with minors."

What had possessed her to be so bold? Anna didn't say bold things around guys, not since the old stalker days anyway. But he actually seemed to be laughing.

"That's not even funny," said Irena.

Chen started playing the German hymns and the others went quiet, readying instruments and stands. Anna watched Darien and Irena, noting the intricacies of their little two-person dance that only Irena seemed aware of. Irena leaned in, Darien adjusted his reed. Irena smiled slightly, Darien scratched his ear. If Darien were an Anna Masterpiece, he'd be The Bored Chipmunk. The Gorgeous Bored Chipmunk.

Chen finished with a bom-bom-bom sound. "Alright," said Irena brightly, "let's try this all together now! On the count of three—" A nod towards Darien.

Battle of the clarinets? Bring it on! Anna drew breaths like gulps of water, holding until her stomach strained, smoothing the slurs of her First Clarinet part fluid with her tongue. She noticed Irena doing the same, holding on extra long for dramatic effect. She couldn't curb a glance at Darien. Burnished hair, symmetrical Greek nose. Like Irena, no flaws were detectable, no matter how she looked. Don't look. Irena was looking too. Eyes on music. Music. It was nothing, Anna would say if asked, she was just looking up in a state of melodic transport. Es ist genug. It is enough. But it wasn't.

"Let's switch instruments," said Irena after the hymns.

"And play the same thing?" asked Darien.

"First we'd better see if we can get any sound out of them," said Anna.

Irena offered Darien her clarinet, leaving Anna to hand hers to Chen and accept the trombone. "You purse your lips and blow into it like this," said Chen.

"I know how to blow in a mouthpiece."

But her attempts to control the notes with the slide resulted in random sputtering sounds. Try and it squelched, try and it squawked. Chen had a much easier time getting the clarinet. Well, no one could call it a hard instrument, thought Anna. Meanwhile Irena played an entire, clear melody on the alto sax.

What go-oes up
Must co-ome down
Spinning wheel
Got-ta go rooound

She must have played one before.

"You should try my alto, Anne," said Darien. "It's way easier. It is Anne, right?"

"Anna."

"Wow, I'm sorry."

"No problem. They sound alike."

"Half note versus whole note. One's twice the length of the other. I really should've remembered."

"No, it's fine."

"Irena, can you get Anna a new reed?"

Anna watched her dip silently into the alto case, her face hidden. Deliberately, she was sure.

Accept saxophone, a heavy golden body, its weight unexpected. Tighten neck strap, pulling hair casually away from neck so Darien can see its full slenderness. Lick reed, taste slightly sweetened tongue depressor. Wipe mouthpiece clean of remnants of Irena's spit. Two ways she'd seen people hold a sax: to the side or between their legs. She tried holding it to the side but found she couldn't trust the weight, and switched. Accidentally looked up towards the acute triangle of Darien's chest. Effects like fractals in her pulse. Look down so you can catch enough air to blow into the thing. She hoped she wasn't blushing.

You played it the same way as a clarinet, only spreading your fingers wider and feeding more air. It wasn't hard. Fingers could relax, didn't have to press so precisely against the holes because there were keys that did the job. A G was sonorous, filling the air. It was also a little sharp, so she adjusted. Irena was back on clarinet, showing off her fancy fingerwork with cadenzas and crescendos, but Anna, Anna was louder. She who was sometimes a soloist but never louder. She paused, then tried a scale. A few mistaken notes, the ones that differed, but she figured it out quickly enough.

"Can I try the hymns?" she paused long enough to ask Darien.

"Sure. You just picked up that thing; do you know what the notes are?"

"Sort of," she admitted. "I can hear the pitches but don't know all the fingerings." Fingerings—God, how much more awkward could this get?

Darien seemed unbothered. He leaned toward her, demonstrating note by note. "Here, this one's G—"

She launched into the scale again—the G scale was nearly the same as the clarinet's C scale. Darien shuffled the sheet of hymns onto her music stand. *Es ist genug.* She began. The instrument had a clear tone and crescendoed easily. It wasn't difficult, she thought, a giddy smoothness in her chest. There was something ascendant about it. She imagined lighthouses, promontories, vistas viewed from overhead. When the hymns were done she was ready to play again, to devour the hours in a sound which was simply more.

"Good tone." Anna started, resenting the interruption. But it was Darien.

"Oh. Thanks."

I want to play this. I want to have one. No, not Darien,

stupid, the saxophone! What was Irena doing? Looking carefully down at the floor. Oh. She should have a turn with the alto again. After all, it was a music orgy. Everyone was swapping spittle. Even blondes whose elegance surpassed *potential.*

"We should play the hymns together," said Chen. "We still haven't done that."

The others mumbled agreement.

"I'll count us in," said Chen. "One-two—" They made a muffled entrance, clarinets droning. Dead leaves—insulting— no, honestly, hymns had the energy of dead leaves. Then Anna came in, and found she could be heard even over the trombone.

She gave the saxophone back to Irena to play another jazz tune, Irena whose smile was wary, and let Chen play her clarinet again, Chen whose grin was eager. Darien the jazz man, Darien the prince, whoever he was, watched Irena. The attention he'd shown Anna had been brief and cordial, and couldn't have been more.

She didn't have a clarinet tutorial that day, but she stopped at Michael O'Hara's office during his prep period and her supposed "practice session"—she'd grown too old for teachers to hover around censoring her time. He sat scribbling in his notebook with a stubby pen. She waited for him to look up, glancing at the tiny formations of music notes and words scattered at odd angles, all too small to read.

So this was a creative mind at work. It looked ...messy.

"What do you want?"

"Hi. I just wanted to say I'm thinking of taking up a third

instrument."

"Which one would that be now?" He rolled the pencil between his fingers.

"Alto sax, if the school has any extra. If not, maybe a tenor."

"And you want to do this while you're prepping for a concert *and* have an upcoming solo in my band piece."

"Yes. I need to do something new, or fun, or just—something."

"Well, fine. Go check the shelves. And don't stop practicing your solo."

She found a battered case without an owner, A.S. #8 painted in white on its crumbling leather. The instrument inside was dulled with scratches so most of the original gold tone had turned to muted silver. A dent marked the right side of the bell. Its former occupant had left a pile of colored candy wrappers in the hollow with the neck strap. There was a lot of room to hide small things in that hollow. Or salamanders—she should have grown out of those silly thoughts.

She tried it out, having persuaded Michael-never-Mike to sell her a reed. The sound quality was as resonant as the other's, or more. The thought crossed her mind that maybe instruments got better with age like cheeses did, and she laughed at its absurdity. Occam's razor: the older instruments were probably just better made.

Alright, Anna, a license to be loud! Now better practice some piano. She'd wasted enough time—

On the piano bench, she opened A.S. #8 and sent a high G keening to the ceiling.

7

Grandma waited with a plate of shortbread and a teapot. At least she had the baking part of grandma-hood down, thought Anna wryly.

"What's that thing you're dragging, Anna?"

"A saxophone." *What does it look like, a weapon of mass destruction?*

"How many things do you play now?"

"I'm just starting on this one."

"Don't get distracted from the piano now," Grandma raised a finger. "Your mother got distracted, and look how that turned out. But you don't just have talent. You have time."

Anna thought of all the time her mother had spent, on a failing relationship and on her. "It's music," she told her grandmother. "It's the same thing."

Grandma gave a huff of discontent. "I hope you'll stick around for a while and not run off to your father's place. I have plans to take you shopping."

"Yeah, I'll do it," she said, aware of the edge in her voice. "But I've got to do my book report tonight."

The house smelled like disinfectant, also Grandma's doing. Shopping and buying. Anna's friends would envy her, but she hated the idea of trailing a griping grandma through the mall's dully lit stores with their vapid, tuneless music. She poured herself some tea, grabbed a piece of shortbread, and moved towards the stairs.

"You're going to eat that messy food in your room?" Grandma called as she climbed.

Too late.

She didn't like writing reports. Who really did? She read over her notes, hoping they'd start going together at some point, unsure if any of them made sense.

Book Report: The Pigman

(In margins, a jowled pig, feet deep in mud, top hat on head, straw sticking out from its mouth.)

Thesis: Love is ~~the main force in the book but~~ *But the characters just die don't they*

All the characters the Pigman loved die except for the kids but then he dies so it's like they've traded places

Book is honest about stuff, not always flattering (Pigman's name, Pigman is big kid, parents are lame)

Real thesis: Love is a force that promises meaning but destroys it things substance. It wrecks the stuff it makes happen?

"Anna, come down and help me set the table!"

She drew a line through "Real thesis" and went downstairs. Her mother was home. Mashed potatoes, salad and ham were served. After dinner she would give the book report a break and brainstorm excuses for getting out of the house. Then practice.

Mom had other plans. "Anna, I've got something in my room I want you to have a look at." She only had things in her room for Anna to look at when some Christmas article of clothing was slightly too small—daughter-sized. But there was no clothes pile on Mom's cream-colored quilt. The room was as always, immaculate. Carpet, curtains, bureau, everything was "creamy white," the color she'd painted the house after Dad left. Anna saw little difference between that and the dingy white it had replaced, but apparently the house was "so much fresher now." There was a doily on the bureau topped with a carved wooden bird, a Botticelli on the wall, and beeswax candles in the window. A well-dusted shrine not meant to be touched, but no clothes out anywhere. Strange how this one slight fact could be unnerving.

"You're smart, Anna." Mom's fingers briskly sorted her own hair. "You're good at planning things, right?"

"What am I supposed to say to that—no, I'm stupid?"

"Be serious for once. Alright, sorry for babbling. But you know Tom. My mother doesn't know he exists. We made plans to get together tonight and I'm wondering if—well, since your grandmother goes to bed early there's probably no need for you to do anything, I'm fairly confident but—"

"You mean you want me to cover for you?" Anna's laugh was abrupt, incredulous.

"Well ...yes. That is what I'm asking." Mom laughed, a small lost sound, and turned towards the window.

Would Grandma say this was another instance of her daughter getting distracted?

Anna imagined herself telling Irena: My grandma wants to take me shopping and my mom wants me to cover for her while she sneaks out to have sex with her coworker dude! No, she wouldn't tell Irena. Not Sarah either, who would make too big a deal of it. Darien would think it was hilarious, if she knew him better. Stupid thought.

"It shouldn't be too hard. I should be able to get out fine."

Funny, Mom talking about having to "get out" of her own house.

"I'll leave early in the morning so it will be alright."

"No worries, Mom. I'll make sure your hot date is kept top secret. I'll do a better job than the CIA, even." She flounced out of the room whistling the tune to "Love Shack."

"Anna," a thin voice followed, "please try to be quieter."

A love shack is a little old place where

We can get to-ge-therrr

Love shack bay-ay-beeeee

She slammed the door to her room where two clothes piles had heaped up in the corner, not yet put away, and papers fanned across the floor. She plugged in her earphones and turned to Wagner's Ring cycle. "Love Shack" superimposed itself on the operatic words.

Huggin' and a kissin', dancin' and a lovin'

Wearin' next to nothing, 'cause it's hot as an oven

Her mother had had sex before, obviously. Otherwise she wouldn't be alive. She reckoned her mother hadn't had sex in a lot of years. No wonder she was turned on by this Tom guy. At Chen and Michelle's birthday sleepover (a no-guys affair), Sarah had tiptoed down into the basement with a story of overheard groaning and grunting in the master bedroom. The twins had exchanged horrified glances. Knowing Sarah, she might have made it all up. She'd imitated the sounds: "Uh, uh, ooh! Oh oh oh oh!"

Tom would bend towards Mom at the door, take her coat, place it on a wire hanger in a closet full of hunting jackets. He'd usher her into an immaculate creamy-white house with IKEA furniture. He would have baked some lasagne in the oven even though it wasn't his forte, or maybe grilled some sausages for their midnight meal. If he really wanted her, both. She'd insist on having some fruits or vegetables and he'd drag out a bag of sorry-looking McIntosh apples, on sale for $2.99, that had gotten bruised in the trunk on the way home from the grocery. Tom would suggest they go to Kelly's Restaurant the next time they got together and Mom would stammer some excuse. It wouldn't be safe to make out to her own offspring's romantic piano tunes, she'd think.

"None of that, then," Tom would croon into her ear. During dinner they'd gape and giggle at each other. He'd feed her a sausage, which would make her think of his dick. They'd put dark chocolate in each other's mouths and get it smeared all over their faces. Maybe lick it off. Who knew translators' ideas of foreplay? He'd undo her bra right in the dining room, suck on her breasts, and come up with a sound like a plunger unsticking from a toilet.

Anna's insides curdled.

She would spend the rest of the evening in her room,

not planning, not working (except the music which shouldn't count anyway), listening for footsteps.

Now Brünnhilde sang:

Bang, bang, bang, on the door, baby.

That song was really fucking stupid.

Chapter 6: *Washing Machine*

Age Six

It was jacket weather, trees and ground collapsing together in waterfalls of sun-colored, fire-colored, tiger-colored leaves. Liss stood on the grass hill that had almost completely turned brown, the one facing the school or away from the school depending which way you looked. Liss looked away, towards the oak tree and the four pine trees and the road where cars move like snails. Away so the sun shimmered and blended the edges of her into the edgeless scene.

"I'm the Queen of the Castle!"

Anna wanted to be the Queen of the Castle, but Liss was the one who'd made the fort. Liss was the one on top of the hill and she was the one looking up, behind.

"What do I get to be?"

"You're the Dirty Rascal!"

"No I'm not!"

"You are too! And you know why? 'Cause you're not tough enough to beat me!"

Another Anna rushed up the hill, barrelled into Liss and started punching. Another Anna was six feet tall, as big as her dad, and stood there with the sun coming from her body. Another Anna knew exactly what to do.

"Look," said Liss to Anna, still on the low ground, "you

don't even know how to fight. That's 'cause you ain't got any sisters."

"Ain't isn't even a word," said Anna. That was what her mom said.

"No, it's ain't *ain't* a word. Everyone knows that."

Anna's stomach felt like a sewer pipe. She noticed something climbing on her shoe. It was a red ant—she must have stepped on one of their nests! She screamed and jumped away.

"What's wrong?" Liss turned to face her.

"It's a, it's nothing, just an old red ant."

"You better be careful, you know how they bite. Those things could kill you."

7

They had started doing journals in English class. Anna hated her handwriting which looked like threads pulling in all directions. She spent most of her time drawing pictures. After the date (she couldn't tell if the 7 was backwards or forwards), she took her red crayon and outlined a giant insect. She gave it a pair of crunching jaws and tried to make the eyes look mean. In a speech bubble she wrote *I kill yo yuo* –that didn't look right, so she wrote in her name instead. *I kill yo yuo Anna.*

After that was chorus: "Everybody on the risers!" Sopranos in front, Anna and Liss side by side. They were learning a song about peace with words in Latin. Anna wondered if Mr. Wilder, the teacher, could speak Latin or just sing in it. What country did people speak Latin in? Maybe his family came from there. The kids were noisy with their words she could just half-hear and their snorting laughs and one or two with gum which wasn't allowed, Mr. Wilder calling "Spit that out in the garbage can!"

"I got gum too," Liss whispered. "I'll give you some after school."

"You're not sposed to," whispered Chen beside them.

"You weren't sposed to hear," hissed Liss. "And plus gum's fine for after school."

The song went something like "Donanoby spachum pachum." The words on the page didn't look quite like that, but that's how they sounded. Liss's voice was loud, like her mother's. It cut across the others in a lighthouse beam of sound. No, a lighthouse beam wouldn't be so much like the crystal in the breakfront, wouldn't be so see-through and breakable, wouldn't rise quite so much. Copper hair and a shirt that showed her collarbones and stage lights just bright enough to read what Anna could read of those funny words, just enough to make Liss's face look soft and bits of gold catch in the little threads sticking out from her clothes. Something lightened in Anna's ribcage. She felt a need to press against the air. She pushed her voice up and up, following Liss, trying to be more than what she heard. And her wave-like voice was loud, so loud she was bound to be noticed, pronouncing Spachum Pachum with every sound perfect from her lips. She was above, hovering up there with millions of stage lights, where the tips of curtains hung just at the edge of sight.

She ended a beat after the rest of them, showing how long she could hold on.

Mr. Wilder kept her after class. She waited, pulse ticking

like a sped-up metronome, as everyone else ran and shuffled noisily out of class. Liss put gum in her mouth on the way out and handed some to Michelle. Anna probably wouldn't get any now.

"Anna, your singing is lovely." The teacher, a wall with curly hair and a tie, was right in front of her.

He'd noticed how far she'd gone. Maybe he'd seen her fly to the curtains for a moment. Had she been like Liss? But Liss hadn't been kept after class.

"You know when you're playing one piano and your teacher's playing the big one, how you try to match her notes?"

"Yeah."

"As I've said, I'd like you to do this with singing. We're a chorus, and the point is to have a sound that blends together, not to have one person stick out. If someone's too loud or off key or something, it makes the whole thing sound bad. Listen and try to match the people around you."

She hadn't been off key! She wasn't stupid, she knew that much. Did she sound bad? She needed to ask people, 'cause the Chorus teacher didn't know anything.

She thought of asking Liss or her mother, but she couldn't ask someone who sounded like lit-up glass or someone who sounded like an ocean. She could ask her father but he might yell.

Mom sang in a choir at church every Sunday. She wore her best dress and stood in the back row. Anna usually had to go to Sunday School where a grumpy lady told a Bible story and the kids, louder than Anna wanted them to be, colored pictures. In the stories people had weird jobs like selling doves at the market and raising sheep. There weren't any dove-sellers on P.E.I. If they were good, these people were forgiven and sometimes brought back to life and given feasts, but if they were bad—

On Sunday nights she dreamed of hell with its tree-high tongues of fire, of sin that burned like coal in everyone's hearts because some old relative way back when had eaten a poison apple. If life was such that some great-great-grandma doing wrong could mess up her kids' kids' kids forever, there was no way she was getting to Heaven. She did too many things wrong. She snuck candy when she should be doing theory pages and stayed up in secret to play with stuffed animals and sometimes even lied. She broke the lamp in the living room while running through and was horrified by the small glass icebergs that fell to the floor—she sinned without even trying. She dreamed of the devil's shriveled red monkey face, his sharp-toothed grin that could chew her to pieces.

Sometimes while coloring her pages, she heard the organ chiming through and the choir with it. She heard her mother's voice, clearer and more on key than any other. On holidays she could listen to choir and organ, that strange giant piano, up close, proud and solemn in her family's wooden pew. The choir was dignified, like a row of candles. She wished she were as old and beautiful and important. She wanted to play the organ someday, but of course she wasn't pure enough for a church ritual like that. It wouldn't be right to have an organ player who dreamed of the fires of hell every week, who was secretly scared she was going there.

"Come to my house after school," Liss asked her. So

Anna went to Pine Grove with a little yellow note in slanted writing she couldn't read, and the secretary with big shoulders wrote her a pass for Bus 54.

"Got any candy, Joe?" Liss yelled as they climbed the bus stairs. The driver held out a bag of licorice nibs. Anna had never had a bus driver. Such a wonderful thing, a man in a pointy blue hat who gave out candy.

Liss grabbed a handful and started towards the back. Some loud older boys had claimed the back seats, so they sat two seats in front of all the noise. Liss snuggled in by the window, leaving Anna to squeeze between the seat and a curved hump that jutted up from the floor. Her legs had to rest on top of it. But at least she had the candy, a few bright pieces closed in her fist. She'd make them last 'til Liss's house.

The bus played country music, the kind her dad listened to in the truck, a song about a sad girl. Liss sang along to all the words, though it was harder to hear the light in her voice over the dull radio. "Come on, Anna, you gonna sing?" she cut in during the middle. When Anna did nothing, she broke back into song. Anna couldn't see much out the window, but what she did see was great, the bus's extra height turning tractors and barns into farm toys.

"Bump!" yelled the kids around them, and the bus lurched and Anna flew a little off the seat and her legs fell hard on the solid curved hump and her hand uncurled and the candy bits bounced on the floor. Her legs hurt. She looked at her hands which were red and sticky. She licked them. "Bump!" She was thrown up again and back down, landing into Liss. "Ow," they said at the same time, then laughed.

Liss grabbed Anna's hand and nudged her. "This is our stop." Anna was glad her hand was licked clean as they skipped into the yard. A clipped lawn with short clipped trees, a driveway made of pebbles, a big gray house, a porch with potted flowers and chairs. The window on the door looked like a fan with flowers drawn in the glass. Anna wasn't sure exactly how to tell an old house from a new house, but she thought this one looked new.

"Hello," said a face at the door. Liss's mother didn't look like her at all. She was round and white like a biscuit, with her blond hair up and fancy work clothes on. Then Anna remembered that Liss was adopted, and noticed the two little bodies in the background. The twins looked like her mother, except their shirts were pink with animal faces on them. When Liss's mom told them to say hi, they darted behind her and stood watching from across the room.

The inside looked new, too, but it had cabinets of old stuff—flowered dishes, little glass angels, paperweights with more flowers in them (some even looked real). Liss grabbed Anna's hand and pulled her into a room-sized explosion. Footsteps followed them.

"This is the playroom," came Liss's mom's voice while Anna gaped. "I'm sorry it's messy."

It was huge, white and unfinished, with slides and Barbies and stuffed animals and pieces of costumes and giant trucks clumped on the floor. In one corner was a pretend oven with too-bright plastic foods that could fit in Anna's hand, in another a puppet theater with hollow felt animals slumped on the floor in front. The walls were splendid. Colored markers had drawn and written all over them. *I was here, L.M., Love,*

Piece, Shcool is garbidge, MOZART ALWAYS, handprints, squiggles, cats, trains, dinosaurs, and the smallest wall covered in music notes.

"You can write on the walls?" asked Anna.

"Yeah. We got lots of markers and stuff." Liss balanced to the corner through the mess and rustled through a pile of puppets. She came up with pink, orange, blue, green, red and black. "What color d'you want? Dibs green."

You weren't allowed to write on the walls, not anywhere that Anna knew of. But the twins stepped up and fought over the orange. Anna backed away from the screaming into a wall with a train and squiggles chugging across it, but Liss dropped the markers, grabbed the twin punching the other and pulled her off. "*You* take the red, Katie." She forced a marker into the girl's hand. "And Cassie, you take the pink." Liss stuck the orange in her own pocket. The twins went off to scribble across the back wall.

The world and its rules had done backflips into crazyland. Anna took the blue and started to draw a castle. It looked like a box with funny pipes sticking out. She didn't want to scratch it out because it was on a wall. How did you spell castle again?

"Come listen to me practice." Anna frowned at the lopsided castle. She didn't want to just leave it there, but she followed Liss.

"Mom got the piano the year before I was adopted," said Liss. She led Anna to a music room where it stood between music stands and violin cases and drums. A lace cloth sat on top of it, and on top of that a statue of a man's head, glaring.

"How old were you?"

"Just a baby. I don't remember anything." She said that

proudly. "The twins are in piano too. Mom uses these tapes on them because she wants them to learn to play faster."

"What tapes?"

Liss settled herself on the piano bench, not listening. She played some scales, then began a Mozart minuet. Anna couldn't remember which one it was, but she recognized it as something she'd practiced with Mrs. Hobbes. Liss missed a note and started again. Her hands dragged too much. "Try it faster," Laine would say. It was an easy song.

I'm better at it than she is.

Anna found a chair and sat. It was across the room, had a music stand in front, and wasn't very comfortable, but where else could she go?

Liss turned pages noisily and started another song. Still dragging. Anna wondered about the tapes. Would they make the twins better? Had Liss listened to them too? In the corner was a piece of furniture with shelves of music books on top and shelves of tapes stacked on the bottom, hundreds of shiny cases. Liss's mom had so many more tapes than her mom did. Was she allowed to look?

I want to play one.

Liss's hair glowed in this light too, but it didn't look magical. Her back was so thin. She kept playing, song after song. Anna was bored.

I want to listen to some real music.

She thought about building a real castle on the hill in the schoolyard. It would have tinted windows like Uncle Theo's van, so she could see out but no one could see her in there. She'd wear a blue cape that sparkled like the sky and eat candy on golden plates. She'd keep a tape recorder and headphones inside and decide what rules to make for the world. She wouldn't allow there to be bugs.

"Now I'm gonna practice violin." She hadn't realized that Liss had finished. "Listen to this." Liss put the instrument to her chin and sat in the chair beside Anna, which also had a music stand in front. "This is a chromatic scale." She, Anna, knew what a chromatic scale was. She wasn't stupid.

The violin hummed through semitones. It fit against Liss's chin as if it had been built to go exactly there. Then a song that Anna didn't recognize, mostly in key and quivering slightly the way violins did, coming from a honeysweet hollow caveplace no piano could. Liss who could play two instruments and sing. No wonder Anna was better at piano. Maybe if she'd had Liss's mother she would have been able to do more things. Maybe if she'd had special tapes. Or maybe she'd never have been able to.

I'm bored, she tried to pretend, tried to wish herself back to the castle. She heard the twins screaming at each other. Footsteps came into the room and Liss's playing stopped.

"Are you girls hungry?"

"Yeah," said Anna before she thought whether that was polite.

"Good, I've got cookies and milk on the table."

The cookies were chocolate chip and dry, all the same roundness and size. Anna wondered what was wrong with them. Oh yeah, they probably came from a box.

Something scratched at the door and Liss's mom got up to open it. Black fluff bounced in, jumped up, and pressed its paws against her. Liss broke off a piece of her cookie and held it under the table. Anna waited for her mom to say something.

You weren't supposed to feed animals junk food. But the dog pranced over and grabbed the piece of cookie in its mouth without a word being said. It dropped the piece on the floor, leaned its head down, chomped and gulped.

"How do you like school, Anna?" asked Liss's mom.

Anna found herself answering a bunch of questions she didn't really want to answer. Where did she live? What did her parents do? How long had she been playing piano? What kind of music did she like most? She didn't know what to say to that one.

"Anna likes everything," said Liss. "Like me."

Anna pictured the house as a washing machine. People like Liss were drawn into the middle of it, tossed around with toys and dogs and music stands and soapsuds, and came out clean.

"Let's play Land of Music," she said, not wanting to think of washing machines.

"No, that's for the grass fort." They were standing in the living room next to the music room, a round place with bookshelves and squishy blue furniture. Liss spread her arms above the corner easy chair. "This is my beauty salon. Do you want a haircut?"

"Sure. How much is it?" Anna sat down.

"Free for you, ma'am. Wait while I get my things." Liss went off and came back holding a spray bottle, a mirror and scissors.

You aren't going to really cut my hair

"You'd look lovely with a little trim on that side" and Liss edged closer, sliver of metal shining in her hand breath in face broken rhythm hair spilling across Anna's eyes *this is just pretend* snipping sound and something falling in her lap.

Anna screamed.

"Shut up."

Her ribs banged against arms stiff at her sides like a toy soldier her eyes too weak water shivering in them

"You look really pretty. Here, look in the mirror."

Her reflection was forced on her, face all puffed, a chunk on the right side of her hair came down just past her ear when the rest was to her shoulder, too blurred to see right because she couldn't stop crying.

"You said you wanted a haircut. Want me to fix it?"

"No!" *You can't fix it you can never fix it I've come out the wrong end dirty*

"Wanna play Land of Music now?"

She gulped so she could talk. "No."

"Wanna see my horse collection?"

"No."

"You sure you don't want me to fix it?" The scissors flashed again.

Anna tried to think of what could fix it. Not the scissors that had ruined it. The boring aisles of church came to mind, the Sunday School lessons with that cross-voiced lady who had a nest for hair.

"God'll fix it!" she sobbed. The Sunday School lady said he'd answer prayers so if she prayed with a pure conscience and a pure heart, he'd have to listen, wouldn't he, like grown-ups didn't? If it just took him seven days to make the world, hair shouldn't take very long, unless he had a waiting list but she didn't think God worked like doctors.

"God's not even real," said Liss.

"Yeah, he is."

Liss set down the mirror and bottle and scissors. "How do you know? 'Cause your Sunday School teacher told you?"

"'Cause everyone knows he is." She felt her chopped off hair. All wrecked.

"I proved that he's not. I prayed for stuff before and it never happened."

"You probably didn't have a pure conscience when you did it," said Anna.

"Go into church next time and just ask him to talk to you. Say you won't believe him if he won't talk to you, and see if he says anything back."

The chair pressed into her uncomfortably. Her eyes stung like when her mother cut onions too close by. She'd never asked God to talk to her. Wasn't that Interrupting, and Not Polite? What would his voice sound like? A man who'd turned into a burning bush, and terrified shepherds, and flooded the whole world—she wasn't sure she wanted to know. Thunder shivered her mind. He would be mad, probably, and what would he do then?

"Anna, you OK?"

In the Castle of Treble Clef, a red cape and solid gold scepter waited for the Other Anna. She moved towards the throne. Fires burned at either side, piled with wood, pulsing to Stravinsky's *The Rite of Spring*. She knew this one from Mom's tapes: the Sacrificial Dance, percussion thunderous. She couldn't get too close or they would burn off layers of her skin. A spark jumped towards her. A gravelly voice called down from above: "God wants to talk to you."

A goblin face moved towards her. She blinked and was back at the kitchen table. Not a goblin—a man her mom had gotten to teach her French. His face looked like it belonged to a cliff, all points and tiny indents. Sharp eyebrows. "Bone-joor."

He wasn't talking about God. He was saying words she couldn't understand.

"Bon-jour. Say it."

A leash closed around her throat.

"Say it."

"Bone-joor." The word tasted heavy, strange.

"Bohn-joooor," the French tutor repeated. "Now body parts. Les yeux." His thin finger pointed at her eyes while his own stared down. "Lez yeuh."

Lez yeuh, luh nay, lah boosh.

A devil face, frowning in judgement.

"Lay sheuveu."

Leaning in, pawing hair her mom had said she'd fix and cut around a bowl until she looked like a boy too shaggy too short

Face with nostrils like caves and clunk of bootsteps in the hall sour somersaults in stomach (didn't know the word for stomach, had he leaned in and said it?)

Body shivered as if something was clawing it from inside

Threw up on the floor.

Are you OK are you OK

Mom saying things like sorry, my daughter must be sick, we'll try again, the devil-voice saying take your time.

Another Anna threw the golden scepter and it clanged

across the room.

Our Father who art in Heaven
She pulled on her tights.
Hallowed be thy name
Buttoned her white dress in place.
"Hurry up, Anna, we can't be late for church."
Thy kingdom come
Buckled her white shoes. Snapped out the door to where the car grumbled, warming up.

No one from school was in her Sunday School class, since Pine Grove was so far away from where she lived. The other kids chattered while she stared at the blackboard with colored-in sheep taped along the side. She could hear the organ going in the church, its full-bodied formal drone. The instrument's wall of pipes scared her, so she couldn't go near without slowing down, without her breath weakening. Organs were instruments and organs were body parts. She wondered about the link between Communion and organs, whether the instrument was a body the way the wafer and grape juice were, what it would do to the body of someone who played it. When would she get to play it? Did it have something to do with the voice of God?

Don't think about God
Ask him
Wait

Wait til after Sunday school, til after the teacher's mouth had stopped moving, til after the board had been erased, the page with Jesus colored in, til the other kids stopped talking and went out to the yard to play tag, the grown-ups went out to munch on cookies and slurp coffee and stand in little circles.

The church emptied out into the reception room and the sun-soaked yard around it. Anna moved into the space that everyone had left. The church was vast and hollow and everything pointed up—the wooden cross by the altar, the praying hands on the blue-swaddled statue of Mary, saints bending to perform miracles across the stained glass windows with peaks like daggers, the angled ceiling so many feet above her head. The organ with its pipes that could swallow and fit her inside, light glowing off them slightly blue. By the altar, another statue of some saint lying on a coffin, carved from gray stone.If she spoke to God, the saint's sleeping eyes would open and that massive robed body would grind up from its uncomfortable bed. If she spoke to God, Mary's head would raise itself and stare. A wind would ripple across the altar, and what would it do when it hit her? The organ, like a vacuum cleaner, would bellow and suck her in.

Her skin prickled.

She stood in front of the altar in the coat of her body, shivering.

Chapter 7: *Progress Donuts and Jubilation Fried Chicken*

Age Sixteen

Hey Liss,

How are you? I know we haven't talked in a long time but

Hi Liss,

Or are you going by Felicity now? Let me know because I don't want to use the wrong name

Dear Liss,

I'm sorry for not writing earlier. I was depressed and

Liss,

I was a jerk and I'm really sorry

Anna crumpled the papers and looked at them sitting on her desk for ten full minutes before she threw them away. She hadn't been in contact with Liss for over a year since Liss had moved anyway. This was a distraction from her mom's freaky sex life, a distraction from Darien (and thinking of her mom's sex life was leading her to think of Darien now—just great).

Maybe she could get his attention. Hang out with Irena whenever they had plans to get together. Moral support, yup. What did Irena have that she didn't? (Beauty, curves, elegance, cool, everything.) Well, what could she do about it?

Get some sleep, Anna, her mom would say if she could hear. If she wasn't off...fornicating somewhere, presumably with better things to think about.

Check on Grandma.

Or not. The living room didn't have a door, and her grandmother was hopefully sleeping. Waking her would be a huge mistake. She couldn't hear snores. She didn't know if Grandma even snored.

She'd done one hour of clarinet practice, one hour of piano, not as much of either as she was supposed to. She hadn't touched the saxophone since—she stared at the stuffed cat by her pillow. She was so tired.

She woke up to yipping in the next room.

"And why'd you come in with all your clothes on? Why's your hair all messed up?"

Stretched and shook her head free from her crossed arms. She'd fallen asleep at her desk. Pencil marks streaked her forearms and her book report notes were smudged.

"It's the middle of the night and you can't even let your mother sleep?"

"Look, I'm sorry. I wasn't sleeping well and needed to go for a walk."

"Oh, I believe that alright!"

"Well, I did!"

"Where were you?"

"Out in the woods."

"Carrie, that look on your face doesn't say woods, it says sex."

This wasn't supposed to happen. Anna had been on guard. If she'd been doing her job, Mom wouldn't have been found out. But what could she have done? Stayed up all night and kept watch on every shadow in the house? Stood outside the door and came in with her mother when she arrived, so things might look suspicious but innocent?

Ridiculous.

Her mother asked too much. She, Anna, had concerts to prepare for and book reports to write and...living to figure out.

"How many times have you done this to me? How many times? Your own mother! Alright, if you won't treat me as your mother, at least treat me as a house guest. Can you. At least. Find. The decency?"

Anna grabbed some clothes from her drawer and slunk toward the shower.

"I was hoping at least one of you girls would turn out right. But first you leave a good school to run off with some vagabond, and then you sneak around like a teenager on me! What happened to my little opera star? Huh?"

"I have a perfectly good translating job that pays the bills better than my voice ever could've! And as for my love life, that's my business, not yours!"

On the way to the bathroom, a clatter that may or may not have been a dish breaking. Then Anna heard nothing because the water was on and running like a warm motile envelope over her body. She scrubbed her stomach. She scrubbed her legs. She scrubbed and scrubbed between them.

That day she pulled her hair into a French braid and went to lunch with Irena and Darien. Only the three of them.

Told herself to *keep a cool head, keep a cool head,* hard to do with Darien's jokes and her own nerves quavering. He smelled slightly spicy and wore a gray plaid shirt. She counted glances. He didn't seem to look at Irena more than her. He didn't seem to look at her more than Irena.

"So Irena says you have a big concert coming up, Anna?"

Irena was telling him things. When? Where? Things about her—an advantage. Had he asked?

"Uh, uh, yeah." The sounds tripped over each other. Stupid!

"That's awesome. I mean, you aren't any older than us, right, but you're doing a concert with a symphony and everything?"

"Yeah."

"What's that like?"

"It's great," said Irena, smiling widely. "She's doing a full programme. Laine, you know Laine, is going to be in it too, but Anna's the star, of course."

Anna hated herself for looking down and picking at her salad.

"I asked Anna."

Unable to look up from the pale vinaigrette-spattered leaves in their plastic dish, she said without thinking, "Actually I'm nervous."

"You'll do fine."

God! Why couldn't she just look up? She did, and her eyes went immediately back down.

This wasn't how it was supposed to happen. This wasn't who she was supposed to be.

She spent arpeggios thinking about her inability to carry

on a conversation. In music she was fine. Rehearsed the trouble spots in her pieces over and over again. But her fingers kept tripping and slipping. She binged on the saxophone and its sound, slacked off on the clarinet. Hey, at least she was practicing another wind instrument, keeping her chops in shape.

She had a shift at Tim Horton's that night, and her mom had to drive her. They left Grandma at home to watch *What Not to Wear* on TV and scoff at the poor participants' fashion choices. At Kelly's Anna had to dress up for "entertaining," but Tim Horton's required she wear a blue and tan shirt, a name tag, and a stupid little hat. The Small size was too short for Anna, so she'd had to take a Medium which hung off her arms. Sarah would have rolled up the sleeves and secured the sides with rubber bands, but that wasn't allowed.

She punched in her time card in the back and went out to the counter, where Mike lounged on his elbows. She stood behind the other register.

"Hey," Mike grinned. "You missed rush hour. Go make some new chicken salad, will ya? We're almost out."

She went to the walk-in fridge. When she'd started working there she liked to imagine it was a giant metal cryogenic unit, but now it was just another boring refrigerator. She took out the chicken, celery and mayo and went to the tiny back room to mix them. She glanced back at Mike, chewing on his lower lip.

This was not a place to think about Darien. This was not a place to think about the concert or the solo. This was a place to not-think. (The image of a red bedroom flashed up as if on a screen. The idea of her hands peeling boxers off.) This was going to be an awesome chicken salad. For other people to eat. Because she knew the chicken had extra chunks of fat in it. Was bred like that. It had probably had part of its beak cut off and been raised in a cage, immobile. Her dad wouldn't eat it, if he lived in his ideal world. Her dad's boxers were faded and had holes in the elastic. Tom was probably an upgrade. Ew, why on earth was she thinking of that?

Back to the counter. She felt her elbows sink against the hard top and stared.

A bald man shorter than Anna stood in front of her, rocking slightly.

"Hello, how may I help you?" she asked. Upward inflection on the ending.

"You wouldn't happen to, uh, you wouldn't have the directions for Dusty's Fried Chicken, would ya?"

"Oh, uh, sure. You go out to the right—"

"Wait, go slower. I need to write them down." He fished a crumpled paper and a pen from his pocket.

Mike sauntered from his cash towards the customer. "Sir, would you like to order something from our menu to tide you over for the ride?"

Dusty's was only five minutes away. He sure was trying.

"Uh, no thanks, I'm just fine."

"Are you absolutely sure about that?"

Anna drew him a little map and let him turn his back from the counter. "Would you like to try our donut of the week?" she remembered to ask then. They were all supposed to.

"It's the Maple Rainbow," said Mike. "Ten percent of the proceeds from its sales go to the Tim Horton's Children's Camp."

The man nodded curtly and left through the glass doors. Mike rolled his eyes at her. "People suck." He reached into the display case and grabbed a Boston Creme.

"Hey, you're not supposed to eat on shift," said Anna.

"Yeah, yeah. If this was my restaurant, people would eat all the time. It would show everyone how good the food was." He bit into his donut and licked a splat of cream from his lips. "And it would have a better name than Tim Horton's. Like, "The Taste of Super Awesome." He flashed his fingers in the sign of a gun.

"Uh, yeah," said Anna. "I'd go there."

"Of course you would. 'Cause you're super awesome."

She knew Mike had dropped out of school a few months ago, and wondered why. Maybe he just didn't like it.

At home there was a note on the counter. *Out tonight. Please feed bird and wash dishes.* Grandma was sitting at the table, playing Solitaire. She didn't notice Anna coming in, still wearing her silly Tim Horton's uniform.

"I brought some Timbits," said Anna, setting the box of extras on the counter.

"Your mother's out again."

"I know, that's what the note said."

"How could she do this to me?"

Anna opened the box and grabbed a glazed circle.

"Her own mother. Staying at her very own house. And she won't even tell me who she's with! She always had big dreams, Carrie. Could've been a *great* singer. Drawn the crowds with that clear little soprano." She spread her skinny arms wide, a gesture that was almost comical. Anna observed tiny pouches of flesh hanging from them. "And what did she do? Marry a hippie farm boy and end up putting papers into French for the government out in the middle of nowhere. And now she works in a cubicle and talks through earphones! Now Louise was always lazy. But your mother wasn't."

Anna couldn't pretend to eat anymore.

"At least Louise has a husband with a reputable job." Grandma lowered her voice. "Your mother doesn't have good taste in men."

Anna tried to think of a way to leave the room without looking rude.

"And here she goes, saying she'd be glad for me to visit, and she leaves me to sleep with some stranger! Warm welcome, isn't it?"

And she leaves me with this insufferable grandmother and a note telling me to do all the chores, thought Anna, anger rising.

Grandma looked at the table, momentarily, then cast her gaze back up. Her thin eyes locked onto Anna's. "Tell me you won't end up like her."

Anna squirmed in her chair. "No. I mean, I won't."

"I bet you're sick of her too."

Anna said nothing.

"And he said if it was his restaurant, he'd call it The Taste of Super Awesome!"

Darien and Anna chuckled simultaneously.

"And wait 'til I tell you about my crazy grandmother! I'm not sure she's all there, if you know what I mean." Anna twirled a finger around her ear.

"Why, what did she do?"

Anna didn't know what was happening to her. Yesterday she had scarcely been able to speak to Darien, and today she couldn't stop talking. Words spilled from her mouth, emptied themselves from the pressurized vault of mental storage. She laughed out loud for no reason but relief.

"It's too bad Irena had a skill test this lunch break," said Darien.

"Yeah. Too bad."

"It's nice to hear you talk, though."

The old Anna was suddenly back, her eyes stuck down at the plate of cafe club sandwich slightly nicer than yesterday's salad at Dusty's.

"Irena talks a lot." He shaped his hand like a puppet, opened and closed its mouth. "Blah blah blah. Blah de blah de blah. And you just sit there and go 'Huh?'" He made his other hand into a puppet and cocked it quizzically.

Between hysterics, Anna noticed that Darien's plate was already empty. She had only eaten a third of her food so far. "And you just sit there and go 'Om nom nom!'" Her hand made giant munching motions at her sandwich.

"Maybe I should open a restaurant too, eh?"

"Maybe you should. What would you call it?"

"I think I'd name it like one of those Chinese places. Let's say... Love and Peace Diner. Or Progress Donuts."

"Or a fried chicken place," said Anna. "Jubilation Fried Chicken!"

"You'd need an opening ceremony for that. With fireworks."

He was too good to be friends with her. But here they

were, acting like friends already. Neither could stop talking.

So Darien had grown up in Ottawa and gone to another music school. His parents wanted him to play concerts and get famous and have babies who'd become doctors. His mom had run off with a real doctor. So his dad had found a new job on the island, and he'd been given a choice—stay with his aunt and uncle and keep going to the same school, or leave and try to get into Pine Grove. He'd been bored for too many years, was lagging behind his class, unsure of himself, so he left. He already liked the beaches here. Since moving, he'd heard his dad talking to his sock drawer. So he'd stayed behind the door and listened as his father called the furniture by his mother's name. So Darien hadn't trusted sock drawers since then. He laughed (Anna disbelieved the laugh). He asked for her story.

So Anna tried to talk like her grandmother: *Anna, what are you doing in those scraggly clothes? I need to take you shopping.* She told him about her mom having a boyfriend and her dad having a girlfriend. She talked about feeling stifled in that spacious house. How she didn't know where to go but her dad's. How she wanted to run, but it was fine, and why was she telling him all this?

"So go to your dad's house."

"Yeah, I think I will."

"Don't think it, do it. I always think it—that's a Darien mistake. You don't get very far when all you do is think."

*

Dad lived downtown, within walking distance. Books on her back, clarinet in hand, Anna motored down the sidewalk past the tan rows of cheap apartments and the McDonald's and the Wendy's and the shopping mall with the kite logo which had shut down a few years back and still stood empty.

Her dad rented a second-floor apartment a few blocks down. From there she could smell traces of salt water and chemicals from the French fry plant. She rang the doorbell, staring at the peeling paint as she waited, trying to divine patterns.

"Hello?"

Dad wore a black t-shirt with a hole in the sleeve. He had always been like that, preferring to wear the same rag-ready clothes from the top of his drawer even when he'd just had new ones bought for him. Mom had made sure he'd dressed appropriately when needed, and scolded him for wearing things with holes—not the new woman. Dad had lost some weight, cut his bangs, and let the rest of his hair curl halfway to his shoulders. Mullet time, thought Anna. Her next Masterpiece would be Dad's Bad Hair Day, sure to make Darien laugh.

"Anna. What are you doing here?" His frown wavered into a half-smile.

"Just thought I'd visit," she said. She must come over less than she realized, judging by his awkward posture and darting eyes.

"Well, don't stand on the doorstep. Come in." He made a little sweeping motion.

This was not her mom's place, so she didn't have to follow her mom's rules. Anna wore her shoes into the house, sauntered through the narrow hallway past his new girlfriend's welcome mat and into the kitchen. As her father watched, starting sentences he didn't finish, she poured herself orange juice in an old trade show mug. The fridge was mostly empty, the cupboard full of jars. The girlfriend spent days of the summer pickling the vegetables Dad grew in his community garden plot or the living room or anywhere else they'd fit, or congealing jam made with fruit from the You-Pick. The rooms in the apartment were dusty, the sink piled with dishes. Anna slung her school bag and clarinet case onto an empty chair. "Anything to eat that's not pickled?"

"You can look around."

She took a second look at the rows of jars. "Apparently not."

"There's bread on the counter. Stop being difficult."

Difficult? That was the girlfriend talking through him. She cut herself a slab of whole wheat and covered it half in raspberry jam, half in blueberry, dipping from two different jars. She was hungrier than was reasonable. She'd have to have another piece, and another, and another, and maybe a plate of acidic veggies. Yeah, wonderful cooking. She gulped down her juice. Her stomach churning with the surge of something more than hunger, she walked towards the living room.

"Stop!" Dad held out his hand, brow furrowed.

"What?" He didn't seem angry. Worried, maybe?

"Don't go in the living room."

"Why? Don't want me to ruin your yard sale furniture?" She raised an eyebrow.

"Just wait. I'll go with you."

Dad marched brusquely past said yard sale furniture and Anna followed. He pointed to the old toy chest and she noticed a cage on top with something in it. Something squeaking and scrabbling with claws. Anna screamed.

"Shh, it's OK."

Dad knelt by the cage and clucked. With one hand he opened the top, with the other scooped out a foot-long hairless rat which clambered readily onto his shoulder.

"Isn't she beautiful? Her name's Lucy."

Anna edged as far away as possible.

"Don't be scared. She won't bite. Will ya, girl? Yeah, you're a good girl." He made squeaking sounds and stroked the rat's head.

"Um, hi Lucy," said Anna. "Does she, uh, come out of the cage a lot?"

"Yeah, sure, when Gwen's home we sometimes let her have the run of the house. She's very friendly."

"Cool." She tried to sound nice. She really did. It was hard to do when she'd started things off by screaming. Her insides twisted as she watched the rat's wormy tail wrap around her father's shoulder.

He frowned. "You sound disappointed."

The rodent made a noise and she edged back. "You could have warned me there was a rat in the house!"

His hands curled and uncurled. "I thought you'd like her. Thought she'd be sort of a surprise for you, you know?"

"Yeah, she was a surprise alright." Anna stalked back into the kitchen. Now for that plate of pickles, and that rat had better go back in the cage.

Thankfully, Lucy was gone when Dad joined Anna in the kitchen. "How's school?" he asked. He didn't use to ask her such stupid questions.

"You know, good."

"How's work?"

"Fine."

He sat in the other chair, said nothing, did nothing while she finished her snack. She took out her history textbook and started reading one of the sections, trying to imagine that Louis Riel was fascinating. She supposed that when you thought about him he kind of was, what with his deterioration into madness, eventual claim to be a prophet, and insistence on renaming the days of the week while there was a rebellion to be managed. For whatever reason, he thought he had a calling. Back in the Liss days she would have related to that.

"Aren't you supposed to be practicin' your songs or something?" He sounded more curious than pushy.

So many songs. She felt tired just thinking about them.

"I can do it later. Hey, can I have a driving lesson?" That was one advantage to visiting her dad—his ease with teaching the ways of the road. She set up lessons with him now and again. Today was not one of them, as was clear from the way he cradled his head in his hands.

"Not tonight," he said. "I'm tired. More work to do in crop inspection here than back out West."

"What if I come tomorrow?"

"We'll see."

She was grateful to the Department of Agriculture people out West for firing him and precipitating the divorce. He'd had the brains to find another job. It seemed there was no way parents could stay with one thing anymore, even Sarah's mom who'd worked with the school board for thirty years. The economy wasn't much worse than usual, but it was never exactly nice.

He leaned on the table, elbows forward, trying to think of what to say. She wasn't helping. But she had nothing to say either. They had grown strange around each other. *Have you called yer mother yet?* That was the thing she knew he wouldn't ask.

He could see she wasn't looking at her textbook anymore.

"You should practice your music, eh?"

"I'm still hungry." She grabbed more bread.

"Gwen's coming home and making supper. Don't spoil your appetite."

Her mom called anyway, mid-bite. By the time the phone was passed to Anna, Mom sounded hysterical. "Why didn't you tell me you were going to your father's? I was so worried something had happened! Are you going to stay the night? Is there someone to drive you home? You don't have clothes there, do you?"

Anna kept nothing in the apartment, which had only one bedroom and an air mattress for guests.

"If you can pick me up this evening, that would be great."

She hung up and practiced her boring clarinet solo, then the band pieces. There wasn't a piano in the apartment. Well, that was just too bad, she thought, but her fingers arced themselves unstoppably into movement. She wanted to play Wagner, if nothing else. She was rehearsing fingerings on the tabletop when the girlfriend came in with two plastic bags.

"Hi, honey!" Dad rushed forward and she hugged him, reaching up to smash her lips to his while squishing the bags against his back.

"Hi, Gwen." His voice softened. "How was work?"

"Lucas is really coming along with his reading. And Matt,

of course, is a holy terror. I'm trying to think of a way for him to keep his participation up without disrupting the whole class."

Gwen was small and round, her hair flyaway with white bits almost indistinguishable from the blond. She hemmed her pants herself, always an inch above the ankle.

"I see we have Anna here," she said. "C'mere, sweetie." She insisted on a hug; it felt like being enveloped by bread dough. Once she finally let go, Gwen reached for her bags. "Let me show you both the things I bought today. You'll like this." She pulled out what looked like a miniature blue leather belt.

"What's that?" asked Dad.

"It's a little leash for Lucy, so we can walk her. And look, I bought her a collar too."

"Let's try it on her." Dad's face held a childish excitement. Anna stood back as they brought out the rat, fitted her with a harness, and allowed her to roam around the living room, taking turns to hold the leash. Gwen picked up the rat and talked to her: "Lucy-bear! Aren't you a good little baby? Hm?" She tilted her head up towards Dad and they grinned at each other.

She'd never seen them yell at each other. Just smile. Was the girlfriend—was Gwen—safe here? Did she have something that Mom didn't, enough to keep her father happy and his anger at bay? If she did, did Anna hate her?

Too much thinking. Anna went back to the table. This time, Louis Riel was fascinating.

She asked for another driving lesson and was refused,

despite the glow of rat time. She gulped down Gwen's chicken wings and homemade coleslaw. When Gwen tried to pawn off some hand-me-downs on Anna—old jeans and a faded blue tank top she'd put on too much weight to wear—she politely declined. Even if she wanted them, they wouldn't fit, but judging from her own wardrobe, Gwen had very little concept of whether clothes fit a person. She and Dad settled on the couch to watch sitcoms, him groaning softly about how his back hurt, her reaching out to rub it while he curled like a contented rodent. Anna's skin itched.

"You two look so cute together," she burst out violently before thinking. Bad idea, Anna, bad idea.

"Thank you," said Gwen.

"Shouldn't you be doing your work?" said Dad.

Her fists bunched under the table.

"No, really, look at you. Attached at the hip. You even have your own kid, never mind that it's bald with a disgusting big tail. Isn't the nesting instinct great?"

Dad lurched from the couch towards her, abrupt. "You shut up."

"Hank!" Gwen squealed. Her hand stretched out and flopped back like a doll's; he was already out of reach.

"You didn't have to come here!" Her father stood near her, breath steaming in her face, eyebrows glowering down.

Anna glowered back.

"You're right. I shouldn't have!"

"Then why did you?" He grabbed her shoulders roughly.

"Hank, stay the hell away from her!"

"You shut up too," Anna shot at the couch.

"Don't!" Dad could handle insults, but a shot at his

girlfriend was a different matter. His eyes registered the imprint of her sting. His face drooped. Then he shook her, but not too hard. His hands were unsteady. Anna grabbed them, thrust them off her shoulders (limp sweaty noodles), whirled and gathered her stuff. "I'm going to the community center," she yelled, and slammed the door.

She had to collect herself before remembering which way to walk, though she'd done this many times. She looked emptily around the blank-faced apartment buildings and the children playing basketball in one of the yards, faced the wind, then spun and faced away, eyes suddenly stinging.

What did you think you'd find by going there anyways? Domestic bliss? Yeah, it's there, but not for you. Nothing for you, just rolls of photographic negatives when you try to remember the Mom and Dad and Anna and tape recorder and Liss times. No color photos to show you what you want to think you had.

The concert would happen in less than a month. Anna would star in it.

The community center was open and had a slightly out-of-tune piano she secretly liked working with because the sounds were muted. That gave the instrument a mournful quality and, more practically, meant she could play as hard as she liked. She used the center payphone to call Mom and ask to be picked up after a couple hours of practice. She was being demanding. Hard to handle. Her mother on the other end sighed heavily.

There was no one in the room but a couple guys her age playing pool. They'd heard her playing before and politely, or apathetically, ignored her. Anna took out her sheet music and started practicing. The smallest things could affect her playing. Tension could slow and murk her mind. But after shouting, her arms and pace were free.

Something has broken and maybe it had to. In a month I'll be staring into stage lights. She gathered the notes like scattered papers. The more she played, the more existed around her.

Chapter 8: *Ay-a*

Age Six

Dear God, are you real? Please tell me if you're real. Say something or do something so I'll know you are. Anna knelt and clasped her hands in front of the altar. *Liss says you're not. But you're listening to me, right?*

From the wooden floor, much closer to the front than she was allowed, she could see the hanging Jesus's nostrils. She fidgeted, then remembered not to. She hoped God wouldn't hate her. She did everything wrong. She didn't know how to fix it. And staring up at the statue of Jesus's body drooping from the cross, she knew one thing suddenly. That body was useless, dead, and even when woken back up, it walked around for a bit and then went right back to die. Those arms stretched out, the dead doves that were hands, wouldn't save anyone. The body, even as a statue, was too heavy and clumsy to be any help. At Communion that's what they ate and drank, the body and the blood, the things that were heavy, drooped and died.

Please Dear God, say something.

The wood pressed dents into her knees. And why shouldn't she fidget? The church was a body too, made from the bodies of trees. The statues were bodies of rock and plaster. The dead saints wouldn't get up. The Mary statue wouldn't talk. She could see little worn-out lines in the paint on Mary's face. She could see through the saints on the stained-glass windows, trees shining through their flat faces and their dead miracle-making hands. They weren't going to be any help either.

She looked up at the organ with an unafraid face. Waited against miracles for it to make sound. All she heard was the laughing of church people outside after the service, too loud, as if twisted through microphones.

Last chance, God.

She waited. Maybe she wasn't listening hard enough, or listening with the right part of her. She strained to listen beyond what she could hear. Sat very, very still. All that came down was part of Beethoven's Ninth, which she'd been practicing, and it didn't come from somewhere else but spun out from the ears in her mind.

Her parents, the priest, her Sunday School teacher, everyone would say she was wrong if they found out what she'd done. They'd want her in the booth to confess. If they asked, she'd say a string of prayers by memory. But she wouldn't tell because if there was no one to listen, there was no one to catch her. The hole in her stomach told her that Liss was right. Sitting on the floor and listening so hard she was dizzy, she felt nothing but the building and the ceiling and alone.

She walked out into the churchyard where a story called God wasn't.

The French tutor came again and then didn't come anymore. When she shivered into tears during practice, Laine asked why.

Don't tell. Don't tell don't tell they'll hurt you.

But Laine kept asking. And Laine was different. The church didn't want women to act like men, it wanted them to marry men, and certainly not women. She'd heard Laine had a girlfriend. She kind of wondered what a lady's girlfriend would look like.

So she told everything.

Laine sat and let her cry. She wasn't a hugging person.

"It's hard," she said when Anna came up, hiccuping. "That happened to me when I was eight. And then I learned that other cultures have different gods."

Laine told her about the Greek gods she'd learned about in school, great humans with superpowers who lived on a mountaintop controlling thunder and taking sides in fights down below. She talked about Glooscap, the Trickster sent by the Creator to help the Mi'kmaq people, who flew with the island Minegoo on his back and placed it in the sea to be their home. She talked about gods from Africa and ancestors from Australia and those who created the Floating World in Japan.

"The Christians only see one side of God, and seeing and listening to just one side can hurt. Think of all the wars that have been caused by people only seeing one side. The divine has many faces." Laine's straight-backed distance was somehow more comforting than touch. "Maybe you'll find one that no one has seen before."

She wasn't going to say "Liss, you were right." She said instead, "This grass fort is a mountain."

"What?"

"This grass fort is a mountain. Like the Greek people had. And our own gods live here."

"What?"

Anna knelt down in the pillowing grass. The fort was small, its walls were small, it wasn't on a hill, but she pictured it swelling and swallowing the trees along the fence. She pictured a woman on top of it—not Liss, not Anna, not Another Anna or anyone she knew, but someone else she couldn't quite see clearly.

She told Liss about the Greek gods on Mount Olympus, using a thundering voice. She told Laine's stories about gods and goddesses who turned people into trees and deer, and about a man who fell in love with his reflection.

"They're not real either," said Liss.

"So?" said Anna. "Let's make our own gods and goddesses."

Liss leaned forward. "They'll have to listen to us then. They won't leave us for someone else to take."

Anna wasn't sure what Liss was talking about, but she nodded. "You know how we have hymns?"

"Yeah."

"Well, some people have chants for their gods like that. Like singing stuff that doesn't always have words. Laine said so." She felt proud, like an explorer bringing back jewels from a journey.

"Like what?"

Anna made something up, humming and spreading her voice into an ahhh, shifting slowly up and down in pitch. She spread out her arms until her body was a cross. She felt dumb at first, until power collected in her arms and played her.

"So let's chant like that," said Liss. "Once we decide on our gods."

"Yeah."

"This one's for the thunder god Bojo!" yelled Liss.

It sounded like a clown name and Anna giggled. She saw some bigger kids turn to look when Liss yelled, and was embarrassed but only a little. "Lalalalala," Liss began and Anna joined in harmony. It didn't sound like they were chanting to a thunder god. Maybe to a dancing god. Not right.

Anna tried the next one. "Oo-ba. Oo-ba." Liss fell over laughing before she was able to join in.

The chants took on sillier sounds. "Bla ra ra." "Hoo oo oo." They stopped calling out the names of gods and other kids stopped watching, bored since nothing but weird noise was going on and music school kids were used to that. Someone started a boom box, blaring a song about a tattoo that was louder than them anyway. The first girls who'd been looking ran off to join a skipping rope game.

When they ran out of ideas, they started chanting "Donanoby spachum." It was a song about peace, but didn't feel any more real than the sounds that meant nothing.

"Ahwahwahwah," sang Liss after that.

"Ayayayayay!"

"Ay-a, ay-a, ay-a!"

Anna liked that. It had a rhythm to it, like drumming. And it sounded almost like her name. The woman on the hill that was their fort swelled into focus. She was tall with long hair, her face cloudy, and Anna couldn't tell the color of her hair or skin. Her eyes matched the sky. Her body, as thin as a tree, was covered in a pile of glimmering patterned fabrics—red paisley, blue and green mottled velvet, gold striped, transparent and glimmering. All Anna could see of her motions was an ocean of fabric rippling.

"Ay-a's our goddess," said Anna. She wasn't brave enough to yell it over the playground, but she said it.

"The goddess of what?"

"Of music, of course."

"Not love?"

"We can make another one for love. Music."

"OK, the goddess of love is Sava!" Liss spread her arms.

They made gods for good luck, for school, for smartness, for family, for beaches, for trees. They made gods for Anna's house and Liss's house, laughing, and forgot them. Anna was still watching the rippling cloth. When Liss suggested they chant again, Ay-a is what Anna chanted.

Mom was going to be late, so Anna waited on the hill, this time alone and at the highest point of the grass that was turning brown. Higher than the fence, higher than the swing set, higher than the school! The queen of the castle, surveying her lands. She watched the ant people get into their cars and the caterpillar buses crawl out. She felt her jacket grow longer and longer until it draped to the ground. She felt layers pile on top of it until her body was covered. They weren't as heavy as she'd expected. Light enough to move easily. Lighter than her regular clothes. Each piece of fabric that brushed her skin sent a different song into her.

She couldn't help it. She twirled and twirled in the brown grass that smelled like leaves, fasterfasterfaster wobblingneverfalling. Her own power made her dizzy.

Ay-a rode in the car to school. Ay-a stirred marshmallows in her hot cocoa and told her not to be scared on the sledding hill. Ay-a told Anna her hair looked better now that it was almost at her shoulders again and wanted her to put a ribbon in it.

Ay-a had a song about herself that she shared with Anna. Ay-a, ay-a, stars in my body, stars in my soul. *Ay-a, Ay-a, music's my both things until I get old.* Music was body and soul, not some angry God who made rules to hurt people and got hung up on a cross. Music was what could save people. Whenever she heard the organ, the tape player, the piano, Anna knew that.

Anna shared Ay-a's song with Liss. They waited until the hill was clear of people to run from the grass fort and sing it there. Liss shook a tambourine she'd brought from home and they were powerful. But that only happened one time. Liss liked Sava better. "Sava moved into my house," she declared one day. "She made it so my sisters will fall in love with the neighborhood boys when they grow up. She made it so the mailman will fall in love with the library lady." She giggled. "I told her to make my birth parents fall in love with me enough that they'll want to find me. She said if I'm good for a whole year, it'll work."

The snowdrifts built little nests on the side of her house. She pressed her ears to these holes and listened. They sounded like the ocean inside a shell or the noise in her ears underwater, only quieter. They reminded her of Ay-a's voice, which she couldn't quite hear the way she could a real person or a song, even a song in her head (since she had to have heard it first for it to be in her head). It was more like hearing the idea of what she wanted to say.

Gods wanted sacrifices. Not just the God in the Bible, but the other gods Laine told her about. It seemed to be a rule. With her mittens, Anna chipped bits of hard snow into animal shapes and offered them to the homes of Ay-a's voice. A cow went into that hollow in the snowbank, an icy sheep into the next.

As she placed the animals carefully, she prayed for the Christmas concert. Laine had her performing Vivaldi's Spring, a real arrangement, not the easy version. She'd never performed before, not on a stage in front of people she didn't know.

Mom had her count two hours of practice every day. Usually Anna played longer anyway. One day she was so nervous she played until supper and again until bedtime. She couldn't get into the music. She had to. Her mind kept crawling in one direction, her hands in another.

"Hey, aren't you tired?" shouted Dad.

She wasn't in the music so she heard him. Yes. She was so tired. Thinking that, her body fell forward onto the keys.

"How about I carry you up to bed and tell you a story?"

Anna collected her voice and managed a weak "Yeah." This was good Dad. This was OK.

Carted up the stairs, she didn't see her father looking back and her mother throwing him a grateful look.

Dad left her awkwardly to change into her pajamas and brush her teeth, then came in without a book. "Once upon a time," he began, sitting on the bed and holding one of her teddy bears, "there was a troll who lived underground. His name was Grunt." He wiggled the bear around and grunted.

At first Anna thought about being watched by millions of heads in seats, about playing a smooth perfect season through the room, about her hands slipping and freezing as everyone laughed. But the story was too interesting. "Grunt's tunnel was a special tunnel. It had a farm inside. There was a pasture full of grass where the goats lived. And there was a cubby where the mushrooms grew. Grunt collected the goats' manure to feed the mushrooms. Yup, he fed them poop." Anna cringed. "Sometimes Grunt's troll neighbors would visit and they would share vegetables and play their loud troll drums and sing their loud troll songs. And they lived like that for years, happily, until one day some *really* loud trolls came into their tunnels."

"They drove in on humongous farm machines, squirting chemicals that made the other trolls cough. They wanted to buy all the farms, but Grunt and his troll neighbors said 'No, are you crazy?' The next day, the noisy trolls mowed one of their farms down, *clickety-clackety-clunk*. But Grunt and his friends fought back. They broke the big machines and used the parts to build barns. One of the noisy trolls, a lady, saw what Grunt was doing and started to fall in love. She borrowed one of his loud drums and called a meeting. 'Citizen trolls, your farming practices are ruining the land!'" Dad waved his hands and pounded them against the bed like a drum.

"It took some black eyes, but finally everyone listened. The really noisy farmers joined Grunt and his neighbors, working with tools and animals until every tunnel farm bloomed with mushrooms. And all the trolls used the rest of the machine parts to make loud instruments they played at Grunt and the lady troll's wedding." Dad took the two teddy bears he'd been wiggling around and made them kiss each other. "And they lived happily ever after with their troll babies. You tired now?"

"Tell me another story!"

"No, you're yawning. Tomorrow night." He tucked the teddies next to the pillow. "Maybe someday we'll have our own farm like that. Whaddaya think? Sound like fun?"

"Kinda."

"Don't worry, I'd take care of the goat poop. You could take care of the garden. Hey, how about making a garden this summer? Wanna do that? You can decide what to plant where, and we'll go buy the seeds together. Whaddaya think?"

"Sure!"

Anna was happy until her father left. Then the thoughts returned.

Metronome. Hands. Phrase. Pause. Phrase again. Fingers tripping over each other.

Two hours almost up.

Go... a little... faster.

❧

Backstage, Anna's stomach crawled with salamanders. She had on make-up and lipstick for the lights. Her mother had put it on, although Laine had said she didn't need to wear anything. The mirror showed grown-up and beautiful. She didn't feel grown-up and beautiful. All she could see now were the heavy black curtains and the kids behind them and the music book in her hand. Her parents and uncles and aunts and cousins and grandparents on her dad's side were out there, watching and listening to a plinking song. Anna moved towards the wings and spied out. Chen and Michelle were playing a piano duet in their frilly pink dresses. Her dress was blue and flowered, just as nice. She wasn't jealous of them now. She tried to think of Ay-a but the goddess was as silent as any other made-up god.

She tapped her own song on her leg, stumbled, tried again, stumbled again. Her hands wanted to play what she heard.

The plinking ended and applause swelled the theater. The clapping made the stage floor vibrate, or maybe she imagined that. She heard Laine announce her name.

Right foot, left foot. Step on stage. Hold book tight. Count steps. Don't look out. Look at the way the yellow line across the stage is overlaid by scuff marks. Look at the piano. Stand in front of the piano bench. Look at Laine's feet in their man's shoes.

No way not to see out, now. Laine's feet a direct arrow. Behind them, a blinded busy space with heads' outlines. Blink. Like a painting, not like people. But they were people and they were watching. An animal jumped in her stomach and squeezed her ribcage.

Curtsy, holding the lace at the tip of her dress. Set down and open music book. Sit on piano bench. Wiggle. Breathe. Breathe. Breathe. One-two. One-two. Arc fingers over keys.

Begin.

Flowers bounce up right away. Calm down a little. Splay open their petals and nod around. Birds trill from fingers. Begin to stroll down the driveway, purposefully, towards the bus, no, towards the carriage waiting to drive her to the castle. This spring has no mud, only pussywillows and once in a while, dark clouds. The wheels do not get stuck. Get out in front of the quiet stone, so quiet that entering makes her nervous. Someone sweeps past in tulip-red velvet and she's in a ballroom that is at once a garden where new things poke up pianissimo. She doesn't know who that woman is—Ay-a, Caroline, Laine, Liss? Other women wisp in, dancing. Dance into a square that faces inward.

Scoot off the bench. Turn towards painted faces, the light so flaming white she can't even see them now. Curtsy. Feel the clapping fortissimo in her body.

She is Anna again, and it is done.

There was more left to the concert, but Anna wasn't scared. She had a lot of listening backstage to do, Liss's violin solo (beautiful), more listening, and near the end Chorus. They all took their places on the risers, used to it. Liss nudged Anna, who caught her nervous face and smiled back. For the "Donanoby spachum" song, Anna sang too quietly to hear if she was blending, or even if she was making sound. She wasn't going to be too loud this time. Liss, just as dressed up as her—lacy white dress, necklace that looked like pearls— was a beautiful singer as always. Her voice reached the ceiling where stage lights came down and left them snowblind.

They sat backstage while parents moved out into the lobby. George, a violinist in their class, fiddled with his bowtie. An older student Anna didn't really know walked by, probably on the way to the fountain. "Great performance," he said to George. George just sat there, still fiddling with his bowtie, looking like a surprised dog.

Liss walked up to him. "An-y-thing boys can do, girls can do bet-ter!" she singsonged.

"No they don't," said George.

"Yeah we do. Look at Laine. She's a girl and she's in charge of this place. And my solo got more clapping than yours did. I counted."

"Oh yeah? Well—"

"Yeah, and girls smell better too," said Anna, making things up.

"Yeah, well, well, we're smarter."

"Not true. Look at the musicianship here and stuff," said Liss. "See if you don't believe me. And you smell awful." Power rose in Anna with each sentence she spoke or heard.

George's face crumpled.

"I'm a better violin player than you. So there!" Liss darted out into the hallway and Anna followed.

Anna didn't hear it until the roses her grandparents had bought her (Good job, Anna) were brown and dry-stemmed and most of the petals had fallen to the table. Finished with practice and walking to her bedroom, she passed her parents'. Horrible sounds came from inside, like animals getting kicked. Not a human kind of screaming. The door was white with nothing on the front, just the plain knocker. She couldn't move. She looked at it. A horse's shriek. Thudding.

She found her feet and ran to her room and slammed. Grabbed armfuls of stuffed animals from her pillow and looked around at the light blue walls with music notes stenciled in a border. Safe safe safe safe safe. Safe?

Suddenly she was no longer sitting in her safe blue room or standing still inside the halls of time where memories froze in pictures with the colors just a little too flat. Spinning upside-down, she was catapulted through their painted frames. Only the hollow beating, beating through her body. Unsteady rhythm she couldn't count into or out of. No sound at all.

Chapter 9: *The Space Between*

Age Sixteen

A Night in Tunisia spun on CD, Dizzy Gillespie's bright trumpet sounds rising through the bland practice room. Anna cradled the sax's golden body in her lap and listened. This guy threw in all kinds of fancy blue scale riffs and grace notes that weren't marked in Darien's Basic Jazz for Alto Sax book. The melody strolled along over the half-step-up, half-step-down bass line—wandering some faraway marketplace, the smell of fish, the glow of lanterns—and slowed to an almost mournful ending sequence.

She took up the horn and began, smooth as butter. No low notes, thank the gods. She struggled to puff up her lungs enough for those. Next to her, Darien nodded approval. At the first twelve-bar blues break, her mouth seized. Quarter rest, half rest, whole rest—she knew the scale by now, dammit! But what to do with it? Darien offered a strained smile. OK, she could play a long G. Could try a little syncopation up the scale, and then what? Another pause. The twelve bars lapsed by, marked only by Darien's steady foot-tapping.

Darien picked up his alto and joined her in the twelve-bar interlude. It was all Anna could do to squeak out the sound, hiding beneath his surer notes. His turn next. He started with a high glissando into a low long tone, his face serious despite slightly puffed cheeks. Then a little cadenza (did they call it a cadenza in jazz?). Next, part of the melody line distorted in a minor key.

Enough already, she wanted to say. She'd lead him to the gym for a round of 21. At least then she wouldn't lose so badly.

They finished. Anna laid her sax down and rested her head on the seat back. "You're getting it, Anna," said Darien. "You just need to work on letting loose for the solos. Don't think about it. Just see what comes to you."

"What comes to me is brain freeze."

"Aw, you just need more practice. Come on, let's go to the piano room. I want to hear your concert pieces."

She played Beethoven's Piano Concerto No. 1, to remind herself that she could do fancy fingerwork. During the spring-blossom beginning, she caught Darien staring open-mouthed. She gave no response but carried on, softened by his awe.

At a sleepover at Sarah's house, Anna found herself sitting apart from the others. "I got a new eye shadow kit," said Michelle. "Anyone want a makeover?"

"Yeah, and I've got a curling iron," Sarah enthused. "We should curl Chen's hair and pretty her up!"

Chen wanted to try on Sarah's green minidress to complement the makeover, so Irena tightened it around her much smaller body. "God, Chen, you're so skinny. I'm so jealous."

"I don't think this thing fits."

"Here, try this." Irena snatched a striped halter dress from her own bag. Michelle brought out a belt to gather it around

Chen's waist.

"So, Anna," leered Sarah, her curly grackle head suddenly bulging into Anna's space. "You're spending a lot of time with this Darien dude. Is it serious?"

"I don't know," she shot.

"Ooh, Anna's mad," Michelle singsonged.

"How can you not know? Has he shown any interest in you at all? Has he hit on you or tried to hold your hand or something?"

"That's my business." A sudden clump of worry sunk in her gut.

"I bet he's gay," said Irena.

The conversation moved on to the spiked punch Michelle's boyfriend said he'd brought to a party, and to what color eyeshadow matched the halter dress on Chen. Anna, distant in a beanbag chair, thought Irena must be right. If Darien was straight or bi, his attention would have stayed on Irena instead of her, and he wouldn't keep asking about her friends. Would it be possible to make a gay person straight? Most people were somewhere in the middle of the Kinsey scale rather than strictly at one end, if sex ed was right. That meant most guys could, based on probability, fall for a girl. But she didn't want him to be rough and horny and loud like other straight guys, Michelle's boyfriends and their gangs, who leered at girls in the halls. She didn't want him to leave her and chase Irena.

"Did I tell you I caught Mike making out with a student?"

"Mike O'Hara the clarinet teacher?"

"No way!"

"Yup. They had their tongues in each other's mouths and

everything. I wonder if he sleeps with her."

Chen's hair was half in ringlets. Anna watched the others as if behind a thin curtain. She pictured their conversation as globs of glue adhering to things that didn't matter, their bodies glistening shells. They stood in a vacant but tangible place, and here she sat on the beanbag chair caught in her own inane swirl of thoughts. There was nothing to keep her grounded, and the ground beneath the other girls rested on air.

I have nothing in common with them.

A familiar feeling, heavy and unstill, surged in her gut. Gods, her body was starting to shake now. She blinked and a tail of fabric shimmered in the corner of her vision. She was seeing things that weren't even real! She flailed against the feeling that tracked up her neck in spite of her. She didn't want this back.

"Hey Anna," said Darien, holding a barely nibbled sandwich, "is something wrong?"

"Why?" She poked her empty tupperware tub with a fork.

"You're just slumped and nervous-looking at the same time. It's a weird combination. You should go look in the mirror or something."

A flash of glitzy fabric passed and she looked up startled, but it was only a girl's t-shirt.

"It's the concert," she lied.

"Yeah, of course. I was wondering if you'd get nervous. Would you feel better if you went to practice? Or if we did something entirely different and forgot about it?" He offered a grin, playful but non-expectant. Supportive. She couldn't *stand* how he looked when he smiled. She looked around at the cafeteria instead, a windowless white rectangle with Milk and Canadian Cheese posters on the walls, a couple snack and beverage machines in the corners, a small lunch line and a fridge, identical heads bobbing listlessly at the long rows of tables. They only ate there half the time, and it was still too often.

"Let's go to the practice room," she said. "But first, finish your sandwich." He did this in a few quick bites.

꙳

She arced her fingers over the piano and the shivers started again.

"Jesus, Anna!"

She tried to take a deep, shuddering breath that didn't go any further than shallow. She thought of the hazy crowd she'd soon sit before. Mostly unseen, while the lights misted her eyes and the clapping buoyed her. A hundred people's breath hung on her sound. In this picture Anna poured herself into music so complete the rest of her life capsized into that moment, smoothly polished music that seeped through the audience and spilled out aqueous. Anna Masterpiece #587, the one she'd never be able to draw. But maybe she could live it.

No, of course she couldn't.

She looked towards her audience of one, felt the familiar sting, and tried not to be turned on. But maybe that would help. Maybe it would make her music stronger.

Her fingers hit the keys for the Chopin, a funeral march incongruously made denser by the wanting, more mournful by the impossibility. Her fingers marched on polished ivory, mindless, resonant, heavy-hearted. And then and then and then.

Had she played this well before? She looked up—a mistake. Darien watching made her hands shake until the funeral song broke up into a sick and twitchy too-slow dance. Damn damn damn! She stopped and rested her hands in her lap, but they kept shaking. Her shoulders quivered slightly.

"Are you feeling alright?"

"Yeah, I'm fine." Looking at Darien only made it worse. Some dark appendage shook through her, trying to grasp outward and latch on, to crush and be crushed. But Darien was standing a few feet away, holding himself physically distant like he always did. She could not direct her eyes at him.

Her mouth dropped open. "Will you play with me in the concert?" she blurted out.

"Anna."

Her cheeks heated and her eyes bore into the floor.

"I'd love to, but that's ridiculous. You already have your program, and who's ever heard of an alto sax playing with an orchestra?"

"We could fit you in!" Her eyes flashed up and focused on a face that hazed as she looked too hard.

"I'd ruin it."

"That's *stupid*."

"Look, in case you haven't noticed, our abilities lie on drastically different levels. I may be better at saxophone than you because you just started, but on the whole— If I had the same kind of talent you have—" here his tone rose and his hands sliced through the air—"I think I'd be the happiest man alive."

7

Anna got a package in the mail from Gwen, sealed with duct tape. She sent those sometimes. This one contained a case of half-used eye shadow in varying shades and a compact of purplish blush. Leftovers.

"Let me see what you got in the mail, let me see!" Hank hung over her shoulder, girlishly excited. "Oh, makeup!"

"You can borrow some, Mom." Anna rolled her eyes. "Or you can have it if you want."

"No, of course not, it's yours to enjoy." Mom riffled through the package and spread the contents across the kitchen table. There was a tiny bottle of perfume hidden in the newspaper on the bottom and a few used postage stamps, still attached to scraps of envelope. To recycle, said a notepaper note wrapped around them. *Happy birthday*. Anna's birthday was in the summer.

"What's she doing sending old postage stamps?" Mom pulled out a twist-tied plastic bag full of gummy bears. Beneath it, a worn brown skirt.

"Betcha your whole salary that rag won't fit me," said Anna.

"Betcha you're right." Mom shook out the skirt and held it up.

"Think it'll fit you?"

"Don't. Even. Think about it!"

The skirt was shapeless and looked like it could fit a Mom and a half.

"That woman!" Mom sighed. "Is she quite alright?" After

a few seconds, she broke into laughter. Anna, relieved, laughed just as loud.

"What do you expect from someone who walks a rat on a leash!" Anna burst out, each word progressively funnier.

"And she wears your father's baseball caps to church, you said!"

"And she said soap operas were called soap operas to sell more soap!"

"No wonder she's with my ex-husband!" said Mom. "They both seem to be missing a few marbles."

They collapsed on the table, amused and out of breath.

"I should vacuum," said Mom. "But I don't feel like it."

"Screw vacuuming. Try on some of that makeup." They giggled again.

"I wonder if any of that would look decent with my blue dress," said Mom. "I want to wear my blue dress the next time I see Tom. You don't think it makes my chest look too flat, do you?"

"No, of course not. It's better than mine."

"You'll grow."

"I doubt it."

"You know, *could* I use a bit of that makeup? Would you mind?"

"Go ahead."

"Alright. I'm going to get changed into the blue dress. Tell me if it makes me look fat too. Be honest." Mom rushed up the stairs. She emerged shortly in said blue dress, a high-necked navy thing with a skirt that almost reached her knees and a sash around her waist. "It probably needs some jewelry. What do you think?"

"Jewelry would be fine, but you look stupidly good, Mom."

She hoped Tom deserved that goodness, that he had a gentle voice and touch.

"Not fat?"

"Don't be a moron."

Grandma had taken the plane back, and it occurred to Anna that this was the reason Mom was more relaxed. Giddy even, with all those dates. She stood in front of the living room mirror, fussily pushing her hair to one side, smoothing it back, worrying a silver ring on and off her finger. She daubed light blush onto her cheeks, lined her eyes, opened the case of eye shadow, hovered with her finger paused above it. She selected the silver. Smoky streaks took shape along her eyelids. Anna wished she'd inherited her mother's beauty. Makeup finished, her mother tilted her head one way, then another, frowned, adjusted an earring.

"Can I take your picture and sell it to *Vogue*?" asked Anna, trying to sound playful but feeling too tender to crack a smile. Beneath her jealousy was a soft and surprising flash of affection.

"Don't be silly." Mom took on Anna's breezy tone.

Anna wondered why her mother didn't hug her often. She just didn't, that was all. It wasn't her thing. She couldn't remember having wondered this before, but the distance between her and Darien, who of course was gay anyway, and the apparent closeness between her mom and Tom, who she still hadn't met, brought the question to mind. The space between the two of them was suddenly tangible.

"How old were you when you had your first kiss?" asked

Anna. Sure she was past her own, but before that first time she hadn't thought to ask. Her parents had not been sexual beings then. She felt herself blushing, squirming.

"Anna," Mom laughed nervously, "that's kind of a personal question."

"OK, sorry."

"Look, you should try out some of the makeup."

Anna gave in and fetched her own makeup kit. One of the colors in Gwen's old case was a distasteful shade of turquoise. If she was going to use makeup from the girlfriend, she might as well use the worst of it. She tried a spot just above her lashes. It looked bold, a graffiti stroke. A familiar thing lurched inside. *Ay-a, Ay-a, stars in my body, stars in my soul.* She smudged it along her eyelids with abandon. Then some purple mascara she'd gotten as a birthday present from Sarah and never worn. Then spots of the purplish blush, which looked closer to a shady rose when worn. Her pulse sped.

"What are you doing?" said Mom.

Putting on makeup. What does it look like I'm doing? But Ay-a wouldn't let her toss out that answer. She spurred Anna to open the expensive citrus spice perfume she saved for special occasions and daub it liberally behind her neck, at her wrists. She felt solid and daring. Ay-a was back, dressing Anna in shimmering gold before Anna could stop her. Ay-a, the silly creation of her childhood. Maybe not so silly. Silliness didn't feel like this. She took some eyeliner and traced a reckless swirl to the side of her right eye.

"You look like a circus clown."

She gave herself a critical survey. She didn't look normal. She didn't look like a clown. She looked like a young, bizarre rock star. A canvas that stared in defiance. A warning sign.

Darien, watch out, said Ay-a in her head. *Beauty, you'd better believe you have a chance.* The goddess gripped her shoulder, then gave her a shove.

"I'm going to play my saxophone," said Anna.

"Honey, your clarinet solo's in just a few days. And there's the piano concert you should be preparing for. I don't want to worry about you. And as for that funny eyeliner—"

Anna swept her makeup and the girlfriend's—hell, it was hers now—into her bag. She took a breath, strode up to her mother, and set a hand on your shoulder. "Nothing to worry about. I'm on it." Mom's shoulder was worryingly thin, but warmer than she'd expected.

I live on my own terms, said Ay-a as Anna dressed for work at Kelly's. Makeup should be formal if she wore it, she'd always assumed. But there was no *rule*. Her hands were on the turquoise and then it was on her eyelids, tracing thin lines underneath. Bright red lip gloss. *Next thing I know, I'll be going to work naked.* She did feel like a layer had been peeled off. She loved being seen onstage, admired for her music, but that was a kind of attention she could control. With rocker make-up on, she shed her usual armor of invisibility. Her boss's brow crinkled as she entered the restaurant. Customers stared at her more today, now that she was a look along with the sound.

"Hey baby, can you play a Mozart song?" called out a man over his plate of roast beef with a side of canned peas and carrots. So she was a "baby" now? She wasn't sure she liked that.

When she'd started the job, she chose all her own pieces.

She still did most of the time, but once she'd played *Moonlight Sonata* when a co-worker yelled out asking her for it, and word had spread that Kelly's pianist could play songs by ear and take requests. She held a grudge against the *Moonlight Sonata* for what it had led to. Even when it got her tips, she wasn't fond of the schmaltzy pop tunes people wanted her to play. Surrender was alright on days she hadn't already played their stuff, but once a sentimental couple had requested "My Heart Will Go On"—a song from years ago, romance long aged to stale cheese. Of course, she'd done it.

She liked Mozart's Piano Concerto 5 and launched into the first movement, wishing the restaurant smell less like fries with the works. This was what it meant to be an entertainer, she supposed, instead of a musician.

Sarah liked the turquoise eye shadow and doll-spots of dark rose on her cheeks. "Sex-ay!" she sang out.

"I dunno, honey," said Irena. "I'd tone it down a little." Anna's gut lurched, and she took note to put it on heavier next time. Laine grinned during their lesson. Darien didn't comment, but he seemed to stare at her a little more.

The girlfriend came with Dad to the concert. Mom didn't bring Tom. Why was she so secretive? Was she shy? Ashamed that even in this town some miles from her own where everyone knew everybody's business, people she knew would see her and find out she was dating? It wasn't too big of a scandal, Anna thought. So many parents are divorced now, and how long did they bother waiting?

Or maybe, after all those years with Dad, she was simply scared.

Ay-a stayed unfortunately silent. Anna tried to imagine her talking but it was her own voice, not Ay-a's, that resulted. *That's alright, Anna, you'll do fine with the solo* sounded hollow.

Stage lights. The band crowded together in chairs and sweater vests. Irena and her perfect breasts in hers. Darien behind her. Look back and he's busy scanning his music, a serious shadowed face too drawn in to look up. Rustling pages. Requisite tuning. Raised baton.

Rest. Rest. Rest. Rest. Wait. French horns sounding. Wisp of flutes. Long tones for a few bars. And continue. And continue. Follow the notes on the staff paper, follow the baton, stay tuned to Irena, and continue. Band song feels like a drone and she's not sure why. Caught in a hive of bees and nothing more.

Play the solo. Mild earthy clarinet sound, finger pads trilling rapidly. Michael O'Hara a dot in the audience, never Mike and probably looking proud. She's done, they're clapping.

She knows she can't connect her mind and fingers. Keep on playing like nothing is unusual. Finish the O'Hara song and start the circus-like march. Then another. And another. And another.

"Anna, your technique was great," said Mr. Haslam afterwards. His penguin eyes aglow. No lying in his countenance. Anna felt herself a shell.

"Hey, congratulations." A wrapped square pressed into her hand by Darien's larger, warmer one. "I've got to leave with my dad before he causes trouble, but you were amazing. See you tomorrow."

He moved towards the exit.

Anna recovered her breath. "Thanks," she said once he

was too far away to hear.

She tucked the box into her bag with her music folder so Mom wouldn't see it. Opened it at home, behind her closed bedroom door flashing warning signs that reminded her to peel the tape with care and not tear the bright blue paper. It was a box of chocolates. A very small one.

Dear Liss,

I'm going to start pretending to write you letters that I'll never actually send you. Maybe this is stupid. But I don't care. I'm not going to cross anything out. I hate my jobs. My mom's acting like she's my age now that she's got her Tom, and she's hotter than me too. No wonder she's getting laid. And you see, there's this boy. He's probably gay. I ~~still wonder sometimes if~~ I I don't want to hope too much, but I want to believe in the hope that I have anyway. Because I've fallen in love, again. You know what that's like. I bet you're with someone now. ~~I wonder what would've happened if~~ You're another one of those people who's hotter than me. And has better luck. But I shouldn't say that because of course I'm lucky to have my musical talent and blablabla as people keep reminding me, even though I didn't grow up with those teaching tapes like you and your sisters did. And even though I've gotten too old to be a real prodigy anymore. Or maybe I still am? I wish I was. But music isn't drawing me in the way it used to. It used to be a perfect world that I basically lived in. Yeah, you know this already. But I had my nice life for the most part, until I realized how wrong it was between my parents without me knowing it. It let me just be completely into the music and it was a miracle thing, practice was never boring or a chore. Now it is a lot of the time and instead I get addicted to... other things haha. People said I did a good job on my solo but it didn't feel like it at all. Anyway, I wish I knew what you were up to in your magical life (something brilliant, I'm sure) but I'm not going to write you a real letter and I don't even know where you are if I did want to send one.

Anna sat outside in the schoolyard, her felt jacket buttoned. It was leafless and getting colder. That morning there'd been frost in the yard where the garden used to be. She didn't want to wear gloves but the air was slowly numbing her hands, so she dug the thin gloves out of her pocket and put them on. She watched the little kids in the side yard play skipping and clapping games and push each other down the slides. There were more little kids playing king of the mountain out front. Grass forts had dwindled now that the grass was brown and snow was anticipated. Out back, a circle of older kids played anime card games beneath a pine tree, groups meandered across the grounds and loitered with their backs against the school, a couple made out in a corner. She'd watched these things forever. She wondered what it would have been like to go to different schools as she got older like the public school kids did, for elementary-age kids to be a source of nostalgia rather than a screaming physicality a few feet away. She didn't feel connected to these kids and their games. Of course, she never had been.

Ay-a had walked this schoolyard. Her varicolored shimmers of fabric had trailed the yards of browning grass, her feet never visible. Anna was going to be a real musician soon, a real concert performer. Going to see if the prodigy luck that had tailed her so far would hold. True, she was off or clumsy sometimes and had to polish her pieces, but it was her facility people like Darien liked, the way things came too easily. Like having a bowl of chocolate ice cream and a spoon placed in front of her and having the instinct to eat. It seemed a separate thing from her, a fluke that she could play so well, an accident of genetics that her pitch was apt and her fingers could move fast. Anna was a spectator to this with her want and fear and scalding need to be alone.

Things that seemed immovable ended all the time. Her parents had ended. Liss's attendance at Pine Grove had ended. After all these years, faced with the need to sit among an orchestra and play for real, Anna wondered if her fluke would end. And what if it did? Would the work she put in too lazily be enough? It wouldn't. She was either going to luck out as she always had, be caught by the net called talent that protected her, or she was going to fail. She tried out the idea of failure but couldn't visualize it. Its hovering elusiveness disturbed her. It was there, there, there. But what, exactly? Something she knew but couldn't believe in, something she couldn't touch.

But what if Ay-a knew how to meld with the keyboard? What if her bones were unbreakable, her substance unmeltable? Anna had never thought these things, but they felt true. Ay-a didn't question. The goddess that had once stood tall seemed smaller today, her hair a dark cascade against copper skin. A surge of joyous disturbance rose in Anna. The part of her that wondered about failure watched this and tried to analyze.

Ay-a and failure stood on two sides of the playground. Wagner swept between them, splendid.

Mom was out again, and it was by pure accident that Anna discovered the tapes, looking around to see if the old, overfull, underused part of the video cabinet had anything she hadn't watched or would want to. She never looked there, and doubted it. There were old Barney tapes, a few documentaries about sustainable agriculture and opera and some fancy dollhouse, videos labeled "Anna piano age 5," "Anna piano recital age 7," "Anna learning clarinet." She took out "Anna piano age 5" and turned on the old VCR. A tiny girl with chipmunk cheeks sat on the piano bench in this same living room, the TV fuzzing gray bars across the screen. Her fingers, small and perfect, trickled over the keys in "The Waltz of the Flowers." Dad walked across the screen and she winced. Even back then, the piano was in tune—the younger Anna had made sure of it. Her older self waited for her fingers to slip. They did not, even at the end of the piece where the child's motions seemed for a moment uncertain, then recovered gracefully. Anna wanted to slap that girl.

Before putting the tape back, she rummaged behind the front row to see if there was anything else interesting. More home videos, documentaries, old musicals—and crammed in the very back, some DVDs she hadn't seen before.

Cum to the Doctor's Office.

Oh. My. God.

Mom had porn. Her mom had porn?

Unpleasant imaginings of Mommy-and-Tommy replayed in her mind. The question of whether her mother masturbated on the sofa, and when on earth she'd find the time. Perfect blackmail material, if ever needed. Disgusting, but she had to watch this.

The camera fell on a Photoshop-smoothed man and woman in stilted dialogue about a doctor's checkup. A cut and they'd left the waiting room. The woman lay prone on the sterile-looking white bed of an examining table, naked, her round breasts too obvious. Soon the man was naked too, still talking about check-ups and proper pelvic function as he climbed on top. They were long-limbed rubber things. They reminded Anna of beached whales. The man inserted—close-up on pucker and tube sliding inside—and they started bouncing. The penis went up and down at a silly rate. Boing, boing, boing. The woman panted feebly. Anna felt her cheeks go red. Her eyes were stuck to the screen.

She watched a young gay couple. One of the men was built like Darien. Rather, he was the same height, and had the same angle to his jaw. It wasn't much, but it was enough to transfix. The other man put a stethoscope to his bare (shaved?) chest. The camera tracked their muscles' contours. The other guy had a tattoo and wasn't bad looking either. His biceps reminded her of Ed—she had to stop thinking of guys she knew! The stethoscope came off, Ed's hand reached to stroke Darien's cheek, and their lips locked. With their slow-motion kisses, Anna's hand moved unthinkingly to her own cheek. The tiny details of their faces as they moved, the forehead creases, blinks, the sound of breath, the angle of Darien's jaw. She couldn't stand it. Her head was a whirl of crescendoing cadenzas, measures running prestissimo, too fast to recognize, electric. It was the first time something new crossed her musical synapses, if this was new. Was this something in her possible, uncovered? But then they were fucking. Buried under the grunting bicep man, the slimmer guy's resemblance to Darien was obscured. And then it was back to some stupid guy and girl again.

Her mom wasn't going to be back that night. She'd practiced enough. She paused the DVD and went to the kitchen to microwave herself a bag of popcorn.

"My mom watches porn," she said to the potted African violet on the windowsill. "Can you believe it?" The violet didn't return her incredulous laughter.

Of course she didn't say anything about the porn. Part of her was ashamed at her discovery, at tangible evidence of her mom's sex life, at her occasional enjoyment between the revolted giggles and the distraction of popcorn. If Mom knew Anna had found the porn, she'd probably guess Anna had watched it. All the better to keep it secret, since there were other nights Mom would be gone, and other tapes. Might as well watch it, urged a sly voice. Maximum value. Fun for the whole family!

But there was the concert to contend with. Five-year-old Anna from the home video could have done as well, she figured, as she was doing now. Nerves messed her up. Her fingers ran too heavy or too light. "You have other things on your mind," said Laine. How's your sex life? Anna thought to say, but didn't. Laine naked with a stethoscope was a disturbing, if not entirely unappealing, picture. And she was pretty sure she found herself blushing around Darien, inadvertently picturing him kissing a guy who looked like Ed. She wondered about the music she'd heard, pictured a score labelled *Doctor Porn Symphony!*, but her usually great musical recall failed this time.

Ay-a lived in her, and those old desires singed more than ever. Which was, when she thought about it, encouraging. If she wasn't dead, her music wouldn't be either. The next time Mom was gone, she resolved to practice all night.

"All night?" asked Darien. "You serious?"

"Yeah." She found herself glaring at him. "Hey, you wanna come over?" Another outburst, Ay-a's doing. That damn invented goddess was saying things without her permission. This wasn't good.

"What?"

"When I'm practicing. Or something."

Foot. In. Mouth.

Ay-a cheered her on.

"All *night?* I don't think—" he paused, and his face darkened. "Maybe I will. Would be nice to get away from my place. If it's OK, though, I might have to bring a sleeping bag in case I get too tired."

No need, we've got a fold-out couch you can use."

"Oh. Thanks."

She introduced Mom to Darien in the car. "My friend from school." They shook hands, she thought, with too much politeness, but Darien seemed too mild to arouse her mother's suspicion. Not that there was anything to suspect. Mom insisted on taking his coat to hang in the closet, and cut him a flower-shaped spread of apple slices on one of the fancy plates while he answered questions about his saxophone playing, favorite musicians, and where he'd moved from. Then she drove away.

Coolly, Anna tidied the counter. There was so much to do, stray dishes to put in the dishwasher, crumbs to wipe, a smudge on the counter to clean up. She was suddenly embarrassed of the house that Darien was looking around curiously. The pictures on the walls were too pretentious. The kitchen too chaotic. The living room furniture too high-backed and cold, sterile as if unlived in. Darien was quiet while she cleaned. She thought, I'm acquiring Mom's nervous tics. She didn't like it.

"Are you going to practice now?" Darien's voice seemed cold, cutting as it did through the silence, its first words coming like a scold.

Words clamored forth about everything else. "Hey, have you ever had a garden in the spring? We used to have one all the time til Dad moved out, and I miss it. Even though the raccoons ate the corn and the carrots never got very big. I think I'm going to plant one this year again." She hadn't thought of doing that before, but in that moment it seemed extremely important.

"Oh, cool." He was distracted—just what Anna had wanted to happen, without realizing it.

"And you know what's hilarious? I found some DVDs in the video cabinet—"

"And?"

"They were porn! My mom has a porn stash!" She wanted to swallow her blurting tongue and melt into the flowered floor tiles. But Darien laughed loudly.

"Your mom? I don't believe it!"

"Look, I'll show you." She'd misstepped, but had to go through with it now. She led him to the video cabinet and pulled out the discs. "See, it's stupid doctor porn." She was too caught in her own discomfort to notice the way he shifted nervously and his eyes rolled elsewhere around the room. She had to keep moving. She put a DVD in, feeling something frantic in her chest. They settled on opposite ends of the couch with a few feet of space between them. This tape was a new one, and it began abruptly with two blonde women necking.

Their panting was heavy, their smacking obvious. Black lace lingerie clung to their contours. The camera closed in on their lips, dewed over, dancing wetly. *Was this what we looked like—?* A pair of women and their tumbling hair. *We could have been so glorious.* Anna froze. Make one move and she would shiver. Her stomach churned. She didn't want to remember.

Ay-a was the dark grabbing thing in her. There was no separation. She needed it. Her gaze lurched towards Darien. The space between them hurt.

His body was strangely tense. Sitting erect. Ha ha.

Turn off the movie. He's uncomfortable, and it's rude.

Grab him.

He doesn't want you.

Yeah right, Liss would say. If I were her, I'd just reach over and find out.

Carved jaw, shadow of hair, downcast eyes. Valkyries crescendoing.

If she didn't do something right now to break the insufferable space, she would have to damage something. Take angry bites from her upper arm. Kick the garbage can as hard as she could. Put her fist through the TV screen.

If you don't act now, you never will.

She lunged across and traced an S on his cheek. Her movements were abrupt and hungry. She swept an arm around him and pressed her lips against his cheek, kept them there shaking, then pressed them to his lips. She bent her body to his and held herself there. Felt his chest against her breast, raw skin under shirts. Didn't wonder about him but bent for another kiss, and his lips kissed back. Her tongue broke into his mouth and did not surprise him. He breathed heavily like a surfaced diver. Their hands roved across each other. Strange places like the underside of her arm tingled. Was this what drugs were like? She was insatiable and sated, the sensations half excitement, half relief. She felt an incredible lightness with that distance gone. She gulped it down, moved away to pull off his sweaty shirt. She traced and kissed the contours of the muscles underneath. He made no move to take off her shirt, so she pulled it over her head. She hesitated in her embarrassingly plain cotton bra, then unhooked it. Shirtless, she curled against him. If Darien heard the porn stars' gasping, if it worked as background stimulation, she wouldn't know. All that surrounded them had ceased to exist.

So she didn't notice the door opening, or Darien's eyes going wide, or the voice calling "I forgot the cake, Tom and I were going to have it for dessert." She noticed Darien pushing her away, then she was face to face with Mom, gape-mouthed, watching her topless daughter making out with just-a-friend on the couch, with one of her own porn tapes grunting on TV. Mom shrunk back.

Darien was the first to speak. "I'm sorry," he said. "I'm extremely sorry. We haven't done anything wrong."

"Get your hands off my daughter!" This was redundant, as his hands had left Anna minutes ago.

Anna was frozen, but Ay-a reacted. Indignation flared through her still-present shame. Anna brusquely pulled on her shirt and stood up in front of Mom. "Look who's the pot calling the kettle black."

"That's different. We're, we're, consenting adults, and we've been seeing each other for a while!"

"So are we. And for your information, this was my idea."

"You'd better not be having sex at this age."

"Who said anything about sex?" Her hand flew to her hip. "By the way, those are good porn tapes."

Mom stood there gaping like a goldfish. Anna felt Ay-a solidly behind her, a flare in her near-black eyes. She pressed a palm to Darien's shoulder. If need be, she would protect him.

Chapter 10: *Garden of Moments*

Ages Seven to Thirteen

Anna was nine when time caught her knowingly. She made a list of it afterwards in her journal.

Location: Classroom

Time: Recess, approxamitly approximately 12:15 PM

People in the room: Nobody

The room was empty as a slate, everyone else having chewed up or packed up their sandwiches, made a game of slam-dunking baggies in the garbage can or in a crumpled hoop around it, and stomped out booted into the snow. Anna had two bites of ham sandwich left and couldn't decide whether or not to eat them.

Liss leaned over and kicked her. "Let's *go!*" What would happen, Anna wondered, if she sat there and said nothing?

"You can put your sandwich away! You don't even like ham, you said so. And I have to tell you my dream."

Sit there and say nothing.

Liss stared for a long moment.

Say nothing.

"What's wrong with you today?" Liss whirled around, lurched towards Sarah Gates, and grabbed her by the arm. Anna heard her say "Come on then, let's go build a fort." Sarah looked surprised only for a minute. She was a head taller than Liss, and followed her quickly. Anna watched the two girls walk out to the hallway, Liss's skirt flouncing from speed.

Two bites of sandwich. Maybe three if she ate them small. That would make it last longer, this moment she was alone in the classroom, paused between decisions.

She saw kids out the window having snowball fights and playing tag. She saw Liss and Sarah walking arm in arm. She could stay in this empty classroom all recess and do what she wanted. Imagine she was in another world, and keep the quiet to herself. Sneak into a practice room like the older kids and play the piano. Go join Liss and Sarah at the fort they'd said they'd make.

Or she could get up, go out, and leave them.

She looked to the shelf beside her where a pile of scribblers, the class's English journals, waited for the teacher to correct them. Anna's was in the middle, with a dark purple cover. She looked at the thin book buried in the pile of everyone else's writing as if it didn't matter. It would matter. It *would*. She would remember it forever. She would be grown up and look back on the pile of scribblers on the white shelf and this moment when she was nine would be alive for her and she'd be inside it again. She saw the scribblers in this present now, and she saw them in the present of her future, looking back. She couldn't see what the future was, or who she was in the future, but it was there in the room. She was 19 and remembering, 29 and remembering, 69 - an old lady - and still remembering. She saw the purple cover and remembered it forever.

She'd written about her Life's History in that journal. She pictured the moments she had and hadn't written about as capsules spread out in a garden. Each contained a flower or a few. They were translucent but she couldn't touch what was in them unless she got close and put herself inside the glass. Against a green expanse the flower-filled capsules looked like tiny paperweights or bell jars, even flying saucers. Inside grew tulips, forget-me-nots, lilacs, roses, daylilies, trumpet vines, morning glories, lupins, wisteria, covered with the tiniest shards of ice. The capsules too were frosted like sea glass, filling the space inside with illusionary mist. She wasn't sure if they quite touched the ground. This moment of the purple scribbler would soon be enclosed in its own capsule, and she'd be in another clump of flowers. But she saw the garden spread across the spaces where the desks sat. All the moments were alive for her now, present.

There was the time when Mom started her job outside the house. "I'm not used to working with *people*," she said. "It's been so long." She had a habit of chewing on her lower lip whenever she was about to try something new. Stirring the batter the first time she tried carrot cake, "à la homemade" she said in a voice like the Tide commercial lady's with a thinly stretched smile, she bit at a flake of mouth skin. She rubbed balm from a tub that smelled like pine needles onto her lips every night. "Axle grease," Dad called it, but Mom bought Anna some and made her put it on too. Anna wondered what her mother's lips would feel like if she didn't use that thick smelly gel.

"I don't want to go to work tomorrow," Mom said, knitting some white thing or maybe it was the color called eggshell or cream, Anna's eyes couldn't tell the difference. She remembered a dream where mothers had compound eyes like giant horseflies, and she was frozen in their kaleidoscope stares. The knitting needles clicked too fast. Mom slipped a stitch and fumbled to rethread it. "If only that opera company— And I barely remember what it's like to have a boss. I've got to start making some money for us. But what if— Can't think, can't think. Anna, you ever get so you can't think?"

Anna couldn't think then, so she said, "Yeah."

"It can't be so bad, it's just going to be sitting in a little booth and translating what people say. I've known French all my life. I mean, what's the worst that could happen?" She grinned, as if the sentence were a blanket to hold onto.

"Everyone could hate it. People could laugh," said Anna. It was a game. "All the lights could go out, and—the chandelier could come crashing down and crack your head open." Suddenly Anna was back in her dream, stilled by the leer of compound eyes.

"What's the worst that could happen?" Mom said it again, not as a question but as an answer. Anna stared out the window—snakes could sinew their way across the grassy lawn and muscle through the glass, one would brunt its way into the fridge where they would find it tomorrow curled like a baby, another would drape around her mother's neck like a scarf. She'd walk to her new job forgetting it was there, and along the way it would chew at the flakes on her lip, leaving poison gel for her to lick. Another would get into Anna's stomach while she was sleeping and lay an egg—

"The worst thing," Mom repeated, with a smile that didn't flicker like the commercial lady's. The knitting lay scrunched up on the sofa. She puckered her lips—tasting something milky—no, whistling. Now she was a bird, maybe in her feather-white dress. She'd sung this old song lots of times before, something French about love and a rebellious bird. Anna wondered what there was to whistle about.

There was the moment when Dad stomped into the house with his face crumpled. Uncle Theo, Aunt Bet and the cousins were over. The boys brought their video games and sat playing on the couch. Anna had asked to play and held a controller shaped like a chunky boomerang. "Press Start," said her cousin Todd, and the screen changed from a grid of pick-your-character boxes to a platform where characters walked around. She couldn't figure out which buttons on the weirdly shaped controller made her cartoon princess on the screen do what. She hammered A and B and moved the joystick wildly. The boys seemed to press all the buttons at the same time, their hands were that fast. Hers, so fast at the piano, were clumsy on the joystick.

A giant bug-eating plant with a red cap and white spots walked towards the characters, swinging its leaves back and forth, snapping its jaws. The boys yelled at it as they banged on buttons, "Die! Die!" and their stubby little characters advanced punching. Anna mashed buttons too, hoping they would do something, but her character disappeared offscreen. Suddenly the plant chomped and she saw her princess in its jaws. That's when Dad came in.

His feet were dirt-clouds and his breath was like a horse's after running. He disappeared quickly like her princess— stomped up the stairs (*thud-thud-thudthud-thudthudthud*), then paused, a whole rest. Then *thunk, thonk, crackacrack, fwip*. She pulled her zippered sweater tight around her and shivered as the throb of noises pressed against her ribs.

She ran to the piano. *Thwonk!* A low E. *Thud!* A low G. She pressed her finger to a key and listened as the echo matched the sound.

"Anna, stop that!"

She heard and pressed and banged. Every note upstairs was answered by her angry hands. If she could make her own storm, the other wouldn't hurt her.

She heard the grown-ups talk that night while she sat pretending to review her music theory homework. Something about what an idiot her dad's boss was and the lousy job market and what to do now. He spent five months around the house before getting hired back for a lower-level inspection job in the same department. His face must have been clouded for some of that time, but Anna remembered jokes about the Unemployment Trolls coming to live in the basement and the taste of sausages from the grill.

There was the day when Liss came over to Anna's home forest. Anna belonged there, navigating root systems under the moss, breathing pine. She showed Liss the clearing where she'd kept a stash of all the fallen branches and called it her wood collection until she decided she was too old for that and she couldn't think of a use for a wood collection anyway. On a pale gray rock overlooking a tiny hollow, she'd come to stand most days since Sunday School started, holding onto a dogwood branch that leaned overhead, looking to the sky and praying. Our-father-who-art-in-heaven-hallowed-be-thy-name, it used to be. Now it was Ay-a. Ay-a, help me get a 100% on my Social Studies test. Ay-a, please make sure the audience likes my playing. Please make Laine happy and please don't let my mom get mad at me for finishing the cookies. Ay-a, please make me beautiful and strong and give me a voice like Liss's, even though I know you won't. Anna called this place the Prayer Land, but only to herself. She had to show Liss the rock and tell her how she spoke to Ay-a. She didn't tell her what she prayed for.

Through the carpet of moss she led Liss to the cat tree, the one old oak with a low trunk that she could climb most easily. She'd named it that because she could clamber right to the edge of the largest branch the way a cat could, lie stretched on her stomach and observe the goings-on below, forest movements and beyond them the still lawn with its postage stamp garden and cardboard box house, with eyes she imagined saw everything. On the ground she was smaller and didn't know as much, but she could always climb back up.

"Come up here," she said, and Liss followed her easily through the branches, a darting smaller body. Anna perched on the edge of the widest spot and Liss's face poked out behind her through leaves and their speckled shadows. Anna was thrilled with the knowledge that here, on her own land, she was the leader. Liss settled behind and pressed her hand on Anna's shoulder.

"Look," she said. "We can see everything."

"That's why I go up here," said Anna.

Liss's breath came in thinly, quickened. "There's a little river thing. There's the house, way over there. Look how little the trees are! This is the perfectest thing ever."

Anna didn't know what to say. She'd wanted to be the one

to point things out. But Liss grabbed Anna and pulled her in. "This is some kind of magic, isn't it?"

"The magic that puts us above everything else. Like flying without moving."

"It's *our* magic," said Liss. "And we should do a ceremony."

Anna let excitement run through her and inhaled the smell of pine. Liss placed her left hand over Anna's chest, and with her right, guided one of Anna's to her own. "Do you promise we'll always be in each other's hearts?"

Anna shivered—there was a certain horror-movie excitement in the idea of their making vows—and felt epic. She pressed her hand to Liss's, which held it. "I promise. Do you promise?"

"I promise."

"Forever and ever?" asked Anna.

"Forever and ever. Do—"

"Shh," Anna hissed. They sat very still while a squirrel with its wind-up motions moved inches from her knees.

"Now we need to make a sacrifice." Liss's voice spiked higher.

"Not the squirrel!"

"No, stupid. We'll make a man and burn it, like they did in the old days. Only not a real one. C'mon, let's get down from the tree."

Liss climbed down first, and Anna followed. "Is there anything we can make a man with?" asked Liss on the ground, kicking a sapling. Anna wanted to tell her to stop, but Liss started walking towards the house and she forgot about the poor baby tree. She thought of Dad's old clothes, but those would be missed.

"I think we have some garbage bags in the kitchen. And we can probably use rags and duct tape. And permanent markers for the face and stuff."

Mom walked in on Liss taping together a stomach and arms and Anna drawing the most scary-looking face she could imagine. The eyes bulged over sharp eyebrows. The mouth snarled.

"What are you doing?" asked Mom.

"Making a scarecrow," answered Anna. She didn't want to say "a man," because that would get laughed at.

"Oh, cute. Want a hat for it? Some clothes?"

"Yeah."

They got to pick from a box of Mom and Dad's cast-offs brought out from the closet. Liss wanted to give it overalls, a vast checked shirt, and a baseball cap. That was the only kind of hat Dad ever wore. Anna grabbed one of Mom's instead, a floppy felt beige one with a ribbon around it. "That's too girly!" said Liss. "Are you crazy?"

"You picked everything else."

Anna wondered where Liss was going to put the man, but Liss had another plan first. She waited until Mom had gone to her bedroom, and asked, "Where are the matches?"

Anna hesitated, trying to picture burning on the lawn. An image from a nightmare came to mind—the house on fire, red tongues flicking out.

"Don't be a chicken. Where?"

Liss started rummaging through cabinets. She went to the telephone table, where Anna knew they were kept, and the top drawer opened with a creak. "Found them!" Her voice held the same wild excitement. "Follow me and bring the man!"

She ran catlike to the door.

Anna carried the scarecrow out to the forest where Liss ran. She lifted it (it was awfully light) into the clearing with the pale gray rock and dogwood, just steps away from the cat tree. Light splintered down bright enough to drench them, and the ground was red with long pine needles. "Here's where we'll do it," said Liss, and pointed to the rock.

"But this is a sacred clearing," said Anna.

"Perfect," said Liss.

"But we can't wreck it!"

"That's what sacrifices are for. They destroy things so the gods can make better things grow from them. Better things like you can't even imagine better."

"No." Anna's hands tightened on her hips. The man fell to the ground, between dogwood and pine in a puddle, Mom's lovely beige hat spilling off.

"We've gotta do it." Liss propped the man up against a pine tree. Anna couldn't think fast enough to move. She watched wide-eyed while Liss struck a match and held the flame to its body. It didn't take at first, so she threw it down and struck another one. Anna heard rustling, and the stink of burning garbage bags mixed with the sweetish smell of burning sap. They watched flames creep up and lick plaid cuffs to black and shrink the crinkling figure.

The fire was slow until suddenly it was everywhere, lapping against the tree. The pine was burning! Anna yelled and ran to Liss. Stop, stop, stop, she thought, but all she could do was scream. Liss stood in front of the horrible burning mass, still, fire reflected in her eyes.

Mom was running towards them with fear in the lines of

her face. Her old hat rested on the forest floor, untouched.

There was the hour when Anna gave a recital in a blue evening gown made for a nine-year-old that shimmered like night. She wasn't afraid of the stage after so many times on it. Laine sat in the wings, having introduced her, and smiled when she looked back. Anna walked forward to the piano bench and stood a minute looking down at the smooth wood-and-ivory box of sound. She turned and curtsied into the lights. She turned back and sat.

The first notes came in a fast trickle. She was in the music the moment her fingers landed. Her arms roved, and her back rocked slightly. Anna belonged here. She belonged wherever sound was easiest for her.

But music, the kind with clear tune and rhythm and pure shivers—was it ever easy?

Her hands knew because they'd practiced. They traced the paths they'd followed many times until tracks were left. But then came the hard part, a cadenza too fast for her fingers. The thing she'd practiced over and over and often couldn't play at the right speed.

There were seconds when time froze. Her fingers were about to trip. Her index fell on the wrong key. Her ring finger stumbled after, when it was supposed to come first.

Come on, Anna. Come on. Come on.

Her ring finger came first. Then her index. Not on the wrong key. Enough to the left to land on the right one. She kept the tempo, or thought she did, and returned to a slightly slower section. Breathe.

That's when she understood she couldn't fail.

Something inside her kept the music together, and when it was done, she curtsied to an ocean of sound. Afterwards, Aunt Bet handed her a package of chocolate chip cookies and leaned over. "You're a prodigy," she whispered to Anna, "but don't let your mother know I said that."

She looked for her mother and found her talking to Dad. She heard them before they saw her.

"I think she can be what I never could," her mother was saying.

"Is that what she wants?" her father whispered back.

Then they saw her and straightened like statues. "Anna!" said her mother. "Great job up there!"

"Let's get you home and have those cookies," said Dad.

She did want the cookies, even if they were the dry kind, but not as much as she wanted something else.

There was something inside her like an ocean. She nestled into it. She wanted to live in this place where endless music poured, making up every bit of everything alive. She didn't just hear it, she half-felt it with senses she didn't quite have. She'd have them if music was truly her world. She was so close to belonging there, almost at the point knowing, but something held her back. She couldn't feel the music enough, feel it like she so badly wanted to. But out of everyone, maybe she was the only one who almost could.

She was in another capsule now, staring at her dark purple English scribbler in the pile. She could walk away. She could leave Liss who always picked the games and always told her what to do. They weren't tied together. She, too, could find someone else to spend recess with. Could do whatever she wanted.

Flimsy marshmallow forts fringed the schoolyard fence. She passed bigger forts like castles with slides, snowmen of different sizes, a snow bear and a tiny snow dog.

She found Chen in a corner, rolling a snowball. She wondered what Chen was making, and if it would be alright to ask. Other kids and even married grown-ups had more than one friend at a time. Other kids knew how to make friends. Anna didn't really know how. Chen looked up and over at Anna. Anna looked away. She should walk off. It was rude to stare. But she looked back up and kept watching. Chen looked at her again and she quickly pretended to stare at the snow-covered slide.

Chen walked over slowly. "Hi," she said.

"Hi," said Anna.

"What are you doing?"

"Nothing. What are you making?"

"A really big snowman. Wanna help?"

Anna stood there. "Can I?"

"Yeah. You can make the middle." Chen went back to rolling her snowball, which was still small enough to fit in Anna's arms. Anna bent down in her snow pants and packed a tiny ball. The marks left by her gloves made it look prickly. She rolled into a log, flipped it, rolled the other side as Chen pushed the bigger snowball beside her. They packed the bottom ball in with snow—Chen added extra until it looked like the snowman was wearing a skirt—and hoisted the middle on top.

As she rolled a head, Anna found bits for the arms and face: a couple branches by the hill, small twigs for eyes, mouth and nose, pine tufts she stuck on top to make bushy green hair. She had to tiptoe to reach, and her boots sunk into the snow. Clumps of crystals melted against her cold foot.

Anna grinned at the snowman. She liked that the hair was her idea, and that Chen hadn't minded it at all.

The next day, she and Chen started a fort. She watched Liss build one on the other side of the playground, with Sarah. Liss stopped inviting her over. When Anna's mother asked if she still liked Liss, she shrugged.

She almost stopped noticing Liss's soaring voice in chorus, too busy talking with Chen or memorizing the words or daydreaming herself into some heaven beyond the ceiling. She almost stopped minding when Liss got the solos, and in sixth grade she stopped having to take chorus and could pick a music history class instead. Besides, she had her own performances. She played in school concerts and gave recitals in front of clapping faces. She started playing clarinet the year after her break with Liss. Although it was less natural for her to play something that involved breath as well as fingers, she was getting the First Clarinet pieces in no time. She liked owning her own small instrument that she could carry around and take care of. She played the organ at church and occasionally at weddings. It was the only thing she liked about church anymore, and the stuffy loudness of the wedding ceremonies was enough to make up her mind that she'd never get married.

Not long after Mom bought her an electric razor, Chen started hanging actor posters in her locker. "Don't you think he's cute?" she asked, pointing to someone's smile or someone else's bare chest. Anna couldn't see why cuteness was important. She was too consumed with nightmares about growing giant breasts and gorilla leg hair that invariably ended with her parents yelling—at her, at each other, at everything. She wasn't normal enough to care about something like guys, until she saw Ed's cartoons in music history class.

She was thirteen when she and Liss were partnered up for a Social Studies presentation. They had to choose a country to research and present to the class. Liss wanted to do India because she'd decided she looked like a Bollywood actress and thought her birth parents might have come from there. They went to Anna's house and searched for curry recipes on the internet. "If we feed the teacher, he'll love us," said Liss. She looked around the office, where a Degas print hung next to a painting of island lupins, but stacks of Dad's once well-stacked papers had come to overflow their drawers and puddle in untidy heaps on the floor.

"This place has changed," said Liss.

When Mom brought snacks and suggested they take a break, they turned on the TV and watched a blooper show. They laughed as cats toppled out of boxes and football players wiped out on the grass. A kid went to blow out the candles on a blue-frosted birthday cake and his face fell into the frosting. Liss snorted. Anna laughed louder. Liss shoved her and she shoved back. "So why don't we hang out anymore again?" Liss asked.

They made up an India Rap and got an A on their presentation, another memory encapsulated in the Garden of Moments. They fell back into inseparability as if there had been no time out between it.

Chapter 11: *Suspension*

Age Fourteen

At fourteen, Liss came onto the playground humming a Rita Deviant song. Her hair was tied like Rita's, in an untidy ponytail, and a small chain dangled from her jeans. She'd used a lighter to burn a few holes in her black t-shirt.

She collapsed onto the grass. "I can't wait to get my license. The day I do, I'm gonna buy a car and get outta here." Her long metallic earrings clinked as she gestured.

"Where are you gonna go?" asked Anna. They'd been over this before, but the answers changed.

"I told ya, I'm going to Nashville. They record all kinds of music there, not just country. I'm sure there's a band there that would have a spot for my talent." She tilted back her head in mock arrogance.

"Country Western Violinist," said Anna.

"Hey, there are some pretty sweet combos. Not everyone's as narrow-minded as the mainstream." She picked a blade of grass, stuck it between her teeth, whistled. Anna moved her science textbook from lap to grass. She'd taken it outside to study for the test the next day, but it didn't seem likely she'd get much studying done.

"You should hear the music I'm gonna make someday! It'll be like nothing that's existed before." Liss leaned forward, causing light patterns to shift across the top of her head. "People will listen and it will do something amazing to them."

It already does, thought Anna.

"It'll make them laugh and scream and dance 'til they go mad. It'll make them furious. It'll make them know things. It'll make them want to change this pathetic plastic world. Break it apart and put a new one in its place. Rita's got that," said Liss. "You *know*. She's got the soul and she does things to ya. Who needs drugs and all that other stuff when music can break and make you like that?"

Anna didn't get the power in Rita Deviant's songs. For her they were, like many others, mildly energizing and fun to dance to. They had a thumping bass beat, some funky techno sounds, admittedly good electric guitar, and the lyrics were often silly, at best mediocre. Liss's softer voice sang them better than Rita's grating one. Liss began a song right then.

I'm gonna ache I'm gonna take until the break of dawn
We're gonna shake we're gonna quake we're gonna get it on

Here the music broke into instrumentals, guitar screeches and low percussion moans for a full minute and a half. Liss simply tapped her knees intoning "Danananana," then went back to singing.

I'm so hot like you'll never see, hot like you'll never be,
like honey in the club and all the guys are flies.
I'm the star of the human race, gon' take this club to outer space,
and what you're gonna see you won't believe your eyes.

"I had a dream that I was Rita last night," she said afterwards. "It was the best thing in the world."

"What happened in it?"

"I was onstage singing and playing guitar and, well, it was

like one big orgasm."

Anna wondered if Liss had had an orgasm. Probably. She certainly hadn't. Maybe most girls would have by now—she had to look that up on the internet.

But Liss continued the dream, her cheeks glazed in light that came over the hill. "I was making out with people, all these people. And we ended up in this place with an indoor pool, and realized we were surrounded by mirrors, reflecting us in a million directions. You shoulda seen what I saw in those mirrors. Sexy as hell. Rita Deviant, a million times, right there, reflected from my own body. Imagine seeing *that.*"

Anna pictured Liss making out with "all these people"—men in suits, men with tattoos, boys smelling of concert sweat, svelte boys like Ed who carried agenda books and played the piano beautifully. In the mirrors they multiplied to hordes. And there was supposed to be a pool, wasn't there? She visualized men in lawn chairs, doing the backstroke and front crawl and butterfly, having splash fights and paddling around on pool noodles. Two of them wrestled in the water. They had perfect muscles, being figments of imagination. Liss looked as Liss always did—small with a wavy ponytail, and unlike Rita Deviant who wasn't all that interesting. Energy rippled off Liss like heat, but that wasn't unusual.

"Anna," said Liss, "why aren't you saying anything?"

She was embarrassed. Liss tried a few more times to prompt conversation, then settled into Anna's silence. They sat there, people-watching on top of the hill.

Irena strode by, Michelle beside her, both in tight jeans and cute jean jackets. "Preps," said Liss from their vantage point out of earshot. "Sell-outs."

"They're not so bad," said Anna.

"Speak for yourself. They're like walking magazine ads. It's that sort of conformity that's ruining the world."

Anna could see her point, but she liked Michelle's vitality. And she and Irena sat next to each other in Band, and she'd heard songs that Irena composed a few times. Once Irena had given her a piece she'd written for clarinet, signed with a small plump heart on top. She'd played it in her room in the half-light of evening, and it had made her shiver. She didn't trust these girls, but she couldn't look down on them either.

"Look, there goes Lover Boy!"

Liss *would* notice Ed before she did. Luckily she hadn't spoken loudly. Ed was talking with Jacques, a shorter guy in glasses. He was middling height himself, thin but athletic, his blond hair always gelled forward. When he played the drum kit, it swung around as his body got into the rhythm. Ed was studious but not quiet, always cracking jokes in class. Half of them were some twist on the subject matter, so no one minded. Once she'd seen him caricature their science teacher's jowls and too-short pants. Another time she'd noticed a comic strip involving a boy in a baseball cap, a girl with breasts, and a bug-eyed squirrel. "Great drawings," she'd said lamely, and he'd smiled. She had taken to drawing her own cartoons in the margins of her pages, hoping he would notice, nervous he would criticize because she, unlike Ed, was no artist.

"Are you going to do anything about him, or are you just going to keep staring forever?"

Anna shrugged. "You're the one who brought him up. Maybe you should ask him out." Liss, confident and beautiful, would stand a chance.

But she wrinkled her nose. "I don't want him."

"Who do you like, then?"

"Ryan's not bad." She shrugged, leaving Anna disappointed at her lack of grand passions. Then Liss looked away, onto the playground. Anna couldn't tell who she was looking at. "Come on," Liss said then, "at least ask him to dance at the next dance. You're cute. You'll get him for sure."

He was too good for her. But he *had* smiled. Once in theory class, they'd watched a video about composition and his eyes (clear blue) kept flicking back towards her, and each time she looked down. She couldn't remember anything from the video. But she'd probably read too much into the looks, or what she thought were looks. It was like a conspiracy theory— think about it, and you start seeing signs everywhere.

Anna pictured herself in the gym between strobe lights refracting dancers and music blaring from speakers, striding up to Ed:

"Hi."

"Hey Ed."

"Hey, wanna dance?" She couldn't do it. Ed didn't notice her at dances. No one did.

Still, she bought magazines at the corner store, plastered with smiling famous faces and neon pink headlines: How to Get His Attention! What Men Are Really Thinking! She hid them in her backpack from her mother, who probably wouldn't care but Anna didn't want to take chances, and read them in a tent beneath her sheets. Because she was too old to hang a Keep Out sign, she started collecting Danger signs to put around her room. Falling Rocks. Caution: Men at Work. Moose Crossing. The weirder, the better.

The light through Anna's window had dimmed to sepia. She was reading an article with a garish orange headline, How to Decode Guys' Body Language, when Dad lurched through the door. He smelled of sweat. She heard him pause against the wall and could tell he was wobbly.

"Where were you?" Mom called out from the living room.

"With friends."

Don't argue, thought Anna. Don't argue!

"What friends?"

"Oh, you know. The guys from work."

Was that a slur in his voice?

The next week, he helped her with math homework, sitting together at the kitchen table with Coke and cheese and crackers, decoding algebraic equations until they made enough sense for her to solve them. Mom walked past stiffly, keeping her distance.

Two weeks later they were fighting again. Mom shouting as Anna came through the door with her backpack, Dad edging towards her, face like a storm. Anna dropped her bag, ran in front of Mom and yelled in her father's direction, instincts wanting to shield her mother with sound. Her father's hand stung her face. She reeled and white spots fuzzed her vision, mold spattered through the house.

She dreamed of wrestling her father off of his armchair and pounding him against the wood floor over and over. The grimace she'd see. The blood that would come out.

Her playing grew frantic. She tended to the bruise like a perverse medal, caked it carefully with makeup because her mother made her, but told Liss the story. She ran her fingers over it before her piece at the regional music festival, which won first place in her age division. She won at the provincials too. Safe in her room, she pressed her trophies to the reddened spot on her cheek and was soothed by the lingering sting.

"Don't tell me you're going to do it."

"Yeah, Chen, I think I'm going to do it."

In history class, the most sedate, all things monumental happened. Chen sat on one side of Anna, Liss on the other, both watching her intently. She looked down at her paper and scribbled a heart. Another, interlinked. Then another. 1914 Archduke Franz Ferdinand of Austria assassinated. Start of war. Heart, heart, heart, heart, heart.

"He likes you," said Liss. "How can he not like you?"

"What, did you ask him?"

"Of course I did. In gym class. He said you were hot and he's craaazy about you." She grinned.

Anna's shoulders tensed. Heart, heart, heart was all well and good. Nothing frightening in the imagined, the impossible idea of someone like him liking someone like her, someone nothing like Liss, someone caged in timidity and confusion with her flat chest and the dusting of pimples on her forehead. But the thought of Ed, standing in front of her— Ed, in the flesh—

And in a mental flash they sat cross-legged in front of a river, grass on their calves, the sky dipped in gold and auburn, holding between them one of those two-dollar, too-sweet trifle cups from the school cafeteria. Their spoons dipped towards each other. They leaned in, licking cake and pudding. Lilacs bloomed around them, though it was quickly getting too dark to see the purple. A voice much like her mother's sang out, *Je veux vivre dans ce rêve...* Their spoons touched. Their noses brushed. He could move closer, could lean in and kiss her. Not that she knew what a kiss was like except from watching. Not that she'd been touched much, ever, at all.

Chen leaned across Anna, frowning at Liss. "You're lying."

Liss blinked.

"That's right, you're lying. Ed's too shy to call someone hot."

"You'd know," said Liss under her breath.

"Tell me you made that up," said Chen.

"OK. I did make that up. But Anna deserves him, and I know he'd like her."

Unsure whether to feel unnerved or encouraged, feeling instead some uncertain mix of them, Anna tore a sheet of paper from her notebook.

"You're going to do it!" Chen squealed.

"Shh," said Anna.

"I guess we should be doing our work."

But Liss whispered, "You go get him."

Anna wasn't one to chase people. She wasn't one to chase anything. Piano and music school and recitals and concerts and awards were things that just happened. There had been an active agent in her at one time, a goddess or something. But did she even do much?

She wrote across the top of the paper.

Dear Ed,
Hey Ed,
Do you know you have beautiful eyes?

Hi, how are you?
I was just wondering what our homework was for
Roses are red, violets are
I admire your study skills

"Ooh, study skills," grinned Liss.

"I think there are going to be a lot of versions of this note," said Chen, trying not to smile.

I just want to tell you I think you're
I just want to say I
You're an awesome person
I think I really like you

"Put x's and o's at the end," said Liss.

"No," said Chen, "you don't want to sound too eager."

Anna tore out another page and copied the lines she thought were least awful. She signed the note *Anna*. What to do now? Leave it on his desk before class? Then she'd have to find a time when he was gone, since he was usually early. Someone else might see the note, though, and everyone who came early would see her putting it there. He'd show it to his friends. Maybe his friends would see it first. Embarrassment steamed through her. She needed someone who could deliver the note and swear him to secrecy.

"Hey Liss, could you give my note to Ed?"

"Sure thing!"

Liss and Chen beamed at each other. Their eyes passed across Anna as if she wasn't there.

"Be careful on your mission," said Chen.

"Trust me, I'm good at this."

Anna handed the good copy to Liss and fingered the crimped edges of her first draft. She bent a corner. Then she crumpled the whole thing. Liss slipped out after class with the note hidden in the fold of her palm.

She couldn't concentrate on her homework, her clarinet playing, or her supper. Her mind replayed the incident a week ago when she'd run into Ed in the hallway. "Hey, have you read that chapter on Handel?" she'd asked.

He paused to answer her, and his friends paused with him. They didn't exchange looks, so she must have seemed normal, just a classmate asking about homework. "Not yet. I'm half done."

"Isn't it great?" she blurted out.

Great? It hadn't been great. It had been boring. Ed was great. Ed was why she couldn't think straight.

His blue eyes looked decidedly confused. "It was alright." And she started giggling. Giggling! Right there in his face. Her cheeks flushed furiously, and she had to run away.

Liss had brought Anna a folded up piece of paper, grinning and humming. She clearly hadn't read it.

Hey Anna,
Thanks for the note. I'm sorry but I'm dating someone else right now.
Hope you have a great day! :)
Ed

Another Anna would find out who Ed was dating. Liss, who had kindly not looked at the note until it was delivered, wanted to. She wondered aloud if he had made that up. "Maybe he's just not ready for a girlfriend yet," she mused. "Or maybe he likes guys." Another Anna, after finding out the girl, would track her down. Or would convince Ed, by her sheer musical genius and grace on the dance floor and slender long-haired beauty (Another Anna was always prettier), to forget that girl and pursue the more desirable woman.

Anna read and re-read the note. Anna pressed it behind the papers in her binder pocket. The square black letters almost hurt her eyes. Anna tasted imaginary trifle. Anna cried.

"Screw Ed," said Liss in the cafeteria a couple days later. Anna couldn't forget the note, and Liss's lecture wasn't helping. "'Hope you have a great day'— what a tactless thing to say to a woman you've just turned down! And the *smiley* face! Way to make it even better. Yeah, I bet he's gay. That's such a gay thing to do, don't you think? Forget that Ed moron. I bet he doesn't even know how to kiss a woman!" She said this loudly, and Anna was certain people heard. Anna mashed her heated face into the table so she couldn't see who was looking, and they couldn't look at *her*.

"Anna," said Liss sharply. "The problem with you is you're repressed. We need to fix that." She set her face like a stone. Her This Is Important face. But Anna wasn't intimidated, not like she would have been when she was younger.

"And how do you plan to fix that?" she asked.

"I plan for us *both* to fix that. The first step is to get you comfortable with yourself."

"I am." She knew, even better than Liss did, that it wasn't quite true. But she was brave. She'd dared to write that note when so many girls wouldn't. And when she melted into her music, she was comfortable. Her self, her skin, all blurred into the moment.

"OK, if you're so comfortable with yourself, I dare you to chase down Ed and ask him about that note."

"No!"

"And tell me this: would you strip in the schoolyard?"

She pictured herself stripping by the flagpole. A gangly tangle of too-white limbs, Ed and his friends pointing and laughing. Chen yelling, "What do you think you're doing?"

Liss watched and this look overcame her—hurt? Defeat? "Would you?" Liss's This Is Important face flinched and froze, her jaw slightly open. "I said, would you?"

"Of course!"

"OK, then I dare you to do it."

She pictured Liss stripping by the flagpole, bare limbs like copper branches. Ed pausing to swivel his head and watch her.

"Tomorrow."

"I'll be there to make sure."

"You know, we'd probably get into trouble with the school. We could get kicked out or something." Liss looked down at her lunch bag and fiddled with the clunky chain around her neck.

"OK, then," said Anna, finally breathing freely.

The next day, Liss was worse. She brought Anna a magazine with an article on sex positions, and a worn-out swimsuit calendar stolen from her dad's room. "You need to get in touch with your sexuality, that's what I think. If you're this prudish, don't you think you're already behind?" She nodded smugly.

Anna eyed the swimsuit model's lurid tan skin. "Have you

ever ...done anything?" she whispered.

"Oh, lots of times," said Liss at full volume. "With friends, with teachers, with rock stars. It was all in my head, of course. You should try it."

Anna had, sort of. The fantasies were vague, the bodies hard to imagine, triggering revulsion all warped with excitement. But she didn't think of them now. She just wondered if her best friend had ever even kissed anyone.

"I know how we can make you sexier!" In excitement, Liss rose halfway out of her seat.

Anna pushed around the leftover bits of salad in her tupperware tub. "What?"

"We should be a band! We can make punk music and stuff, like Rita. Get a head start for when I make it to Nashville. You know people in these groups have to be sexy or they don't stand a chance."

Punk had never been Anna's thing. And what would they stand a chance for? There was no way the two of them, fourteen years old, would get a record deal.

But Liss would listen to none of that. "What should we call ourselves?" she asked as she doodled on her napkin. The picture was crude, but recognizable. Ed would have done it better. She slapped the thought away. It was a skull in the shape of a heart. Fracture lines ran down the middle, and it was grimacing. Anna related to it.

"We can call ourselves The Beast Beat. What do you think?"

"Um, I dunno. Is that supposed to be our logo?"

"Sure. I like it for us."

"Me too. But it doesn't really go with The Beast Beat."

Anna examined it. A broken heart and death, compactly intertwined. "Heartstroke!"

"*Heartstroke?*"

"I dunno."

Anna looked at Liss and her eyes were strange, open and dark, the irises just a shade off from the pupils, two nested-doll discs hard to tell apart. In that moment they were fixed dead forward, directed at Anna but staring right through her.

"Suspension," said Anna.

"Suspension, I like it!" Liss scratched the name above the heart-shaped skull in pointed letters.

Playing as a duo could be interesting, especially in a new kind of music. Different from band, youth orchestra, and piano duets with Laine and other students. Violin and piano—or keyboard, it would probably have to be keyboard. Strange instruments for punk. They didn't have a drummer, a bass, or even a guitar really. Liss had taken a few lessons and could play it passably, but she couldn't rock out.

A lot of teenagers at school were in bands, and some were already good. A couple of hippie girls sang Gaelic folk music under the tree out front, and some skater kids always reserved a practice room to rehearse their ska. Another group played soft rock covers out back, and little kids gathered around them at recess to make requests. Karen Green's band had recorded a CD and was touring the East Coast. It was like Liss had said about her and sex—the two of them were starting late. They were behind.

But that was stupid. They were already musicians, and this would just be for fun. She imagined Rita Deviant's songs with Liss's violin in the background. Abrasive lyrics. A soaring melodic sear. Soften with Anna's piano, purposefully arrhythmic. Switch to keyboard, play around with the bass setting, make the violin shriek, throw in some riffs off the blues scale. This could work. This could sound awesome.

They met in their favorite practice room, the smallest, with a stack of sound equipment in the corner. They hadn't been in that dim little room for weeks, but suddenly its smallness was exciting, a hideaway, a fort for secrets to grow. Anna plugged in the electronic keyboard and settled herself behind it. Liss perched on a tall speaker, skin glowing from the low light. Anna began to tell all her ideas about their sound.

"You're amazing! How do you think of all this stuff so fast?" She found herself caught between Liss's small breasts in their cotton tank top and a series of spiky bracelets poking into her back. Liss was a tight hugger, and held on longer than most people.

Part of Anna didn't want to answer. She liked being called amazing. "I think I'm just lucky," she said. "Really lucky that I can think like that."

"But you don't really compose, do you? You haven't?"

Buried near the bottom of one desk drawer, between some birthday cards from her grandparents and a seventh grade research paper on lemmings, were her attempts. The waltz she'd written for Laine was flat and colorless, and one of the marches had a few phrases accidentally copied from Sousa.

"I've tried a bit, but I wasn't any good."

"I wouldn't be sure of that."

Anna thought of Mozart. She'd heard people compare

her to him as a kid, when the music she heard traveled directly from ears to fingers. But at the ages she'd been playing by ear and sight reading, he'd felt symphonies siphon through him. Where did they come from? She'd never had access to that place. OK, she'd heard bits in scarce strong moments, mid-leap running through a field of lupins, thinking of Ed, in the afterglow of a recital. Such music seemed to spill from the fibers of the air, sourceless. Maybe it was just stuff she'd heard before and couldn't remember, like the Sousa. She didn't think so. It didn't matter, though, because the sound passed through her as ghostly as it came. Her once-amazing memory was stuffed with other people's songs. If she wanted to do what Mozart had done so much younger, it was already too late, wasn't it? He'd been one of the elect.

Had she?

Liss spoke in a tiny, un-Liss-like voice. "I have some lyrics for us. Sort of. I'm not sure how good they are." Anna noticed the folded paper in her hand, the way she curled in on herself.

"Let me see."

Liss hesitated, made a wavering motion towards Anna and away, and finally held out the paper. She didn't pass it over, but stood with it sitting in her outstretched palm. Anna took it.

It's been so many years since I was swept outside your door.
You gave me life. I demanded so much more.
I needed shelter, money, song.
You couldn't give me that for long.
So you threw me down on the world like acid rain.
I was taken where I'll never see you again.

Chorus:
I'm still awake, watching out the window.
When will you come? I am waiting still.
Expecting you. When will I hear your voice again?
Memories can't tell.
I hope you wish me well.

There probably are a lot of you, a family's a must.
Are you reeking in the rot of you, or smothered in your dust?
Do you think about me ever? Have a number you could call,
hanging on your fridge door? Yeah, NOW you could have it all.
Are you sitting stoned in front of your new satellite TV?
Someday I'm going to find you and someday I'm going to see.

"We need to add to it," she mumbled. "You think it's OK?"

Where had she learned to write like that, with taut lines and feeling hissing out? Liss was a composer, thought Anna. A real songwriter. She felt as though she'd swallowed cough syrup.

"It doesn't sound punk," she said, hoping to channel some of the medicinal taste through her comment.

"Oh, screw genres. We can just be a whatever band." Anna watched to see if she flinched at all. Yes, there was a barely perceptible squint as she spoke.

"How do you sing that?"

And Liss's voice rose in an anger Anna had never heard in all her rehearsed singing, in all her Rita Deviant impressions. Her shrunken presence expanded with each syllable. She paced the practice room, slicing its musty air, her body and voice windmilling wildly. The last verse left her panting, her hair askew. Anna waited until she calmed down before speaking.

"Hey, it's about your birth parents, right?"

"Please don't think I'm lame." Liss had shrunk again, not herself.

"Why would I think you're lame?"

"I've never met them. I've never known who they are or where they're from or anything. Not that it's a big deal."

"I get that."

"No, I don't think you do."

I wish I had *different parents* flashed through Anna's mind, but she wasn't cruel enough to speak it aloud. She searched for the easy thing to say.

"The song's awesome."

"Really?"

"Yeah! Let's add some instruments."

Liss paused. A trumpet blasted in the practice room beside them, through the supposedly soundproof walls.

"Alright, let's do it," said Liss. She placed her violin beneath her chin and Anna positioned herself behind the keyboard. The melody that Liss had just sung nudged at her fingers, but she ignored the itch, waiting until her friend began.

The first line came a cappella. Liss's violin swept stridently after, and only then did Anna feel free to join. She improvised unthinkingly, incorporating some of her earlier thoughts—bass tones, blues scale. She'd never heard rage sound so melodic and pristine. She threw back her head and hurled herself at the keys. Her eyes connected with Liss's, which were narrowed but warmed at the contact. Tendrils of Liss's sound circled spires of Anna's. They were really doing this. They were in it.

Finished, they were breathless. Anna held out her hand for a high five. A tiny static current passed between their fingers.

"You're amazing," said Liss.

"No, you're amazing."

"OK, we both rock."

"We should play our school music together too," said Anna. "Why haven't we been doing that?"

"Yeah, why haven't we been doing that all the time? We suck!" Liss laughed and Anna joined her.

Anna tried to remember her keyboard improvisation on the piano at home. B flat—no, B—no, what had it been? She banged out a couple chords in frustration. That didn't sound bad. Maybe she could add a similar chord sequence.

"What are you playing?" asked her mother. Anna hadn't noticed her entering the room. Her tone was not approving.

"Liss and I have been inventing some stuff together. We've started practicing our repertoire pieces together too." Best to add that, something true and safe. Laine liked her Beethoven renditions, and had suggested the idea of a solo concert. She hadn't yet told anyone, although her mom would certainly approve. The idea filled her with giddiness and dread. She'd screw up. She couldn't screw up. She never had. Little slips, but nothing that couldn't be glossed over. No, she'd screw up. Her luck had to run out at some point. One of these days, warned the familiar surge in her gut, she was going down.

Mom's sigh interrupted her thoughts. "That's great. I'm

glad you can share your music with someone." She paused. "Would you mind folding the clothes when you're done?"

"The clothes can fold themselves!"

Dammit! Where had that come from? Her panic at the thought of failure?

"Anna, what are you being a smart aleck for?"

She looked at Mom across the room. Really looked at her. Her mother leaned against the gray cabinet that held her tapes and CDs. The wood was worn, and so was the expression on Mom's face. There were creases in her forehead and purplish half-moons below her eyes. Strands of hair had come undone from her ponytail.

Anna heard Dad shuffling papers in his office, cursing under his breath. Her father hated his job. He hadn't been promoted since he'd found the new lower-level position, and he missed the extra salary. And her mother ...her mother was so tired. Her head, always held straight, had fallen slightly to the side, and she leaned it against a hand.

After practice, Anna would set the table, then try to finally read through Liss's gift. In her room, the magazine cover blinked neon. Sex Positions to Maximize Her Pleasure!

"I'm sorry," she said.

Chapter 12: *Tell Me Everything*

Age Sixteen

Anna could understand Sarah better now, Sarah who had dated Kyle a year ago and bothered everyone at their lunch table with grinning singsong questions.

"Anna, guess what?"

"What?"

"I have a sexy boy-friend! Anna, guess what?"

"What?"

"I have a sexy boy-friend! Anna, guess what?"

"Shut up."

"Michelle, guess what?"

The space between Anna and Darien didn't disappear right away. But it was no source of embarrassment anymore when Anna, shooting hoops, tripped over Darien's foot. They eased around each other, helped by the knowledge that neither felt the space had to be there.

"Have you noticed the way he holds his head when he looks at you? Or how good of a listener he is?"

A love unquestioned, unmocked, publicized, smooth as something in a movie. Sometimes Anna thought it was too easy.

Laine noticed, like everyone else. "Anna, you're happy today."

"Yeah, kinda." Her smile widened.

"Good for you. Just try not to play that funeral march allegro."

She was used to infatuation being miserable, constricting, but now she felt as free and high as beach air. There was only one doubt—why did he even like her? But she couldn't linger on that for long, as new onslaughts of giddiness swept up to replace it. They kissed in the parking lot in front of the buses and felt daring.

"You're such a cute couple," said Sarah. Beside her, Irena scowled.

"Are you finding time to practice for your concert?" asked Chen.

"Sure, at home." That was a half-lie. Last night she'd only played an hour, then leafed through her old stash of magazines about What Men Really Want and The Ten Best Orgasm Tips. Caution, announced a sign on the wall, but she ignored it. Men at Work, blared another, and she giggled at potential dirty connotations. Yield. Go Slow. Everything sounded sexual.

Dad didn't bring Darien up until one of their weekly driving lessons—now that Anna would turn seventeen in a few months and get tested for her license, her father had begun to schedule them in earnest. Mom wanted Anna to put off driving practice and focus more intently on her music, but she would have none of it. Already Chen and Michelle, Irena and Darien, those lucky souls whose parents had opted for driver's ed, were cruising unsupervised down the highways and back roads of the island. She was the only one getting carted around to parties like some twelve-year old.

"Buckle up," said Dad jovially, although Anna had already fastened her seat belt and he was still buckling his. "Be careful backing up the driveway. Blah, blah, you know all that."

Anna scanned the road behind her as she reversed, glancing at the rearview mirror and shoulder checking nervously. She hoped the car wasn't wiggling too much. She waited until the road was clear before reversing out and shifting into forward.

"Can I put some music on?" Mom never let her, not wanting her concentration interrupted.

"Sure. Just keep your eyes on the road." Dad said this lightly, as if he had no reason to worry. It was one of his good days. Anna turned the radio to her mother's usual classical station, the one she set as her alarm when she didn't use a CD. The road was only mildly busy, not the highway yet. She scanned the bland storefronts, the occasional city tree shedding its tanned or reddening leaves. She was grateful the steering wheel didn't slide like the one on Mom's car. Dad and Gwen's vehicle was new and rather box-shaped— less responsive and gas-efficient than Mom's small car, but faster. Its sturdiness made it more likely to survive an accident should one happen, and Anna had certainly had nightmares of her foot slipping and the car rolling uncontrollably into a guardrail, a vehicle, a logging truck. She would wake with her breath caught in her throat, half-choking while the imprint of her dream car collided with the car in front of it. It passed through like smoke, and the unfulfilled expectation was almost scarier than the hard jolt of a crash.

But she had fewer of these nightmares every week, and her parents trusted her more. Slowly, she was trusting herself more too. It helped that the Darien situation was sorted out—she was still infatuated, yes, but without the tension of waiting. The radio played a soothing chamber quartet that Dad probably hated. Anna turned onto the highway. Driving with her father was nice because he didn't give much direction— turn here, merge there—or destination. There was no grocery fetching at the end of a driving practice, as there was with Mom. Now she drove aimlessly, just to feel like she was heading somewhere. She accelerated. Yellow lines and passing zone dashes scrolled frantically before her.

"So I hear you're dating someone?" said Dad.

Anna started. "Where'd you hear that from?"

"Yer mother. We do talk sometimes, you know."

She realized that her concentration had been lost for a second and she'd drifted towards the center line. She corrected.

"So what's he like?" her father asked.

"Great. Funny. He plays saxophone." The words sounded pathetic, nothing like Darien's excitedly jarring presence. No description could encompass him, but hers seemed particularly stupid.

"Sounds like a saxy guy!"

"Oh, Dad." Her groan was as automatic as his pun.

"Well, I'm glad you've found someone. It makes life a lot more worth it."

Cut the cheesy Hallmark crap. But that was the sort of thing she said to her mother, not her father. She had edges she walked around both, but her father was more dangerous.

They approached the abandoned mall, a listless-looking rectangle with a bright kite on the sign. Dad pointed to the bustling Wal-Mart further down. "Want to practice your parking?"

She wanted to continue scrolling down the highway, listening to the music she'd tuned out. And the car was under her control, so she could. Instead she said "Sure" and signalled her intention to turn into that ugly Wal-Mart's parking lot. She had little trouble installing herself in a space. "What now?" she asked. "Do you want to go in?" The car was still on, the music still playing.

"Well, Gwen said she wanted pectin for apple jelly, if you don't mind. You can wait here if you want."

"No, I'll come with you."

She kept her eye on him, watching for abrupt movements.

They walked past a middle-aged couple dressed in orange and pink. The woman's backside was broad, and both their stomachs protruded. By the door, a scruffy-haired boy tried to tug a teddy from the grip of his tiny pigtailed sister, who was squalling. "Shut up!" yelled their mother, a scowl wrinkling its way across her blank face. "And Taylor, you let go of that bear! If I ever catch you stealing Amy's toys again, you're grounded."

She didn't catch Taylor's reaction as they were walked ahead, past shelves of Christmas candy laid out early. She trailed her father past the jewelry section, past the headgear and women's lingerie, through the low lukewarm store air, towards the rows of food packed neatly in cans and bags. For what seemed like an eternity already, Darien's image had floated to mind in boring moments like this. Her grocery trips had been spiced with arousal, lending a purposeless directness to her step. But these fluorescent lights were baking her. She felt them dull her senses. She struggled for a snatch of music, a glimpse of a gaze, a thought. Maybe she'd see something funny, something she could tell Darien about and they could laugh at it together. But the idea seemed pathetic. What did love have to do with a place like this?

She put down her saxophone to pick up one of the old magazines from Liss, hidden among the dust clots under her bed. Blow-His-Mind Blow Jobs, page 167. *Reading ahead, are we?* Ay-a grinned. She was always amused. Anna hated her mockery. She tried to summon the goddess's face and visualize herself punching it, but Ay-a's nebulous features had given way to Liss's narrow ones.

Another Anna hesitated, then punched anyway. Her fist met laughing smoke.

A knock.

Anna shoved the magazine back in its musty place. Her mother's porn stash was no longer secret, but she at least would maintain what she could of her dignity.

Mom pressed a strand of hair back. She looked towards Anna, then down at her wrist where she fingered an elastic band. "Hey Anna?"

"Yeah?"

"I've been thinking—wondering if you'd like to meet Tom."

An upsweep in her mother's voice, followed by a heavy sigh. Anna was glad she wasn't holding anything. She would have dropped it.

"Of course. Yeah. I'd love to meet Tom."

No sarcastic remarks this time. Just a dumb, hazy near-repetition of the phrase and name she'd wondered about since he'd first been mentioned.

Her mother's happiness threaded through the room, tentative and delicate. Anna had allowed it to emerge this time, but she hadn't done anything to create it.

"I'm thinking of inviting him for supper. Does ...would Saturday work?"

Anna assessed her schedule. She and Darien had a date on Friday, she was playing at Kelly's on Sunday, but she had nothing on Saturday. "Yeah."

"Great. How's the piano coming?"

The stupid piano. It had made her mother happy once, her hands, the sound, all those hours.

"Good." She'd been taking a break from it tonight. She'd taken one yesterday too.

You said you'd get around to it. Ay-a tossed her net of hair, laughing again. *Sure you're taking a break. Uh-huh, you so-called prodigy, I believe you.*

She waited as her mother faded back into the kitchen, then stared down her wall. Truth is, Ay-a, she thought, I just can't think about it anymore. It's Darien, and is he thinking of me right now, and does he like me, and will he call, and how do I know it's me he likes and not Another Anna he sees instead? The music just isn't coming anymore. It's like the thoughts have pushed it out, and whenever I put my fingers on the keys they're too heavy to play right. I'm not there. I'm just so tired.

Even in the practice room, Anna was aware of the acuteness in the weather—the constant throb of rain, the wind's terrible song, the unwarmed air pressing in through the threads of her sweater, unhelped by the coldness of the saxophone that hung heavy on her neck strap. She and Darien had gone through the B flat blues scale, the E flat scale (C for altos), a chromatic scale for the heck of it. Now, the twelve bar blues. She kept up the accompaniment, tapping her foot, while Darien soloed. She watched his cheeks puff slightly as he shrilled a crisp high G. A sound that could stare down crowds. His sneakers were fraying near the soles. She thought to nudge his foot with hers, but would that be practical when she was tapping to keep the beat? Was that a squeak? No, only the wind. Suddenly Darien was looking at her. She lost track of the notes she was supposed to be playing. She wanted to pour into him like music, but his gaze was no more accessible than a pane of glass. For a moment she couldn't think. Then she realized with the calm of returning logic that he was signalling her turn to solo.

"Guess where I was last night?" Sarah held court between Anna and Michelle.

Michelle leaned across the dusty table. "Tell us."

"In the backseat of a caaa-ar! And I bet you can't guess what I was doing."

"No way!"

"Yeah way! My cousin was up and he brought his hot friend Steve. He's 19 and in college, and Oh God. He wanted to take me for a drive, and one thing led to another, you know?"

"You're making this up," said Irena, her head held deliberately high. An instant of uncertainty tugged at her mouth before it settled into a firm line. Anna pictured Sarah with her legs spread on dark leather, a lithe muscled guy from one of Caroline's porn videos hovering over her. She grimaced.

"I hope you were safe," said Chen, wide-eyed.

"Well, duh. He had a condom and all."

"Yeah, right," said Irena.

"Did you check?" asked Chen.

"Well, uh, yeah. Anyway, it was amazing." She grinned her grackle grin.

"I wanna hear the details!" Michelle giggled. "How big was he?"

"Michelle!" Irena shot.

"Come on, tell us! What position did you do it in?"

The salt-spotted fast food table was a circle of faces tittering, blushing, leaning, frowning, each girl's expression legible beyond her words. Irena's mixed incredulity and alarm, Chen's plain worry, Sarah's mask of indulgent pride with flickers of something less pleasant—confusion? Disappointment? Fear? Michelle's fist was clenched around her burger, her body straining towards every word that fell from Sarah's mouth. Surrounded by faces, Anna felt the nausea of a world spun out of control. Ay-a stirred inside her, leaning: Tell me more. Tell me everything.

Gwen called to invite Anna for dinner, but (such a relief) she was working at Kelly's that night. A valid excuse to avoid the happy couple and their rat. At the table beside her piano bench (she breaked to drink water) a woman in an ill-fitting sweater set and pearls snuggled against a man with a profile like the side of a cliff, jagged and sharp-nosed. His tweed jacket had elbow patches and her hair was curled carefully, maybe permed. Their chairs were pulled together to enable physical contact. She stroked his goatee; he offered a brief peck on the cheek and squeezed her shoulder. They looked about the right age to have kids, but didn't have any with them. Maybe they doted on their pets instead. There were certainly kids at the table beside them, a black-haired boy and girl thumb wrestling and a baby shrieking in a high chair. "Shh," soothed their squat black-haired mother, trying to jostle the baby into calmness. "Shh." The father looked about the room, attention darting, tension in the lines of his face. A man slumped alone at the next table, poking at his remaining canned peas with a fork. His hair was salt and pepper, his shirt flannel, his belly modest. Maybe he owned some of the same DVDs that Mom kept in the cabinet. A few months ago, Anna might have caricatured him. She wondered what that past Anna would have found funny.

Their shipment of redesigned band sweaters had arrived. Irena and Anna waited for the Smalls to be unpacked from their cardboard box. Mr. Haslam held up sweater after sweater, navy cardigans with gold lettering—Pine Grove Senior Band—and a perky eighth note below it.

"Did I tell you about the new opportunity with Treble Learning?" asked Irena.

"I don't think so." Treble Learning was the company that published their music books.

"Well, Michael told their CEO about my composing, and showed him some of the stuff I wrote, and guess what? They're interested in having me contribute to the music books!

They have to see if their grants go through, but if that works out, they're going to give me a paid contract and everything."

"That's awesome." Anna's smile felt like wax. At least she had tonight with Darien (chatting with Paul in the back) to look forward to. And she had her concert.

Darien's secondhand Toyota lurched down the rutted dirt road to the beach. Ice puddles cracked under the wheels, and Miles Davis blared from the CD player. Darien had an MP3 player like Anna's which he listened to at lunch or when filling idle time, but he liked the old-fashioned way better, he explained—CDs had better sound quality.

"And my dad has an old record player I like to listen to. The Beatles, Joni Mitchell, Bob Dylan, Cat Stevens, all that good stuff. It's kind of amazing that we can still listen to the exact same sounds that were around before we were. And some of the album covers are pretty spectacular. Joni did her own art, the flower paintings and stuff. And she taught herself to play guitar—invented her own tunings, can you believe that?"

"Old music's the best," Anna agreed, thinking of her mother's tapes. Rita Deviant had been all but forgotten on the radio, and her replacements were worse.

"They were so innovative. The 60s, 70s, they were like golden ages. God, I wish we could jump in a time machine and go back to when these people were creating and be part of that."

Outside the window, lawn ornaments ranged in front of a yellow house—a row of sunbonnet girls, a deer curled up beside a dalmatian, a painted boy emitting a yellow arc of pee, plastic pinwheels turning.

"Why can't we create stuff like that now?" asked Anna.

Darien fell silent, his gaze out the window. The car felt emptier. It wasn't because of the Wal-Marts, Anna thought, or the lawn ornaments, or the weather that stayed brown and dull longer before assuming a proper snowy chill. There was plenty of new beauty evolving, if people knew where to look. Some of Surrender's stuff. Irena's little pieces. The bands that met in practice rooms and later went on tour. The sounds that filled Pine Grove every day, if you let your preoccupied mind be sensitive enough to hear them. Once, every note she heard from the tape recorder or the piano or her mother's mouth had been an entity with weight, leaving an impression in her brain. Even a jingle on TV—she remembered more ads from her childhood, sound by sound and word by word, than she knew of the modern ones. She heard much less, now. Could she have played by heart what Miles Davis had just played on the CD? Probably not.

And Darien. What was it that had made his shoulders slump? She wanted to hug him. She was too shy. Her arm hovered between them for a minute and settled in her lap. The small trees along the road, which she used to see as big trees, were blotted with shadows. At the end of the little road, she noticed the slate blue line of water.

"I used to love coming to this beach," said Anna, remembering warm summer water and easily caught hermit crabs, and Dad calling out to her with pails and shovels. "My dad and I went clam digging here a few times."

Spires of goldenrod in the ditches had dried and iced over. The marram grass was bent.

"I like how hardly anyone comes here," said Darien. "It's not like the big tourist beaches."

"Or even the one with the little river by my place," said Anna. "Too many people swimming and kids running around. Ever notice how beaches attract the cheesiest colors?" She talked to build something between them, to fill something, to make up for their hesitance in touching. "It's always something too bright, like neon orange swimming trunks and lime green umbrellas with little smiling starfish on them. And there are all the bad smells like sunscreen and beer that get in the way of the salt air. The beach would be so much better if it weren't for the stupid things the people bring." She realized she was talking like her mother.

Darien parked at the end of the little road. Neither made to leave the car. Her friends' date stories played in her head like a slow-motion film. Michelle getting fingered in the abandoned mall parking lot by moonlight. Sarah fucking the older cousin's older friend. Even Irena had claimed an episode, although she wouldn't share the details. Chen had looked around and retorted, under her breath but fiercely, that she'd kissed a stranger on a Greyhound bus trip. Sarah had set down the curling iron to high-five her.

Looking from one stubborn shining face to another, Anna had felt less daring than Ay-a wanted her to. She'd told them about finding Mom's porn, about inviting Darien over and taking off shirts. "I'd love to see what's under that shirt," Irena had said.

"Ever feed the seagulls?" Darien interrupted her thoughts. It took a moment for her mind to settle, and she had to replay his words to know what he'd asked.

"Sure, on picnics."

"Well, I brought some old bread."

He pulled a bag from the trunk. They set their sneakered feet to sink in the sand, and he split the contents of the bag between them. The beach's remaining gulls flapped around them, squalling. The ocean was so slow this time of year that it was almost still.

"Here, catch!" Darien ripped a chunk of bread and tossed it towards the water. The birds took off, two squabbling as they reached the food. One grabbed and gulped, thrusting its head back while the bread lurched down its gullet. Really, thought Anna, they were as loud as the bad colors that people brought to the beach.

They took turns tearing the bread and sending the gulls into a frenzy. Darien's movements were simple and sure, not at all like his approach to Anna. She was almost glad when the bread was gone.

They walked towards the ocean, past shell-speckled rows of pebbles frozen in place, crunching dried seaweed. Anna grabbed a stick and drew in the hardened sand "A+D" inside of a heart. "Let me have a turn," said Darien. Underneath the heart, he wrote "4ever." They walked towards the waves, gray and scarcely lapping at this time of year, their capacity as heat sinks long since exhausted.

"I'll take my shoes off and run in the waves if you will," said Anna.

Darien looked down at the sluggish foam-frothed ripples.

"I don't really want to."

"Me neither," she admitted.

Why didn't he ever call her beautiful? He wasn't one to

say that sort of thing, maybe that was all, but she wished he was. He'd put "4ever" underneath the heart. So, no running hand in hand through those miserable waves, freezing and not caring. Would she have him forever? She wanted to own him, to trickle in through his skin and devour him from the inside. *Make a move. Don't move.*

They sat on a large knobbly log and leaned into each other. Darien was the first to kiss, and they continued.

The table was covered in lace, the good china set out, and Callas cheeping loudly against the *Moonlight Sonata*, of all the clichés Mom could've chosen. It reminded Anna of work at Kelly's, which didn't sit well with her appetite. Mom had put in some effort, but nothing ostentatious. It struck her that the effort was for her, Anna, instead of for Tom—a pantomime of decorating for a special guest, when Tom had surely seen a less-than-perfect version of the house many times while Anna worked.

"I think that's him." Mom trotted to the window and Anna, who hadn't heard anything, followed. A dust brown pickup truck was pulling into the driveway. Mom ran to the door while Anna watched the passenger clamber out. He was ...teddy-bear shaped. His gait was slow and rolling, and he wore a collared brown shirt with jeans. Not the sleek officious translator Anna had imagined. Not the type she'd expected her mother to date.

He disappeared from view, and the door opened, and Mom fountained into his arms with a gushing greeting Anna didn't catch. In an equally fluid gesture he wrapped around her. She huddled in his arms as if used to snuggling there.

She caught sight of eyes, Tom's facial expression so soft Anna wondered if her vision had gone blurry. Melting. Yes, they were melting. When had her careful mother ever melted?

She separated herself after a prolonged hug (too long, Anna thought). "Tom, I want you to meet my daughter Anna."

"Pleased to meet you." He stuck out a pretzel-dough hand and bowed slightly in her direction. Her grip was firmer than his. Benign. Unscary.

"Nice to meet you, too."

"You look so much like your mother."

Anna stuttered: "Well, well, thank you." What was that supposed to mean, if she looked like the person he wanted to screw on a regular basis?

"I've heard good things about your piano playing."

It was up to him to keep the conversation going, it seemed. But Mom interrupted: "I hope you can make it to her concert next month." She started chattering about the orchestra and the dinner of marinated salmon she'd made for them. She led Tom to the sofa where they snuggled again, and Anna sat stiffly in the rocking chair. He rambled about his niece who was learning to play piano, and the little songs she insisted on playing whenever she could find someone to listen. He reminded her of her father on a good day. And, a little bit, of Darien.

Chapter 13: *Family*

Age Fourteen

"You tell her."

"No, you fucking tell her."

Anna clutched her clothes pile harder in reflex, and stopped halfway up the stairs to listen to the yelling. Her eyes settled on the painting that hung along the staircase—a woman on a dock, facing a sea of high crests that had always reminded Anna vaguely of horses, white dress and taffy-colored hair torn back by wind. The clouds were heavy and the watercolor had blotted in certain places, turning the subtly darkening storm into clumsy ink blobs.

"I thought we'd agreed it would be you." Mom.

"Hey, this was your idea. And you're the one who gets to keep the house. The least you can do is explain yourself to your own kid!"

On the distant rocks (a thinly painted brownish jut) stood a gray lighthouse, thin and spired as a narwhal horn. Its beam was watery, and there was no reflection.

"Shut up. Just shut up."

"No, you shut up!"

The thud of something solid against the wall, then Mom's shriek. Had he pushed her?

She couldn't move. Couldn't.

She was darting up the stairs, heart overheating. Pounding on the door. The clothes slipped from her grip and crumpled in all directions on the floor.

"Come in!" Mom, afraid.

"Oh, Jesus," Dad groaned as she stepped inside. Mom was leaning against the wall, her hair undone. Dad stood with a fist dangling by his side, as if he didn't know what to do with it. The covers were a mess, the floor littered with quilt and pillows, the bureau with papers. Both parents were breathing heavily.

Anna took three steps into the room, walking deliberately around a pillow. Anger flared in her face. "So what's up? What do you guys have to tell me that's important enough to fight about?"

Her parents glanced around all corners and angles of the room and even at each other. Almost allies in their fright, their glances never connected.

"Your mother wants us to get divorced," Dad said finally.

"I thought we'd agreed on this."

"Yeah, but it was your idea."

"Well, you've been—"

"So that's it," said Anna. "Why couldn't you just both tell me some nice, peaceful time, like over supper?"

"Well," said Dad.

"Well, we were going to," said Mom.

"That's OK. I heard it was Dad who was moving out."

Before they could answer, she was running to her room. One door slammed behind her, then another, and she pummelled her pillow like a toddler. She felt like swearing, but only strangled sobs came out. She sounded, she thought, like a chicken dying.

It was usually Liss who led them to the practice room, but that day Anna took her by the arm and steered through the dazed cafeteria crowds, past the gym, through a little beige door to an unplugged keyboard—

"What's up with you today, Anna? Jesus."

She realized she was holding Liss against the wall, paused (hands latched on wrists), and breathed.

"I need to escape my house."

"What?" Liss was too startled to struggle.

"My parents are getting divorced and I wish I had somewhere to go while they yelled and banged around and figured out what the hell they were doing. What the *fuck*!" The words felt like fire in her throat.

Liss wrapped an arm around her (she must have let go while swearing). "Dammit, that sucks! But it's not like they got along anyway. It'll probably be better to keep those beasts in separate cages, ya know?"

"I know. I don't know why I'm upset!"

"It's normal. Probably something weird happens to your brain chemicals when you're shocked."

What was lost anyway?

She felt lost.

What was there to regret?

She felt regret.

"I wish I didn't have to stay in the same house as them while they figure out how to, how to, take this parents thing apart!"

"Hey, listen. I bet you don't. You can come stay at my

place until your parents have everything sorted out."

Anna looked at her earnest face. "You've got to be kidding."

"You know my mom, she'll say yes, and my dad will have to agree. We can practice for our band, get ready for a life of adventure."

Tension trickled off her. She breathed in thirsty gulps, and some remote voice in the back of her mind wondered why she'd been so upset.

"Liss, I think I love you or something."

At that, she went quiet. Anna didn't mind. Her gratitude flooded the room.

They moved Anna's suitcase into the spare room, which had none of the decorations that Mom lavished on hers. The bed was covered in a faded blue quilt, a square boat in the middle of a very practical lake of bureaus and night tables and stacked transparent boxes of wreath-making supplies from the classes Liss's mother used to teach. "Bounce on the bed," said Liss.

"Would your mom be OK with that?"

"Of course!" Liss clambered up beside her. "This one has the best spring in the house." She bounced a little to demonstrate, her dark hair floating and falling. Anna laughed and tried a tentative bounce. It was a springy mattress, definitely better than the ones in hotels.

"Come on, you've gotta try harder than that!"

"I feel like I'm on vacation," said Anna.

Liss grinned lazily. "Welcome to the time of your life."

They somersaulted and wrestled until Liss pinned her

down. Anna, breathing so hard her lungs hurt, looked up at a face that was childlike and stubborn and pitiless. A sudden laugh burst out and they fell over each other, giggling.

They went to the playroom where the toys had long since been replaced with a yoga mat and exercise bike, a karaoke machine, a stack of board games, and the twins' transparent boxes of jewelry making supplies. The walls were still full of jottings and doodles, years added to years. The twins Katie and Cassie and their friends had chosen a corner for a list of "THE HOTTEST GUYS" now that they were twelve and thought themselves grown up. Liss had corrected her own childhood spelling—*School is garbage*. Between a set of initials and a heart-petaled flower, Anna saw a drawing of a blue box with pipes sticking out, the castle she'd sketched in first grade.

"Write your name on the wall," said Liss. "You live here now."

Anywhere specific?"

"Nah. Just pick a place."

She looked for the family members' signatures. *CASSIE MAC*, she found in pink polka-dotted block letters beside the list of guys. *KaTiE MaCkInNoN* was written underneath, even larger, in green. The twins had tried to make their signatures different, Katie slanting her letters where Cassie rounded them, but the writing still looked alike. *Liss MacKinnon* was written in cursive scrollwork in the top right corner of the living room, a foot removed from the other writing. She must have stood on a chair.

Anna MacKinnon. She couldn't write that. *Anna Stern. Anna C. Stern. Anna Caroline Stern. A. C. Stern.* Which sounded most like a professional musician? She wished she had a symbol, some mark to distinguish herself. She settled on scrawling her usual signature, Anna Stern, in the white space by the mostly blank right corner. She drew a Yield sign with a quarter rest in the middle, and beside it, Suspension's heart-shaped skull.

"Hey, sweet, you're doing the logo," said Liss. "I drew one over here." She pointed to a near-identical drawing with Suspension scratched above it, and the lyrics *I'm still awake, watching out the window.*

"Cool," said Anna insincerely, because Liss's logo looked better. But that was a dumb thing to care about. Liss finished off her stylized violin with an arrow through it, and they went into the kitchen where Cassie was feeding the dog.

Liss's mother set out some cheese and crackers. "How was your day at school?"

"Good," said Liss, helping herself to a chunk of marble. "Mr. Rue was really nice to me today." Mr. Rue was her violin teacher, a stout man with thinning ginger hair. "He brought in brownies and said my vibrato was getting masterful."

"Oh, that's wonderful," said her mother.

Did he hug her too? Anna wondered. She'd seen him pull his arms around Liss before she left her lesson once, his eyes aglow in their folds like a patient father's. Liss had fit in his grip just so.

Cassie looked up from beside the chomping black dog and said, "When do you think you'll be ready to do a concert?"

"Pretty soon, he says I'm ready. You're going to come, right?"

Cassie regarded her sister with round eyes in a round pink face. She was a sturdy girl, her hips beginning to curve, blond hair clipped just above budding breasts already the size of Liss's. "Of course! And if Katie wants to skip it to hang out with her dumb boyfriend, I'll drag her out!"

Anna's stomach twitched. She shouldn't be hurt, but there'd been a thrill to being the only student in her year asked to perform her own concert. Liss too? Now the idea was suddenly commonplace. Liss stood with a floaty grace, and Anna was diminished.

"Laine thinks I'm ready for a concert too," she said, out of stubbornness.

"Oh, awesome!" said Liss. "We should ask if we can do one together! We could play some of the duets we've been working on, and we should talk them into letting us do 'Acid Rain.'"

Anna watched Liss's mother pour herself some orange juice, which she did briskly. Cassie washed her hands and settled at the table with a plate of crackers. She might be a bold talker but her motions were timid, her hands making the smallest softest rubbing motions under the spray of water.

"What do you think?" said Liss.

"Yeah, I'll ask Laine."

She thought of breaking her word, but it wouldn't be fair to Liss, who dared wonder if they could play one of their own compositions. She liked the idea of being associated with such a piece of sparkling originality, even if it was Liss's originality.

They finished their cheese and crackers. "We should practice now," said Anna.

"Aw, honey, take a break," said Liss's mom, swooping to squeeze her shoulder.

"Yeah," Liss chimed in, "you're on vacation, remember?

One day off won't kill us!"

Anna stared into her empty plate as if some answer would show itself in the cracker crumbs. It was hard not to think of her father, stumbling on the stairs and yelling with a murky voice that wasn't his. It was hard not to think of her mother, leaning against the stairway, holding her head. It was hard not to think she might be hurt right now, there might be blood and it wouldn't be the first time. If there was, it was difficult to think of whether he'd meant to cause it.

"I know what we should do," said Liss. "Remember the good old days when we watched *Titanic*?"

"Oh God!" Anna laughed in embarrassment. They'd gone to the theater during an on-spell of their on-again, off-again friendship and gushed over Leo DiCaprio's face on the screen. They'd made a plan to go to Hollywood and kidnap him and kiss him like crazy, which was about as far as their girlish imaginations wanted to go. What was the other thing they'd planned to do, marry him together and have a honeymoon on the water where they'd all drown holding hands?

"We had these goddesses and stuff back then," said Anna, "didn't we?"

"Oh yeah! I think I remember chanting."

"I had the goddess of music, and you had Saya, the goddess of love. No, it was Sava, mine was Ay-a."

"Yeah, now I remember."

"And we tried to burn an effigy at my place."

"That was fun." Anna felt again the stab of fear, saw again the flames reflected in Liss's eyes and her mother running. "We made everything epic back then," said Liss.

They had, hadn't they? Anna remembered the pale gray

rock and her prayers holding the dogwood branch, the clearing she'd called the Prayer Land, her perch on the cat tree, Liss's prayers to Sava to be loved, and the swish of Ay-a's glittery clothing on the hill. "I wish we still thought everything was magic."

"You know," said Liss, "why the hell not? Why not resurrect the goddesses?"

"Could we believe in them now?" Anna heard her parents' shouting, saw their stricken faces, far more real than Ay-a had ever been.

"Couldn't we?"

Liss's grin lit across her face.

She stepped briskly to the video cabinet and put on *Titanic.* They watched under her patchwork quilt, a medley of crimsons and yellows. Lovers on the screen who hadn't yet met. "Why are you watching that old thing?" asked Cassie, passing through the living room.

"Because we want to," said Liss.

"Whatever." Cassie shrugged childishly and retreated to her room.

The dog came to curl between them, and Anna scratched the ruff of fur behind his neck. Liss's mom came with a bowl of chips. Liss's quiet furtive dad came home from his late shift, took off his boots, grabbed a glass of milk and disappeared into her parents' room. Liss stood on the far arm of the couch and flung her arms out in mimicry of Jack and Rose. "I'm flying!" she said. Her shadow cast a cross against the wall.

"I wish humans could really fly," said Anna, "not just in airplanes." She paused. "But of course, if you get to fly you end up dying, like Icarus did."

"Wasn't he the guy who got barbecued?"

"Yeah. He drowned just like Jack."

"I wonder what it would be like to know you were going to drown," Liss said, and her muscles assembled themselves into a brave face. The image of Liss's corpse drifted to mind, emptied, rotting among kelp. Fish swam over to nibble her sightless eyes.

Liss moved on to talking about the couples on the Titanic, now buried under the sea. "Sava would protect their souls," she said. "She always guards those in love."

They were having too much fun with their solemnity to giggle. Grand images scrolled across their minds—billowy blonde Sava underwater, Ay-a on the half-sunken deck, folds of fabric trailing into the ocean. The dog jumped off the couch and they edged closer, holding onto each other like survivors. Anna was enveloped in a rush of heat, a flare she didn't want to go away.

After the credits, Liss flipped to a music channel. They watched Rita Deviant strut down an alley while her newest hit played in the background—a straightforward major-key thing about stalking all the shadows, thick with electric guitar and percussion. Rita's black-dyed hair hung over her face in a jagged bang. She wore way too much eyeliner, Anna thought, and she was glad that Liss didn't. Her hips swayed - *one-two, one-two* - jangling a chain at her pocket, too sassy and perfect to be unchoreographed. Behind her, two shadowy men exchanged something under their coats.

"Anna, don't you just want to be her? Don't you want to have those sexy hips and move that way?" Not waiting for an answer, Liss took up a pillow and sang into it like a microphone. She swayed her hips, pausing now and then to sweep her arm towards some immaterial audience: *"In the shadows all the talk is behind closed eyes, secrets and lies."* She paused for the backup singers on TV to hiss *"Secrets and lies"* in a breathy bass tone meant to sound sinister.

The beat picked up, becoming dancy. Liss grabbed Anna's hand, tossed the pillow to the couch, and swung her around. Anna let herself be carried by the motion. Round and round went the plush blue room, the couch with the gold and red quilt on top, the smiling blond family photos with their single dark face blurred into streaks.

They strolled arm in arm towards the smallest practice room, Liss carrying her violin case. She opened the door briskly and froze. Anna peered over her shoulder, straining to see, and Liss slammed the door. But Anna had already caught a glimpse of Ed and Louise, a flute student in the grade below them, pecking at each other's necks. Louise paused to look up, a giggle cracked out, and Ed's eyes flicked towards them just before the door closed.

"Did you see—" Liss began.

"Yeah."

"That preppy Louise kid, I can't stand her. They deserve each other."

"But Ed is nice," said Anna, hurt in the pit of her stomach.

"Wasn't too nice of him to write that tactless note to you. Listen, you deserve better."

Ed's lips on Louise's pale neck. Blonde Louise with her logo jacket and painted nails and what looked like C cups.

Anna wouldn't have wanted to be Louise at any other time. The girl's smug look was too polished and somehow too solid, lacking the ethereality that Anna craved. She was the type who'd win the beauty pageants, stay in town with kids and dogs and a boring job, and make regular hair appointments into her old age. Ed was quirky, sparkly, an original. But maybe all guys went for Louises, no matter their own degree of interesting. Hateful world, as Liss might say. Hateful laws of attraction. And why couldn't she be a Louise, now? Why couldn't she own that veneer of effortless pep? (She was awkward, her motions skirted around things, they didn't swagger. She was a t-shirt and jeans girl, solid colors, mostly plain. She didn't have Liss's style, or her mother's. She—)

They got a keyboard from the music room and went into the practice room next door.

They'd met with Laine and Mr. Rue to demonstrate the duets they'd been working on—some Beethoven sonatas, some Mozart, an Antonin Vaclav piece called "Poème"—and given a vigorous run-through of "Acid Rain"—Anna nervous, Liss's tone never wavering.

"Well, you two seem independent," Laine said, not quite smiling. She never *really* smiled like other people did, but Anna could read her. "With all the competition swirling around here, a joint concert might be a good thing for this school, don't you think?"

"That 'I'm still awake' song doesn't fit in with the repertoire," Mr. Rue objected.

"Nothing wrong with diversity," Laine gazed at him straight on. "Showcase their many talents."

"Well, um, well . . ." he cleared his throat. "I suppose you girls are talented songwriters."

So the concert was on, and their month would be spent in practice, as if there was anything new in that.

Anna couldn't sleep in the spare room. The black gauze of shadows on the wall swelled to her parents' sizes, spindly arms waving at each other, malformed legs kicking. A dog yelped somewhere on the street. A branch clicked against the window with rhythmic gusts of breeze. Click, clack. Click, clack. Anna remembered the sounds of objects launched across the room, of boots on the stairs. If it would shut up, if only it would just *shut up* . . .

She tried to count in time signatures. One-two-three, two-two-three, three-two-three. One-two-three. It had worked as a kid, the blank rhythms soothing in themselves. Now, without music, the concentration dulled her mind into depression. And the only songs she could summon with the richness of every chord and instrument, inflection and crescendo, were Dad's country and Rita Deviant and that stupid *Moonlight Sonata* which she'd played too much to love.

She couldn't sleep.

Maybe if she got something to drink, she'd be more rested. Where was the path from the bedroom to the kitchen? There were no night lights like the ones her mom left on. She felt her way around the hall, bumping into—ouch, what was that?—the sharp edges of a telephone table, and stubbing her toe on a corner. The house was eerily quiet. Everyone else was probably sleeping, and if she tripped she'd probably knock something over with a huge crash and wake them up. Bats could swoop through the window and glide past without being noticed. Someone stealthy could probably enter through the window without being noticed.

Damn, she'd forgotten about that step to the kitchen. There was a tiny bit of moonlight here, so she could see the outlines of cupboards. Were those cups or bowls on the bottom shelf? Should she turn a light on? She wasn't even thirsty. Not worth it to get a drink that she didn't even want, that would just make her need to pee in a few minutes and keep her up longer. She should just go back to the guest room, maybe read from one of the boring school books she'd brought. She wished she had a stop button for her spin-cycle mind. She wasn't even supposed to be here.

Was Liss asleep, and if so, what was she dreaming of? Liss liked to stay up late. She might still be lying there with her earphones on and maybe her notebook open. By this time Anna was standing in front of her door; she knocked. A rain of footsteps and the door opened to Liss in black t-shirt and pyjama pants, hair tousled, MP3 player in her fist. "Hey," she yawned.

"Hey. Can't sleep."

"Tell me something new. Me neither." Liss sprang onto her bed and spread out. Anna lay down beside her.

"Life sucks," said Liss, "oh …97.5 percent of the time."

"Parents suck," said Anna.

"Yeah, a hundred percent of the time." They laughed darkly. "But you know what's embarrassing? I can't stop thinking about my real ones."

"Your birth parents."

Liss went quiet. She didn't talk about her birth parents much, not like she used to. This was the first time she'd brought them up since the "Acid Rain" song, and she shrank against the pillow.

"Yeah. It's so stupid."

"No, it's not!" said Anna. "If I had birth parents, I'd want to find them too."

"I'm the only one in the house who doesn't look like a MacKinnon. Different skin color, different hair, and no one even knows where my real family's from. They probably have traits I have and don't know about. I mean we're all like our parents, right?"

"Yeah, I've got my dad's fat face and my mom's flat chest."

Liss ignored her. "But if I never meet them, there might be some parts of me I'll never know about. I want to know the truth."

Anna, envious, thought of opera plots. Liss could be the love child of great artists, abandoned because their music was much more consuming. Or the illegitimate daughter of a foreign diplomat. She could be descended from Asian royalty. She could be anyone.

"Well, I know exactly how I'm like my parents," she said. "I've got my dad's laziness and my mom's need for everything to be perfect. I get mad like my dad and freak out like my mom. Put them in a blender and ta-da. It's *great* to know who you really are."

"But—"

"And what if you find out they're horrible? What if they're murderers? Will it change you, to know there's violence in your genes?"

Liss looked back with those fierce fox eyes. "It'll change me no matter what. People who know the truth are always superior to people who don't."

Anna wanted to say that only their knowledge was superior, not always what they did with it. But maybe she only wanted to think that because she hadn't stayed to witness the truth taking place between her parents. She didn't want to be stuck between their yelling and hitting any longer than she had to. She wondered if she was weaker than Liss, or if she should tell her—a rebel with a coddled life and functional family—that some truths hurt.

"In two years I'll get my license," Liss was saying. "And I'm outta here. I'll track down where my parents live. I'll bribe the adoption agency if I have to, make them spit it out. And I'll see if I have any brothers or sisters I don't know about."

Anna couldn't look at Liss. The natural place to look away was the door in front of them, and on it was a mirror. She saw the moonlike mass of Dad's face under her own thick hair, her father in drag. Then bits of Mom poked out—the nose, the chin. She tried to salvage a feature that was only her own—her tawny eyes, those were hers—but the mirror was too far away to tell their color.

She was a mix of two broken people.

The only child born to hold and disappoint their expectations.

"Wouldn't it be nice to have a perfect family?" she spat, and was surprised at her venom.

"Yeah," Liss's tone was hopeful. "That's one reason I want to find them."

"Wouldn't it be nice if you could just create your own family and your own place in it?"

"I wish."

"What would it be like, Liss? If you could?"

Liss leaned in, excited again. They were perched on the cat tree, scoping the house and river, making vows. "All artists. No preps. All genuinely brilliant. And of course you'd be in it."

"You'd be in mine too," said Anna. "You're the closest I've ever had to a sister. And I don't know many other genuinely brilliant people. Do you?" Liss shrieked with laughter, like Anna'd known she would.

"Maybe Wagner, if he was alive." They'd taken to his operas that week. Liss stuck one earphone into her right ear and the other into Anna's left. She clicked through the CD tracks until "Ride of the Valkyries" seared in their eardrums. "You should come with me on the road trip. I'll introduce you to everyone as my sister. And we'll find someplace to live far away from here and make music. We'll run away 'til we reach a place where we can become exactly who we want to be. "

"Suspension will make an album and put on concerts."

"Everyone will adore us."

Liss, as always, lent her courage.

"We won't have to call on the goddesses for help." Anna pictured the two of them under stage lights so bright their bodies were absorbed. They trickled upward, merged, flared out into a plasma glow that fireworked above the audience. "We'll *become* goddesses!"

Liss flung an arm around Anna, pulling her in. Her face came so close the eyes blurred together. Anna shut hers in reflex and tasted sugary lip gloss. A soft pillow-like surface moving, then saliva. A wet tongue lunging in her mouth, coiled and slithering. The air was a hothouse. She couldn't breathe properly. A lurch of guilt in her stomach. A flare of heat. Her tongue stirred into motion and pressed back. Stage lights glittered behind her eyelids.

Chapter 14: *Jump*

Age Sixteen

Anna dreamed of Darien's room, which she'd never seen. It was meticulously tidy, with posters of Dylan, Miles Davis, and Joni Mitchell on the cream-colored walls. Wooden furniture, no real piles of anything. A record player and a stack of vinyls in one corner. A music stand in another. Darien sat in a neat wooden chair in front of his neat wooden desk, straight-backed, serious-eyed, looking ahead. Anna had the eyes of a security camera. She watched from multiple perspectives, and he couldn't see her. Where was she? Her sense of self was hazy.

Suddenly she felt a hot hand on her shoulder and Ay-a lurched up behind her—she must be in the room now—as tall as the ceiling, chains clinking between the folds of her many-layered gown. From this angle, her nostrils were flared and terrifyingly visible. She opened her lips which were coated in strawberry lip gloss, and words oozed out—"Move the furniture!" Then they were on the bed naked—Anna, Darien, maybe Ay-a, she couldn't tell—and as they dove at each other Anna could see from the corner of her eye that everything had changed places. Half of the night table stuck out of the bureau, and the lamp was floating upside-down. She was too hungry for that to mean anything. A heat wave rippled outward, visible in stippled light.

Anna knew it was stupid to take dreams as signs. She and Liss had analyzed each other's dreams—Liss's driving a tour bus to LA suggesting a desire to escape while remaining in control and exercising power over others, Anna's giant spiders eating a piano denoting a fear of success. Once she'd dreamed of going to school in an evening gown and diamonds—Liss had said she needed to be bolder.

There was a half hour break between the end of school and concert band. It wasn't hard, not physically, for Anna to go to the pharmacy down the street. She walked the length of the store, scanning every sign, and walked back again. There it was, in a row she'd missed—Family Planning. Everybody was looking at her, the matronly woman with her shopping cart full of party favors, the short balding man with beady eyes holding a pigtailed toddler's hand, the modelesque couple in their twenties leaning into each other's space as they walked without seeming to notice they were doing it. She should just go home. She was a poser, a wannabe, a kid doing what kids weren't supposed to do. But then, this was what her friends did.

There were so many kinds! Blue packages and pink packages and purple ones that reminded her of packs of gum. Extra Large. Sensation Increasing. Ribbed for Her Pleasure. She'd had no idea the condom selections were so extensive—or so expensive. And beneath them, the bottles of lube. As hearsay would have it, she should probably get some of that too. She picked up one of the cheaper bottles, turned it around, watched the tiny bubbles that swished inside, set it down, sighed, and picked it up again. Condoms. Many small colored boxes dominated by letters. She picked a box with spermicide. You couldn't be too careful. She grabbed the closest reasonably big thing she could find—a soft green polka-dotted bath towel—to throw over them in the shopping basket. She imagined herself explaining the purchase to her mother: *You can't have too many bath towels.* Or: *It's for swimming in the summer.* Or: *Here, Mom, I bought you a towel, I thought it was cute.*

They couldn't really be watching her as she walked towards the counter. Surely they were just regular, non-suspicious people going about their regular, non-suspicious shopping. Straight back. Brisk pace. Try not to look suspect. Breathe faster, shallower, than usual. What was the point of buying these things? It was stupid, because they'd probably never get used. Would Darien ever make a move? She didn't have the strength to lunge out of herself that way, did she? She got in line behind only one person, a man in a tuque with a pack of gum. Another person came to stand behind her, then another. Oh god, they were going to see the package, the bored-looking teenage clerk was going to see the package. She couldn't hold her head straight or keep herself from looking at the scuff marks on the floor. They'd judge her from the frozen look on her face, and the condoms and lube were a stupid impulse buy, tokens of wishful thinking that would never get used anyway. They were permission.

"Hello-how-may-I-help-you." The clerk sounded as bored as he looked.

"Hello," Anna mumbled to the counter. The boy bagged the items with no comment, and Anna was grateful. She looked at her watch—almost late!—and ran across the road to school. *Dear Ay-a, please let no one ask me what's in these bags.* They didn't. They were all parading onto the stage to practice, while Anna jammed her clarinet together without greasing any of the cork and had to readjust her reed during rehearsal because she'd tightened it askew. She joined her breath to the others in a German hymn, striving to blend her tone with Irena's, straining upwards and out of herself in a sacrificial smoke of sound.

It had been a long time since Anna could play Chopin's *Marche Funèbre* straightforwardly. The somber chords brought to mind the time she'd used Darien's proximity to fuel her playing. The impossibility of touching him, and the weight of wanting to, had fed the progression of grief. And now ...there was something too appropriate about linking getting turned on with a funeral march. She thought of Sex Ed lectures. Warnings against teen pregnancy. Handouts with grotesque photos of genital warts and herpes sores.

She waited a couple of days to test her courage and commitment, glanced at the unreturnable box of condoms, walked through those school days with cement in her stomach, and waited. Finally she faked being sick and made it to the school nurse's office. "B-b-birth control," she stammered when asked. The nurse squeezed an inflatable sleeve around her arm to test her blood pressure, smiled coolly, and scrawled a prescription. Back to the pharmacy, standing taller in line, repeating to herself that she'd been brave. Damn, it really wasn't difficult to get sex supplies. There were a lot of steps to think about, but sex as a reality seemed frighteningly easier with each one. She pictured Sarah getting fucked by the older cousin's older friend, some beach-blond guy grunting as he pushed her against back seat leather, her collarbones sweaty and mouth twisting. A salty breeze seeped through the half-open window, and the wildness in their faces looked like freedom.

She couldn't muster her usual sarcasm at dinner. When Mom asked what was wrong, she said, "Just worried about the concert" and retreated to the wide room of her fears where Darien moved towards her, shifting from gentle to coyote-eyed. She tried to tune out Callas' cheeping, then realized she'd forgotten to feed him.

Her friends certainly talked about sex enough, but she couldn't drag her secret desires from their windowless room and speak them. Especially not to Irena, who still looked Darien over sometimes. She couldn't look at anything on Mom's computer that might make her suspicious. All she had to read about sex were magazines, which she read repeatedly, scanning for hints.

The music sometimes hindered, sometimes helped. At school Ravel's *Jeux D'Eau* trickled and tripped, fairylike under her fingers. Water games, Mom had translated. She'd played this as a child from one of the tapes at Christmas, looked up, and found herself lifted by relatives' watching faces. Christmas lights illuminated them, inhuman, glowing golden as ornaments. She'd felt warmed and absent.

The little piece was so light it unmoored her. There was an almost unbearable sincerity in the music's desire to empty itself. Much density in the strident notes. A few darker gushes. Light reflecting on ripples, manifold shades of gold and blue unfanning. She played the little river by the beach, the one where she used to collect sea glass and still did sometimes, that tiny hesitant body that staggered into the ocean's gush. She sped up and played a crash. And here she was supposed to slow down, go playful again, but the notes rushed and rushed and her hands flickered out of control.

Warmth. A pressure telling her to slow. Darien's hand pressed to Anna's collarbone. A voice like a heat sink: "I'm worried about you."

Anna let out the ragged breath she'd been holding and tried to compose her features. "Just nervous for the concert," she breezed.

The practice room was a white cell. She wanted him and was oppressed by the wanting. Afraid. She needed to go to the water. No matter that it was ice now. Water stirred underneath. Not thinking, she leaned in fiercely.

"What are you doing tonight?"

"No plans, really."

"Want to go to the beach?"

She seized and kissed him before he could answer.

Bundled in scarves and parkas, they walked deliberately on the ice. The sand had a thin covering, with tiny blots of snow stuck in places. There were fewer seagulls in this season, and no people. The nearest houses, pastel building blocks that they were, stood far enough away, and the sand far enough below the banks of marram grass, that no one could spy on them. The sky was an unforgiving tint of bright ice blue.

"What do you like about the beach in winter?" Darien asked.

Anna didn't know how to answer. Clinging to Darien's

gloved hand with her own, she liked the warmth but wasn't sure she liked the beach right now. It was too bleak, practice room sterile, and she'd come here seeking something alive.

"I was hoping it would be warmer, honestly," she said.

"Yeah, it's freezing out here! I kinda just want to go back to the car."

Anna looked abruptly at his face. Was this a hint at something? "Yeah, let's go to the car." She was crazy to think that. He wouldn't want to.

They staggered back over the beach ice, walking fast but clumsy in their care not to trip. Darien turned the car on, activated the defrost, and a wave of warmth flushed their bodies. Some jazz came on—"Spinning Wheel," a clear bluesy rendition. Anna clambered into the back seat.

"What are you doing?"

"Come on," she motioned, "it's easier to cuddle."

Darien broke into a small smile.

They sank into the nylon, touched hands, and Valkyries mustered in her head. Go away, she told them, go away! They mapped the familiar regions of each other's bodies, all the safe zones. She reached lower.

"Anna—"

She loved his nervous deliberateness. His luminosity. The interruptions in the timbre of his breath.

"We shouldn't be doing this."

"Oh, come on."

She grabbed his hand, moved it to her, and he stopped objecting. She stroked him like she'd practiced, on vegetables stolen from the crisper.

The car was their room, a closed zone, artificial. They

could make it what they wanted.

"I have some, uh, some stuff in my bag," she said. "If we want to go further."

Darien gaped.

"I've started taking birth control and stuff."

"Jesus, Anna."

"What, haven't you ever thought about it?"

"Well, of course, but Anna—it's going to hurt, you know that?"

Anna was impatient. She'd waited, she'd planned, she'd wondered and doubted and sat around enough already. She wanted to grab, demolish, be destroyed. She wanted something to happen, and she wanted it *now*.

"I want the pain."

"You sure?"

"Just fuck me," said Ay-a, her eye glinting over Anna's shoulder.

"Just fuck me," she blurted out.

Maybe it wasn't the best thing to say. He could hardly fuck her while she was rummaging for a condom in her backpack and they still had all their clothes on.

She hadn't thought it would hurt that much. The world contracted and went white. She squeezed her eyes shut. She didn't know if it lasted one minute or five minutes or five hours. She didn't get to watch him come, to know what that looked like.

⸙

Darien's arms close around her. She feels their log-like weight on her back, but she scarcely feels her back. She is Ravel's *Jeux D'eau*, a lightness seeking desperately to escape itself. "Anna, are you OK?" OK. What is OK? His voice reaches her muffled as a canned laugh track.

Open your eyes, Anna. Somewhere there's a person called Anna. Not here. Not now in this car, this room that was supposed to make them what she wanted. What's on the radio? White static. She can't hear a note. Open your eyes, open your eyes. White static in the outer world.

In the inner world, capsules like bell jars or flying saucers spread out in a garden. Each contains a flower or a few. Irises, buttercups, carnations, dahlias, strawflowers. Translucent, closed to her touch, though she has no hands to touch them. The green expanse ices over. The ice cracks until it's choppy. Bullet holes mine the glass. Sound of white static.

Frozen beach. Suspended time. A capsule for the Garden of Moments.

Beautiful.

"Am I beautiful? Am I sexy?"

"God, Anna, is that even a question?"

Open eyes. See Darien. Darien. Here? Right? His face blurs.

"Am I as beautiful as my mom?"

"Are you as beautiful as your *mom*?" Incredulous laugh track. The next question spews forth.

"Am I as beautiful as Liss?"

"Who the hell is Liss?"

"Nevermind! Justnevermind!"

Faces, shapes, return as haze. A sense of legs.

"I'm going for a walk."

"Anna—"

Find the door, throw it open, run run run run breathe don't breathe breathe cold and heat and sweat and slip and land on ass and not feel it and look up into the cold sky. Be cold with it. Ay-a, black curls drenching gold-embroidered fabric, swoops down like a Valkyrie, howls: "You betrayed yourself!"

Leave me alone, Ay-a, I don't want you!

Joints tense from falling and frustration. Not turned on, so far from turned on, still sore from impact, thud, thud, thud, and dissatisfaction. What had she done?

A glimpse of the real world, Darien running through sand towards her, his clothes like hers pulled sloppily back on. Rutted frozen sand, white-coated ocean.

Anna frozen where she'd fallen. Making the effort to blink.

Come back to yourself, Anna. Anna? A tape player that unleashed a fountain much faster than any real fountain moved. A scary wooden box that she could coax sound fairies from, lingering in the air after each piece was finished.

Anna, a mind always swarmed with songs. She could slip in and summon one at need—melody, accompaniment, counterpoint—the whole blend of tones, even when all that came were mechanical marches and staid pop. Herself.

Now, white static. Walls and walls of it mashing into each other. Sound? Sound?

Pulse without rhythm. Cold that has frozen her in place. Panic that coils around and chokes her.

No sound at all.

She's six years old, standing on the edge of the dock at the Marina, watching seagulls quarrel and a jellyfish float up out of season. The wind beckons. She wants to fall into the water, to be swept into its gradually churning power, to erase herself, and she leans. From a distance comes her father's voice: "Don't jump!"

She jumps.

The hurtling displacement of air around her is horrible.

Darien's arms around her. Darien's lucid eyes. Fall leaf brown, mottled light fanning from the center.

"I told you we shouldn't be doing this, Anna. We haven't even known each other for very long, and at our age—it's just wrong."

"But we wanted to."

(*I* wanted to.)

(What the hell was I thinking?)

"You're too good. I shouldn't have let my stupid animal wants take over. I shouldn't have hurt you like that."

He was talking nonsense! It had been her wants, not his, that had lost control. *Hers.* Was he blind? Did everything have to be his fault, even the blame claimed and owned?

"I mean I—I fucked you."

Part of her was in shock, smarting from the pain. Another part was warmed by the word, in a way that hurt a little.

"I don't think we should see each other anymore," he said.

White static. No sound.

"I mean, I'll be there for you if you need anything, if you want to talk things out—"

⁊

The History of Opera. A heavy red-bound book from Mom's shelf, with pages edged in the color of sulphur. She read one sentence.

Read another.

As Clara Schumann grew older, she lost confidence in her compositional abilities, writing: "I once believed that I possessed creative talent, but I have given up this idea; a woman must not desire to compose — there has never yet been one able to do it. Should I expect to be the one?"

Empty marks, flying past like scenery from a car window. She checked the clock. Five minutes.

"I once believed. . ."

She'd been reading the same sentence over and over again.

She went alone to the piano at lunch. She yelled at Sarah and Chen when they tried to follow. No Darien to tell her the three things she was doing wrong and twenty she was doing right. Don't think about that.

The notes of Ravel's Presto came thud, thud, thud. A ghostly body intruding in hers. She had to stop. Her hands fell to her thighs, and she cringed at the contact. Intruders! Shake them off.

She wished she played a subtler instrument than the piano. Maybe the harp. There was only so much beauty she could draw from a run or a crescendo; the sound of banging forte or fortissimo notes was so absolute. It must have always been like this. Why hadn't she noticed until now?

Or the violin. She should have learned to play the violin. And singing, of course. The human voice was one of the world's most subtle instruments, infused with emotion in its natural state. The piano in front of her was a hard black box.

Laine's face was stony. "Anna, listen to me. I know a concert is a hard thing. God, I used to not be able to perform without throwing up before I went onstage! OK, so that's probably more than you wanted to know. But the point is, it's hard for everyone. I know what happened last time and how hard that was for you. And I know you haven't been feeling well lately. But every concert is a new start. And this is a debut for you on a new level. You'll be out there with an orchestra. You've worked so hard for this. And I'll be there for musical support, I guess you could say. And of course your family will be in the audience. I know you can play yourself proud. Have you ever thought about what you're going to do afterwards? You've only got one year of high school left. There are opportunities, Anna, scholarships—if you do well at this, your future will be made incredibly easier—"

Irena held up a contract to all who would pay attention. "They accepted my songs. They're going in the music book!"

"No way!" said Chen.

"I can't believe you!" shrieked Sarah. "Let me touch the paper."

"Our friend the musical genius," said Michelle.

"Congrats, but I doubt anyone's surprised," said Darien. He and Irena had been chatting all lunch hour, and Anna deliberately sat on the opposite side of the table from him.

Not too close, but close enough to watch. She fumbled with her fork and a clump of pasta fell onto the floor. Clumsy! Idiot! She bent to pick it up before realizing how stupid it was to retrieve a dirty lump of food.

Another thing she wasn't supposed to do, but Anna had drifted so far from "supposed to" that she wasn't ashamed to crotch watch. Dammit! He was definitely hard.

Anna tried to rehearse the concert pieces in her mind. She'd been trying since that day she didn't want to think about. That day she'd been abandoned in a world without music, unless she turned some on or played some, in which case she'd hear but it wouldn't permeate. The sound was an external thing that glanced off her without entering. Her blood was cold.

She clutched her music scores to her dark red evening dress, its clean lines a mockery of her recent transgression. When the conductor motioned, she staggered out in a thin pair of glittering heels. She never wore them, and hadn't mastered the art of walking in these things. It was a new stage, the public one where she'd first watched the symphony orchestra perform, watched Laine perform. She'd never stood there herself until the dress rehearsal. The auditorium's black velvet seats were tiered row upon row, and the balconies were vast. With the blue-white lighting so bright, she couldn't tell how much of the space was full. She knew from the dress rehearsal that the sound carried richly. From the other side of the wings, Laine in her black and white tailored suit strode crisply to the other piano. Between them sat rows of musicians in black adjusting polished flutes and heavy cellos.

Some glanced at her as she passed—one face bored, another curious, one smiling in encouragement, one reverent, one inscrutable. Some looked to be in their thirties, others were gray-haired, all much older than Anna. She sat down in front of her piano, the smaller of two grands. A vase in front held a single spire of white gladiola.

Her parents sat in the audience somewhere, pinpricks of light among the indistinguishable crowd. Her mother, crossing fingers for a splendid future, accompanied by Tom, with whom she spent more and more time. Her father, who went through the motions of encouragement, off on the other side with Gwen, who seemed, so far, safe from his anger. Friends and teachers, aunts and uncles, and a whole crowd of waiting strangers.

The orchestra swelled with sound. She heard it reverberate across the tiers of seats through the air and up to the vast ceiling, but she was cold to it. Her entrance came, she knew it, she felt no compulsion. Her fingers fell. She could do this by rote. She'd practiced so many times. The good thing was she felt no fear. Yes, she'd practiced. She'd hit a point where her hands functioned like machines.

On through the Beethoven, while the orchestra hit peaks of joy. The melodies from Laine's side were something she recognized, through her numbness, as beautiful. On through all the Chopin. *Marche Funèbre's* hollowness was hollower than usual. Ravel—the Presto was perfectly on tempo. A bunch of songs played thoughtlessly. Until *Jeux d'Eau*. With the fountaining of notes came a crush of physical pain. Darien advancing towards her. Eyes and body shut tight. Darien telling her to go. Darien blaming himself and refusing to listen to her, the true culprit. Darien hard under the table while Irena talked about her music book contract. What was wrong with her fingers? Presto became prestissimo fingers tripped lightness thudded crashing everyone was wondering what she was doing everyone was wondering what she was doing.

Freeze. *Carnival of the Animals*, now. Pause while string chickens screech back and forth. Pause while aquarium fish glimmer. Play while fossils rattle. Now the pianists, she and Laine and their scales, the most absurd animals of them all. Up and down and down and up, infernal. No cares about speed. Let it pound. Let madness sound.

Imagine hesitant clapping.

Sun filtered bright and tawny through the kitchen's lace curtains, casting tiny rainbows through the prism into Anna's cereal. Anna lifted her spoon and let it slide back down. Lifted, let it slide. She was still alive, right?

"You'd better read this, honey." Mom pushed the morning newspaper against her glass of orange juice, tilting it. Anna caught the glass mid-wobble and let it settle before looking at the Arts and Entertainment page of *The Islander*, where her own face brooded in profile. Her bangs were askew, her mouth too serious, neck vein twisted, hands clenched over the keys. Behind her was a tiny, marionette Laine at a grand piano.

Words rose in disjointed clusters, sticky as junebug legs.

Sixteen-year-old Stern commands an impressive technical proficiency—fails to deliver on her earlier promise—detachment not reflective of the composers' intentions—Ravel's Jeux d'Eau descended into mayhem—excellent rendition of Carnival of the Animals—a consummately skilled performance by Winters.

If only the sunlight would wither. If her mother would just stop looking.

"Honey, you know you need to put more effort in than that. Stop slacking off with that Darien—"

Mom's mouth moved too fast. Her hands folded and unfolded over her perfectly sliced orange.

"I know you're young and need to have fun too, but you've got to be committed to your music if you want to get anywhere. Maybe if you give up your saxophone. I haven't heard you playing it in awhile anyway—"

Gods, how she'd fucked up. Done horribly with her one real chance. There was no way to go back and change it.

"Look what happened to me. You don't want to make the same mistakes as your stupid mother did. Anna, what are you—?"

She curled the paper into a tube and whacked it against the table. Once. Twice. Ignoring the "Stop it!" Her cereal bowl rocked, sloshing milk onto wood.

Chapter 15: *I Cannot Cross Over*

Age Fourteen

The light was fading outside the picture window. They'd spent all afternoon practicing the *Poème* piece as they should—meticulously, in sections. "Polishing," said Liss, "with rags and spit." They went to the kitchen and brought back plates of grapes, store-bought maple cookies, and mugs of milk.

Anna hadn't mentioned the kiss since it had happened. Liss hadn't either. She looked down, away, to the side.

Anna didn't know what to think, or whether the pounding vein in her neck signaled excitement or fear. Whether this was a good or a bad thing. She only knew how to practice. Music was almost like kissing, one person's sound mingling with the other's. But it wasn't the same.

"You guys always have cookies around," said Anna, to fill the space.

"What, is that weird?" Eyebrows raised. A skeptical look on Liss's sharply beautiful face.

"No. Just not used to it."

"Well, in my world we'd always have cookies."

The sky was now a dark electric blue. Bands of curly-edged pink furrowed across it. A Mozart violin concerto—Anna couldn't tell which one, she'd heard it before but didn't keep track of them—wafted down from upstairs. Katie or Cassie's playing. All three girls had been trained with the tapes, and all three sent to music school. It was a lovely song, melodic, buoyant, played with lightness and skill. Just the thing to cuddle on the couch and listen to. She liked the calm, but there was nuance missing. It wasn't Liss's playing.

"I remember thinking when I was little that music could carry you up to the ceiling or the sky," said Anna.

"Who says it can't?"

And their game was on again. "I bet we can play ourselves to Heaven," said Anna.

"We'll squeeze all the power of the world into the music."

"We'll become demons. And gods! We'll go beyond light and dark to create the most omnipotent thing of all—pure beauty that lives only for itself."

"This can be our practice run. So when we do the real concert, we'll own that power." It seemed that Liss's very skin glittered.

"Ay-a. Ay-a. Stars in my body, stars in my soul."

Their hands brushed together, then Anna resumed her piano and Liss her violin with urgent understanding. Their gazes met timidly. Anna saw her own emotions etched in Liss's face.

She played the opening notes. Trickle and sway, and Liss came searing in. So quiet. Keen behind the volume's small space.

They felt themselves drawn tighter, their eyes focused like searchlights across the dinner table, one humming the first few bars of a piece of music as they passed in the school hallway and the other continuing. Anna had never known such delirium, the kind that occupied all attention and desire. They made fun of their homework and practiced and wrote small songs, they cuddled and kissed, and they told each other what their lives would be like once they ran away. Two strands wove together in Liss's fantasies: finding her birth family and playing in a band, and Anna couldn't tell which one she wanted more, or if there was even a difference, so determined was Liss that both would come true. These took different forms from one night to the next, and Anna, who believed most of all in the sanctity of music, its ability to transport, was carried along each time. One day they were living out of a hostel in Florida, performing concerts on outdoor stages under the palm trees. Another, they met Liss's parents in Nepal and studied at a Buddhist monastery, where they reached enlightenment and became pure strains of music ascending to the sky. They practiced, certain this was possible. They spent their nights this way while Anna's parents went to court, worked out settlements, ate dinner at separate hours, and avoided each other as if the house was a war zone. Later, Mom would tell Anna those stories, filling her in on what she'd been lucky to miss.

♩

Before the red velvet curtain rose, they faced each other in the wings, smelling wood polish. Laine and Mr. Rue's reminders echoed:

Liss, don't overdo it with your vibrato. Anna, watch your tempo and don't show off too much. You guys be very careful with the Acid Rain song; you know it's unconventional.

The real Laine and Mr. Rue stood beside them, Laine's hands chopping the air, Mr. Rue's undulating, his mouth crinkled. He was half a head shorter than she was.

"It's our stage now," Anna whispered.

Liss's family waited for the bus together, at the end of the gravel driveway. Katie had on a soccer jacket monogrammed with the name "Logan." Cassie wore a white coat with faux fur trim, and Liss a buttoned black trench. Anna was the outlier, taller than the others and bundled in a boring brown polar fleece. Maybe she should've let her mother buy her a fancy jacket.

Black, silver and red streaks of cars spit past. Anna wondered if any of them had vanity plates cool enough to add to the sign collection she wanted to embellish. She couldn't see from the side of the road. A school bus flashed by but it wasn't theirs.

"This bus takes forever," said Cassie.

Katie broke into song, barely under her breath:

Oh the water is wide
I cannot cross over
And neither do I
Have wings to fly
Give me a boat
That will carry two
And both shall row,
My love and I.

Her voice was velvet-textured, soft and lazy. Compared

to Liss's crystal clarity, it was smoke. A mezzo-soprano. Cassie kicked at stones and looked bored.

"Katie," said Liss.

"Yeah?"

"Decrescendo a bit more. That'll make your crescendos sound that much stronger."

"I'll think about it." Wariness and interest mingled in her voice—*Don't go telling me what to do* blended uneasily with *Thanks.*

"That was really good," said Anna. Oh, wonderful, she sounded like a parent. Really good. And late with her compliment, too.

"There's the bus," said Liss.

"Yeah," said Cassie, "'cause we really couldn't tell."

The school bus flicked its amber lights and heaved to a stop. It was arrhythmic, a huffing creature of bass. They got on. The driver nodded, the engine churned, and the kids in twos and threes in their patched-up seats stared vacantly at them, out the windows, in no direction specifically. Katie and Cassie went to the back, on separate sides. Anna and Liss had outgrown that. They took a seat in the middle. Liss pressed her hand into Anna's. Its weight was comforting. Anna wondered at the fact that Liss, fierce beauty of eighth grade and singer with a voice of crystal, wanted to touch her in public. She felt the impulse to lean in for a kiss, but she couldn't. Not on the school bus, she thought, but maybe she couldn't simply because she was Anna and not her braver friend. While she was wondering, the teasing began.

"Lesbians!" Some sing-song voices behind them. "Lesbos! Lesbos!"

"Ooh, they're in love!"

"Gross!"

The taunters were boys and girls in lower grades. Anna noticed braces and shiny lunch boxes. Their reaction was stupid, but a lump formed in Anna's stomach.

Liss turned and shot the kids a smirk, then bent her lips to Anna's. Dread mingled with that now-familiar fluttering.

"Katie, Cassie, your sister's a lesbian!" someone yelled to the back of the bus.

Anna felt sick.

The *Poème* piece was gentle, intimate, the violin and piano notes drawing close together. They couldn't turn to look, each intent on her own music, but they felt each other's presence magnified. Shadowy figures spread from their bodies like spilled ink. Around Liss, Anna sensed the figure softening. She grew curves, and quivered like water. She pillowed all the hard things in the room. She smelled like vanilla and cinnamon, although that might have been coming from the kitchen. Sava, the goddess of love. Nothing was immune from her touch.

It was time. Anna curtsied, gave the clapping a moment to subside, and settled herself at the piano bench. Then Liss stepped out, swaggering a little. Even her curtsy was edgy. They'd agreed to wear all black, and Liss's sleek dress cut off asymmetrically above her tiny knees. The claps were a drumbeat, summoning them into purpose.

The oversweet smell of cookies rose in the Tuesday evening kitchen. Anna walked in to find Katie reading at the table, pausing intermittently to glance at the stove. A cookbook lay in front of her, with yellowed pages and a brown stain on the open recipe. Cassie sat across from her with a math book, her attention focused on the cell phone she was using to text. The twins dressed with a preteen determination to be different, and Anna observed their outfits as if taking notes. Cassie's denim skirt and pink flower-print silkscreen tee. Katie's oversize brown hoodie over jeans, and the sun-painted guitar pick strung around her neck. Anna suspected Logan had given it to her. Both girls kept their hair mid-length, but Katie had cut herself a jagged bang. Two spring buds, they looked just alike.

Katie rose to take the cookies out. Cassie, finished with her texting, followed.

"God, these smell good. When can I eat one?'"

"Um, let them cool down but—" Katie's head bowed.

"Don't tell me you're going to give them to Logan."

"Some of them, yeah."

"Everything you do is for Logan. Everything you talk about is Logan. I'm fucking sick of you."

You need to get over Logan Disease—that's how Liss put it. Logan Disease seemed perfectly sensible to Anna, kind of like Ed Disease had seemed. It was hard to like him now. God, she'd seen him and that despicable Louise french kissing in front of the buses, their hands crawling everywhere, in full view of the first graders! But she and Liss, now—how did any of this make sense?

"Yeah, well, I'm sick of how you always tell everyone what not to do," said Katie.

"Well, Liss—"

"—does that too. I know. But she's—"

"—not as bad as I am. Yeah, sure."

"It's true! At least she tries to help! You just complain all the time."

Liss sauntered into the kitchen—she must have heard her name. "Hey, cookies, I hope you didn't burn 'em too bad. Have they cooled down yet?"

"I think so," said Katie.

Liss grabbed a chocolate chip cookie and bit. Cassie and Anna followed, but Katie went to get her parents before eating one herself. Of all the young kids to acquire a boyfriend, thought Anna, Katie seemed an unlikely one. What was her secret for being so much cooler at twelve, and so much better at normalcy, than Anna was even now? She heard a slobbery bark. The black dog snuffled into the kitchen and begged, letting its tongue loll out. Surely its pants were exaggerated. Anna couldn't explain why she wanted to strangle it just then.

A figure rose up out of Anna. Ay-a, different than in childhood, no longer a glimmering hug of cloth but faintly sinister, pianissimo humming in a minor key. Anna was intent on the music issuing from her fingers in soft, glimmering runs, so she couldn't make out the goddess's details. She thought Ay-a came from the piano as much as from her—an auditory entity rather than a visual one.

Was there a separation between the small skin-and-muscle body and the larger wood-and-ivory body? Sound winged outward from Anna's chest. *Poème's* serenity made the hairs along her arm prickle. There was something cruel in such composure. She flicked a glance at Liss's sharply cut frame, and saw the music's demonic perfection confirmed in its lines.

Small gods perched on Liss's violin bow, nosed up from the cracks between white and black piano keys, listened from the light bulbs.

Anna glimmered, Ay-a her echo and source. Power danced in her nerves, ordered and electric. Liss had been playing more softly but now she crescendoed. Sava's billowing took on smoke and pain, keening with the hurt of a mother whose body wanted to cradle lost offspring and whisper in accelerando that it would be alright, it would be alright. Anna felt flames close in, like those that had charred their long-ago effigy. This time she wouldn't douse them. The way of the brave, the way upward, was to hold on, hold on while the singe overtook her.

Are you with me? Is this good? Is this so good it's evil? How long 'til we reach pure beauty? We're getting closer.

Even at the apex, the slight tonal slip, the element of doubt. *Are we just playing silly games, wishing silly wishes we should've grown out of?*

It was during the first of Beethoven's three violin sonatas, Op. 12, No. 1, that something snapped. The zing of the stage lights had dulled to a lull as Anna's attention was drawn by the piano. She was playing along as she'd practiced so many times in that bland white room, dipping cozily into the music like she dipped her hands into hot sudsy water when washing dishes, breathing, not thinking of much. Then Liss's vibrato arced sharply upwards, jarring her. How could she so suddenly sound so radiant? Anna's fingers remained on the keys, playing their part in rote. Notes fell like a light rain, but Liss soared beyond them.

Liss was the star, Anna mere accompaniment. She wanted to ascend, but she had to play her part and only hers, or ruin the art of it. They echoed, they conversed, Anna's mild tones stroking the crescendo.

Fugue. Caroline said that in French, it meant running away. *We'll run away 'til we reach a place where we can become exactly who we want to be.*

The stage had been that place for Anna, before. Now Liss was outrunning her. Her body strained for escape.

I'll run away, Liss. I'll run to a place so far you can't catch up with me.

And Anna played in solemn, churchy tones, played deliberately over the violin. No one was there to tell her to blend in or shut up. Liss couldn't tell her that either. Onstage, she was an equal inventor of the rules.

I will give praise from the piano's wooden husk. From the rivulets of blood pumped through my body. From the tension in my muscles pressing the keys. From the strings of my vocal chords, deferred to a stronger surrogate. I will prove myself more devout than you can be.

"How are things going at Liss's?" Mom's voice sounded tinny over the phone.

"Good," said Anna, who couldn't have gone into detail about the kiss on the bus, and her disappointment at being left out while Liss, Katie and Cassie argued without malice, and her nightmares about thrown furniture if she'd wanted to.

"You and Liss are still getting along?"

"Of course."

"Good, I was worried you wouldn't be able to spend so much time together without fighting. Are you practicing much?"

"Of course. How are *you*, Mom?"

"Oh, not the best I've ever been, but I'm alive." She giggled wildly, as if this was some great joke.

Anna couldn't bring herself to giggle along. She hoped that didn't bother her mother. "What have you and Dad been doing, exactly?"

Anna thought she heard a small sigh.

"Ironing out the details of the separation, who's going to live where. I think I'm getting the house so your dad can move closer to work."

"Oh, good. I want to stay with you, then."

"Yeah, of course you will. I mean, I guess it would be good for you to visit your father sometimes—"

Hopefully he's not hurting you. I won't hold my breath.

"Yeah, of course."

Liss was sitting on the piano bench, violin beside her, looking towards Anna and tapping her fingers in her lap.

"I should probably get going soon."

"Alright. I hope you're having fun over there. Call me anytime if something's bothering you or if you want to come home." The weariness in her voice made it clear that she'd rather Anna not call. "Take care of yourself and do your homework on time and make sure you eat enough." She sounded like a caricature of a mother, rhyming off what mothers were supposed to say.

It wasn't technique, exactly, that served as music's ladder

upwards. It wasn't the labor of polish, which added to the beauty of a well-played piece but couldn't fashion a core that wasn't there. It was the interplay of complex sensations and desires, concentrated in a single ever-changing point. Whether it involved a solo voice or an orchestra, a simple melody line or chords and fugues and counterpoints, good music converged. It might storm all around you in whirls of wind and rain and hail, but you could follow it—if only subconsciously—to the pulse at the center.

Anna no longer felt a presence; she became one. She was soft and bitter, and so was Liss, and there was no Anna or Liss. The music breathed, and all the muddiness and sparkle of the notes they'd practiced dissolved. Their state was pre-instinctual. Growing ever more intent, they reached the point of convergence. Seared. Soared.

But in the din of the stage lights, Anna thought of how Liss embodied what those lights tried to imitate, and how much *she* wanted to be that. She crescendoed, upping her game, and Liss crescendoed in response. She added a chord and Liss jumped an octave.

One. Then another. One. Then another.

A few minutes into "Acid Rain"—what was the audience thinking, taken from altered classical to a punky vocal hybrid?—Anna on the keyboard threw herself into improvisation, riffing off the blues scale, her shoulders swaying, head tossing unthinkingly. Boldly, she looked at Liss.

The smaller girl was staring out at the glare-obscured audience, rapt, determined, and then she caught Anna's look. Turning to stare back, her foxy features went fierce. Anna couldn't read them. Hostility? Hard admiration? Liss opened her mouth to sing:

There probably are a lot of you, a family's a must.
Are you reeking in the rot of you, or smothered in your dust?
Do you think about me ever? Have a number you could call,
hanging on your fridge door? Yeah, NOW you could have it all.

Anna felt something crush in her. The desire to outshine weakened to the thinness of paper. This grieved anger lit like lightning, flashed out her fingers in memorized and new configurations. Each key on the keyboard was a small receptacle, holding not a flower but an animal preserved as if in amber—salamander, scorpion, grass snake, rat. Convergence sounded once again.

Anna had one more night at Liss's before moving back. They had a few weeks at least before Dad moved out, but Mom had given her a chain of excuses to return before admitting, with a break in her voice, "I miss you." Dad called only once, awkwardly apologetic, stumbling over his words. Anna told him to leave her alone, and he did. Liss had her happy dog and her happy sisters who finished each other's sentences even when they were fighting and looked up to her even when she criticized them. Mom had a house too big for two and a husband she was negotiating a divorce with. So Anna had to come home.

In Liss's bed that lazy Saturday, snuggled shoulder to shoulder in pajamas, they listened to all of Beethoven's symphonies in a row.

"I can't wait 'til I meet my birth family," said Liss. "I hate my family here."

"I don't think you do," said Anna.

The crowd filtered out to the sound of Wagner's *Ride of the Valkyries* playing dimly over the loudspeaker. People gathered and dispersed like clouds as the Valkyries, long-haired women fierce in golden armour, burst forth. It seemed appropriate. Liss grabbed Anna's shoulder.

"I felt like Rita Deviant up there."

"Really? What about the goddesses?" Anna half-joked.

"Yeah, them too. But more, you know, sexy." She laughed, suddenly nervous, and looked down at her feet. This was strange. Maybe she hadn't caught the competition, or the moment of convergence. What *had* she gotten from the concert?

"*You* were sexy up there."

Anna gaped.

There was an urgency in Liss's voice. "We always talk about those things, but I was kinda lying when I said that Ryan and Josh were hot. Even with the movie actors." She stuttered, but burst on hotly. "You're kind of the only person I've thought that about."

"Not even Rita Deviant?"

"OK, maybe her. But she's a girl too."

"Well, yeah." Anna could think of nothing more interesting to say. She was surprised by none of this, yet she remained surprised by the concert. "Do you think we made it to Heaven on that stage?"

"Of course we did."

Liss seemed so sure. Anna had been sure at some

point, but hollow in the absence of sound and tension and stage lights, she was left suspecting that the magic had been imperfect. Something was always lacking.

Liss seemed satisfied as her arms enclosed Anna's shoulders. She leaned inward—

Lesbians! Lesbians!

In the wake of the kiss, Liss's voice quavered: "I love you."

Anna couldn't assemble her thoughts. She froze. Her eyes shut tight, stayed there, squinted open and blinked.

"No," she said.

"But don't you—"

You love her. You love her. You love her?

"No! You don't know what you're talking about!"

"I don't see—"

Ed and Louise intertwined like a pretzel, so putrid, so normal. Liss onstage, outrunning her.

"I don't want this!"

She unfroze and felt a crumbling around her eyes that signalled oncoming tears. Her pulse beat way too fast. Her feet took off underneath her.

"Anna, wait!"

But as she ran through the halls, she heard Liss's parents cornering her. Her own parents hadn't found her yet.

Anna's feet are pinched in brown flats with little crinkles around the openings that don't match her black tights. The strobe lights in the music room sound like insects. There are cardboard boxes stacked in the back left corner. Laine is not in the office. Anna's left knee bone is pressed against her right inner knee. There is a sound that may or may not be a mosquito. The bathroom is down the hallway, to the left. *Love?* There is a strident reason to be here. Beethoven over the loudspeaker pulls emotion like children pull taffy. Anna distracts herself by noticing the smell of her lipstick. A janitor comes into the music room every day but there are still footprints on the floor which is covered in little uncolorful speckles. Anna wears a black ribbon in her hair from the concert. *Love is too serious.* At a restaurant one time she'd heard a lady with a giant powderpuff for a purse say it's a good thing hair ribbons had gone out of fashion since her time. Taffy pulls are violent. The lighting is much brighter than the stage lights. There is an aftereffect on Anna's brain, a roll of musical negatives. The room takes twenty long strides to walk across. Liss had worn strawberry lip gloss, a birthday gift from Anna. Anna has paced back and forth. *Ay-a, Ay-a, stars in my body, stars in my soul.* The violin case is open in front of her. She really needs to pee. *Liss too high for her to follow.* There is very little shadow cast with all this lighting. There are twelve beige freckles on her right arm. Muscles belonging to something else inhabits it. *Anna running away.* The air tastes like lukewarm water. She has never owned a dog or had a sister. In a taffy pull you yank with sinewed arms and still the candy strings apart apart apart apart. Someone could build a bridge from taffy if the material was strong enough. *Liss running across that bridge, towards her.*

Liss's violin, marbleized wood luminous as eyes. Her foot's proximity. *Liss outshining her.* An inch between sole and polished body. *Liss so satisfied.* Hesitation. *Liss's lips touching her, Liss's gifts untouchable.* Impact before she realizes there's been an impact. Hideous cracking sounds. Again, again, *encore.*

There is a sense of cold grandeur in Anna's eyes. In the keys of every piano are salamanders, scorpions, grass snakes, rats. Anna is made of piano keys. The violin is on the floor and the pinchy flat of her right foot is through it and touching the uncolorful speckles. The music room has windows but they're high and hard to see through. Anna's pulse is doubled where the veins stick out. Beethoven is a musical negative. Everyone had loved them. Past is a negative sometimes set to music. The violin is in two main pieces with a hole scrunched in the middle and assorted splinters. The violin is back in the case on the shelf. It has a name on it. Adrenalin has Anna's veins alight. Liss now owns two halves of a violin. The splinters would be hers too but Anna has picked them up and thrown them on top of the lint and pizza box in the garbage. A piano is too big to stomp through. *Love?* She shudders. A splinter is lodged in Anna's index finger just below the nail.

Chapter 16: *Terminal*

Age Sixteen

The June air was invigorating at the ferry terminal from Vancouver to Vancouver Island. A small bubble world of blue haze and glass, it wasn't attached to much land. The huge glass buildings with lines of trucks crossing between them were islands of their own. Anna and Darien waited.

The break between them hadn't lasted long. He'd seemed happy enough to take her back, and let her cry in his arms more than a charitable number of times.

"Did you and Irena do anything?" she asked, the worry a knife in her gut.

"No," he said, and she really wanted to believe him, but couldn't be sure. In weak moments she was reminded of this.

But she wanted him back no matter how much she'd been hurt by his insistence on a break. Was it love? Was it wishful thinking?

"We shouldn't—I shouldn't have sex with you. All it does is hurt you, and god, Anna, you're too good to do that to."

He looked across at her with some distant, goofy glance, as if she were a statue. A stone thing too beautiful to touch like you'd touch someone flesh-and-blood. She felt neglected.

But she didn't speak of sex again either, because she wasn't sure how she'd feel about a repeat.

When he mentioned going west to work for Uncle Matt and Uncle Parker at their cafe in Tofino that summer, Anna had been jealous.

"You could come too. They're looking for people to hire."

"Really?"

She'd never simply picked up and taken off. She'd never really thought of it—but people could just leave their routines, their lives, travel across the country or the globe and do something else. The idea felt like high tidal waves against her heels. She was young, she had nothing better to do, and nothing that obligated her to stay yet another summer on the island. Nothing!

"Wouldn't you rather go to Montreal?" her mother asked. "You could stay with Aunt Louise. They have more jobs. Maybe you could learn a bit of French. Do they even have a piano at this restaurant?" Not there, Darien informed her, but they had one in the house. Her interest in music had been lackluster after the concert anyway. Everyone said she'd get it back, but when was unclear. Mom tried to push at first, but that just made Anna eat half as much and stay up into the night doing nothing. So she took to saying "Sometimes these things take time," and spoiled Anna with salmon and a new dress.

Dad liked the idea better. He had some second cousins she could look up, and gave her the addresses of Joe who fished and Ellen whose family ran a motel.

"Take these," Mom told her the day they'd left, and pressed a pair of yellowed notebooks into her hands. "Vacation reading, if you're interested. Don't let anyone see them."

She was curious, but Darien's presence absorbed her attention. They flew to Vancouver first to visit his grandparents, who lived on one of those fancy streets of shingle-roofed pastel houses with flowers spilling across the yards. Anna found herself scanning them for clues—the grandfather's height, the grandmother's way of looking downward. How were they like this boy she was dating? When the grandmother said to Anna "I hope you like meatloaf" with a hint of smugness in her voice, and the grandfather coughed into his napkin and rambled about the bonsais he'd grown and pruned (scattered on tabletops, on windowsills, on bookshelves) to a very attentive Darien, she interpreted each gesture as a previously unrevealed hint at Darien's character. They kept pictures of their dead cat on the jelly cupboard beside the family photos. The grandmother's abstract paintings, lumpy tubes and popsicle-colored mountains, clustered around the bonsais. Their record collection was impressive—mostly folk, jazz, and crooning.

"I hope you don't mind sharing the guest room, is that alright?" asked the grandmother.

On separate sides of the bed, neither initiated contact. "I'm sorry my grandparents are so embarrassing," said Darien, his arms crossed over his chest.

"They're not!" said Anna. "They seem pretty cool."

"Oh, good."

"I can see where you got your artistic side from."

"Gram used to sing." He sounded a bit embarrassed.

"No way! I wonder if she'd sing for us."

"Please don't ask."

Part of her wanted to reach across to him, and part of her

was sobered by an old thought. "Sometimes I feel like we're all just made up of parts of our family. Just some repetition of a theme that's been around for a long time. So it's interesting to meet someone's family and see if you can spot the themes."

"Well, yeah, that's how genes work. But the parallels don't always mean much, and it's not like we don't choose what happens in our lives. Look at my crazy dad compared to these sane people. I don't think there's any fate, whether it's genes or God or whatever, that decides what we are and where we'll live and what we'll eat for breakfast. Wouldn't that just be hell?"

"But can you know yourself without knowing your family?"

"Of course," he said.

"Anna, look at me," said Laine. "I read Tom's write-up in the paper, too. That guy finds any reason he can to trash people. And he gave you credit for a good performance in Carnival. That's no small accomplishment."

Fails to deliver on her earlier promise...

Tears welled and stuck and wouldn't fall.

"I ruined everything! I can't go back and change it."

"Do better next time." Laine was gentle and brusque, in that way she had of being both.

"You said it yourself, I can't make up for this. Not after I made such a mess of all those pieces!"

Not after what happened with Darien.

"It's just one concert—not a great one, not an awful one. You have one more year to impress those scholarship committees." Laine's hands navigated a circle in the air. "Now, is there anything you want to talk about?"

"Not really." Her eyes were frozen, the tears suspended.

"You know I'd be glad to talk, if there ever is. Growing up is, well, it's not for the faint of heart, let's just put it that way." Her chuckle was hoarse, half stuck in her throat. Anna felt herself loosen at the seams, felt that terrible sense of grasping and falling, that uncertainty of being solid.

"Look, I was trying to play music and I wasn't even there. I can't even feel anything."

"Yes, that's happened to me before."

"I've wanted to cry all week and I can't!"

"Well, look, here's what I think. Whatever's bugging you, wait it out. Don't dwell on it, don't forget it. At some point you'll be into your music again, but don't let yourself get too far while you're waiting. And don't give up. You can't afford to."

Laine's gaze was sharper than the swathes of sunlight hanging above her.

Anna flushed with curiosity. She was a little afraid of her teacher, even now, but she didn't let that stop her. "What happened that made you not be able to feel things?"

Laine's face clouded suddenly. "Relationship crap. Isn't that the usual?"

Anna started skipping practice sessions. She found herself spending hours she'd meant to sit in front of the piano leafing through something she pulled from the bookshelf— *The Opera Encyclopedia*, or *Art of the Italian Renaissance*, or *Theories of Practical Translation*. She still played most days—ran through scales and arpeggios, polished a difficult section of one of her school pieces with all the interest of scrubbing the floor, scouring an already uninteresting surface over and over in circles. She couldn't play anything just for herself. The thought was like eating dust. Mom worried, but she was busy with Tom. She spent nights at his place. They cooked dinner together, watched movies, and took walks on the wildlife trail. Activities Mom could do with Anna, but she was happier doing them with Tom. She came back to Anna without worry lines, acquired them again, and went back to her boyfriend to remove them. It was good that Mom had someone to treat her gently and bring her joy, and Anna felt nothing about it.

Anna checked her weight one day. She'd lost five pounds without even trying, and she told Chen with a lilt of pride in her voice.

"Anna, you don't need to lose five pounds. You're too skinny already."

The ferry was many-decked, broader than the ones that used to carry her parents and herself to New Brunswick on rare weekend excursions when she was little. She hadn't set foot on a ferry since the bridge had been built. She and Darien ran immediately to the top deck, where the sharpness of the air assaulted her. There was nothing like taking gulps of breath infused with pine and salt water and a strangely tinted cleanness that smelled just this different from home, nothing in the world.

"I'm so glad we're getting away!" She threw an arm around him.

"I'm not sure how much of a getaway this is. We'll have to work regular hours." He returned the contact.

"Some travel companion you are," she grinned.

It was colder out here than she'd expected, and the wind

hurled her hair around her face. She pulled away, unrolled her jacket from her backpack, and shrugged it on.

"The view out here's amazing," said Darien. The ferry was travelling across a bowl of water sunk among rounded mountains, sheer green. The water was dappled where the sun fell on it, and a rich opaque blue where it didn't. The waves were small and regular, tiny folds in fabric. "It never gets old."

"How often do you visit here anyway?"

"Well, at my grandparents', sometimes for Christmas. Tofino, I've only been maybe four times."

The top deck was built to race and pace on. They made their way around it several times. Two small children stood by one railing, their jackets billowing. "We're flying!" she heard one say, and the other answered, "Don't be stupid."

"But look at us, we are!"

She wanted to take the older sister, who was about to protest again, and shake her. She turned on her MP3 player and lost herself in the musk of a cello.

Multicolored packages of lights first signalled the island's towns. The green approached, and eventually a muffled and officious loudspeaker voice warned them off the ferry. Anna looked around the waiting crowd, wondering which faces would turn out to be Darien's uncles, and two men came to pummel him on the back. One of them looked a bit like him, an older, homelier variation—lanky, sharp-featured, with thinning carroty hair that tufted upwards. His partner was stocky with big arm muscles, widely spaced eyes and soft lips that gave him an incongruous look of innocence, and a round, shaved head. They wore cargo shorts and T-shirts. Clasped to the thinner uncle's shoulder, Darien grinned shyly.

The stocky uncle turned towards her and stuck out his right hand. "I guess you're Anna? Good to meet you."

"Nice to meet you too—what should I call you?"

"Parker's fine."

His handshake was gentle and certain.

"Oh, Anna!" The other uncle, Matt, spotted her and swept her up in a hug. He held on with a warmth she wasn't used to. "Darien's told me so much about you!"

"Same with you," said Anna, although she had in fact needed to prompt him to get much information. The uncles had married a year ago, bought a small trailer just outside of downtown and close to the water (which was everything on Vancouver Island, just like on P.E.I.), and turned it into a restaurant named The Breaking Wave Cafe, which they always just called "the cafe." Anna couldn't think of any married gay couples she knew. P.E.I. was pretty closeted. She'd met Laine's girlfriend at a few concerts, a quiet wispy thing, but they weren't married. How would these two live? she wondered, which really meant, how cuddly would they be?

"You play three instruments, is that right?"

"Yeah, but the clarinet's more for school, and I don't have my own saxophone." She should have just left it at "Yeah"— why would he care?

"It'll be nice to have some musical people around," said Matt.

"Oh, come on, you play the piano," Parker interjected.

"Yeah, badly!" They both burst into belly laughter.

Their car was a boxy brown Volvo whose radio crackled as they drove over hill after hill. Matt in the front passenger seat flicked through the stations trying to find one that came through clearly, stopping now and then at something that caught his interest and laughing out, "Hey, this is good!"

"I don't think so," said Parker when a snatch of an aria came on. Anna didn't get to hear enough to recognize it, and she might not have recognized it anyway.

The next "this is good" was a call-in show with some guy who called himself The Love Guru. The caller had a heavy Indian accent and said he was calling in "to surprise my wife."

"How did you meet?" asked the self-proclaimed Love Guru. "Did you just fall in love? Or did someone introduce you to each other and then you just kind of fell in love?"

"You hungry, Darien?" asked Parker. "And Anna?"

"Actually, I am," said Darien. Anna was glad he'd said it first.

"There's a McDonald's coming up if you want to stop for lunch."

Seated with their burgers, the uncles discussed the attitude of the teenager who'd served them ("They need to find some friendlier cashiers. I hope it's not a chronic scowl"), the preparation of the food ("Those fries sure took a while," "At least they put the right labels on all the burgers," "Good thing we don't have to label ours,") and the restaurant's general atmosphere ("Some dirty tables over there," "First lesson for you two—never leave a dirty table dirty," "We're getting new curtains at *our* cafe").

"You see, Anna," said Matt, "all restaurant people are like this. Soon enough you'll find yourself taking notes on everyone else's customer service."

"I've worked at restaurants and never cared that much what people at other restaurants did."

"Ah, but that's because you have no investment in them. At our cafe, everything gets personal pretty quickly."

The uncles, she could tell, were invested in everything, and their interference was something of a thrill.

Matt's next "this is good" was some insipid dance music probably composed a few generations ago. Anna thought about turning to her headphones, and was surprised to realize she didn't want to. She could listen to her own music anytime. She enjoyed this bad music, its poppy crackling a novelty. The soundtrack to a new kind of freedom!

❧

The uncles lived in a small wooden house within walking distance of their cafe, and they took Anna and Darien to see the cafe first. "Here she is," said Parker with obvious pride. It was smaller than any restaurant she'd worked at before, a quaint wood-shingled place with a blackboard full of menu options, heavy wooden tables and benches meant to look more rustic than they were, and a long skinny kitchen. Blotchy abstract paintings decked the walls. A sign outside read "The Breaking Wave Cafe" and sported a painted wooden cutout of a wave in primary blue. Another wave decorated the chalkboard where the menu and daily specials were written.

"Isn't it beautiful?" Matt grinned.

"Yeah, nice place," said Darien.

"And we're going to have a couple more workers here, Bob's girl Jackie from out of town and Kelly from down the road. They're just a few years older than you two."

"Isn't Kelly the girl we met last time we were up here?"

asked Darien.

"Oh yeah, you did run into each other, didn't you?"

"She was the one who gave the guided tour—'And on the left, gentlemen, are a bunch of magnificent garbage cans!'" He smiled, bemused.

Anna went to look around the kitchen. There were stacks of bowls, a shelf full of batter-spattered cookbooks, and two chunky fridges. Everything smelled like dishwater and faint whiffs of edible things—cucumber, ketchup, curry. Something felt both bland and unsanitary about it. It didn't have the greasy, excessive order of some of the places she'd worked, but it wasn't Caroline's kitchen either—it didn't feel warm. *Is this just because I'm away from home?* she wondered. *I'll probably like it eventually. Or at least put up with it. Gotta have a job.* Most of her friends were working this summer too, but Irena had gone to a composing camp in New York. She wondered how Liss spent her summers these days—probably in an even snazzier fashion. She didn't want to think about that.

The restaurant spilled out onto a porch a short walk from the beach. The sand was pale gray like ground-up stone, and the uncles threw handfuls at each other. Anna took off her shoes and stepped into the foam-licked water.

"The waves are different here. Less fierce."

"That's just the weather today," said Darien.

"I love how we're right next to it."

"Yeah."

"It's a prime spot for attracting customers," said Matt. "The beachfront."

Darien caught Anna's attention and rolled his eyes.

"We should probably take your stuff to the house now,"

said Parker.

Anna lapped up the landscape as they drove. Silver sea, rain-laden sky, long fields of yellow grass and wildflowers and finally their small house tucked among them. They carried their suitcases past a fireplace and canvases of incoherent swirls into the spare bedroom. "I take it it's alright if you share a room," said Parker.

Darien looked at Anna. "Of course," she said.

After a supper of organic black bean burritos and berry coleslaw—restaurant food, Matt assured them—Darien chatted with the uncles while Anna wanted nothing more than to collect herself, to savor some quiet in this world of new. She took the notebook her mother had given her and settled in the overgrown meadow that passed for a yard. It seemed to be a diary, in her mom's neat curly handwriting. She'd read one entry per day, she decided, to make them last the visit. She didn't want to miss her mother, but she did, a little. With grass prickling her knees, she began to read.

I met some men at Jana's place today. They were having a barbecue, and one of them wouldn't touch the meat but had made a pizza and grilled it. His name was Henry but he asked me to call him Hank. The other men were Ahmed, Chris, and I forget the third one's name. Oh well. Hank had muscles like a farm worker and longer hair than the others, which was thick, honey brown, and curled past his shoulders. As soon as we met he began to lecture me on ethical farming practices. "I'll only eat meat if it's given space to roam and hasn't been fed chemicals," he said. "I have nothing against eating animals. We're omnivores, after all. But animals are meant to roam around, right, not to be cooped up in cages." I said that was a great idea and I wished I had thought of it, and of course I don't eat much meat in the first place. "Same goes for plants," he said, "no pesticides. There's nothing wrong with a few spots on our food, but there is something wrong with poison in it and the atmosphere. I'd love to have a little farm someday with none of that stuff." He told me about a book he owned called Diet for a Small Planet and said that I had to borrow it. He has a bit of an accent, of the friendly Eastern sort, and inclines his head when he talks—a boyish gesture. Jana tried to flirt with him but I was pleased to note he didn't pay her much attention.

The pizza, by the way, was delicious.

Kelly, a petite blonde firecracker, greeted them all with hugs. "Matt, Parker, how are you! Darien, good to see you again! Anna, it's so great to meet you!" Anna felt thick breasts press against her stomach.

Jackie's arrival a few minutes later was signalled by an unusually loud thump of the door. Kelly threw her arms around the sturdier girl's neck with the same vigour, and there was no confusion over her name because Kelly yelled it so loudly.

"Workin' in the restaurant all day," said Jackie. "I can't wait." She had a voice naturally devoid of any intonations of surprise; Anna thought she was being sarcastic, but it wasn't clear. Her hair was long, tousled, and foggy brown. She wore cargo pants. Not bad-looking, not badly built, but she carried a sense of heaviness that had nothing to do with her size.

"Movies tonight, anyway," said Kelly.

"You bet."

"You guys should come too!" Kelly's sweeping gesture took in Anna and Darien. Jackie didn't smile, but had she smiled once yet?

"OK, first thing." Matt clapped his hands. "Breakfast on the deck. We'll show you what we can do, then we'll show you how it's done."

"Whatcha make?" asked Kelly. "Your waffles with blackberry awesomesauce?"

"It's not called awesomesauce," said Parker.

But the waffles, organic pumpkin muffins, cream-topped berry salad and freshly squeezed lemonade were as awesome as Kelly had predicted. "I can't believe how much food they make," Anna whispered to Darien, feeling foolish enough that she hoped not to be overheard. "Are they always like this? Do they *live* at their restaurant?"

"Well, they kind of always are like this. It's not always cooking, but they always find an obsession and do pretty much nothing else. It's scary."

"Hey, what are you two lovebirds whispering about?" Kelly leaned in their direction, grinning.

"Don't interrupt," said Jackie, her sarcasm a touch more obvious this time. "It's bad manners."

They were given orientation. Parker and Jackie would do most of the cooking, Matt the managing, and Kelly would lead the wait staff. "As for you two," said Matt, "you're floaters. You'll do mostly waiting when the customers are in, and various other chores to keep the place running."

There weren't many customers there the first day, and Anna knew how to wait tables. She'd done it before. Smile, notepad, plate-balancing, routine. She mostly did the needed chores in her own corner, but could hear Matt and Parker, Jackie and Kelly and occasionally Darien as they bantered.

Mine, she thought fiercely when she heard Darien chatting with the other girls, but she tried to check her impulse—it was ridiculous to be jealous because her boyfriend was talking to their coworkers.

Lunch and supper had the lush flavors Anna would come to expect, the restaurant felt more spacious than on the first day, and the music they put on to clean up was jazzy and peppy and genuinely fun. Anna followed Kelly, Jackie, and Darien over to Jackie's place in a sunny daze, making sure to seize her boyfriend's hand. "Hear that brrr-r-r sound?" Jackie pointed to the woods, which were taller, redder, fresher than the ones on P.E.I. "It's an orange-crowned warbler. You can see it on the tree over there, that greenish speck. We have one that eats from the hummingbird feeder at our place. Oh, look, it's staring right at us!" Anna couldn't see a thing.

In Kelly's airy open-concept living room, the girls grabbed bags of chips and watched a road trip movie Anna had heard of but not seen, then a romantic chick flick. The plots were cliché, and the girls made fun of them. "We're all going to end up happily married in the end, once we've stolen back our boyfriends from the supermodels," Jackie quipped.

At this time at home, Anna would be practicing. Darien must have thought the same thing, because he glanced from the piano in the living room to Anna and back and said, "You guys should hear Anna play. She's amazing." He gazed at her with the awed look that he only wore when contemplating her music.

"Oh, what do you play?" Kelly asked.

"Just classical pieces and stuff." The idea of playing here felt heavy. She hadn't practiced for a couple days during the trip, and she liked the lightness that brought the lack of worry.

"Cool." Kelly sounded appropriately uninterested, and the conversation moved to other things.

A green path home. A fresh rain that smelled like rebellion. That night she pounced on Darien, and he was more than happy to reciprocate.

We were riding the ferris wheel and right on top he pulled something out of his jacket pocket and handed me------a box! ~~And it was really~~ Now of course I knew what that size and shape of box was for but I feigned surprise. I really wasn't expecting it now. I took off the silver ribbon slowly, carefully, and the ferris wheel was going way too fast for me to enjoy it the way I wanted to and I didn't see the ring while we were right on top like Hank probably wanted, ~~more like almost at the bottom~~ but it was beautiful. It had a small faceted diamond. The small ones are the best kind because if they're faceted right they're all fire. I could have cried.

The carnie was an old guy with tattoos, puffing on his cigarette, such horrible things for your health!, and his squinty little eyes didn't notice us as we kept on going for another free round. Above the people-dotted fairgrounds, above some of the pigeons even, the motion a slight transcendental wind. I'd like to believe it was our love that made us invisible to the ordinary world.

Between erratic work hours—the restaurant and cleanup often went late, and Matt saw it as a matter of course that Darien and Anna would show up at odd hours when called on to take care of random chores—and outings with Kelly, Jackie and their friends, it was a few days before Mom got hold of Anna on the phone. She asked about Anna's work hours, Anna's diet, Anna's health, Anna's practice habits (she lied), and went on at length about all the music programs and scholarships she should be looking into and activities she should be doing to improve her chance of admission, while Anna tried to imagine the woman lecturing her as a lovesick college student atop a ferris wheel.

She felt guilty enough to play for both the uncles and the girls that night. Approaching the piano, the dread she'd been running from settled over her like a heavy coat. She plucked the keys emptily, but the others couldn't tell the difference.

"Beautiful," said Parker.

"That was awesome," said Kelly, and she turned to Jackie. "Did you see how fast her fingers were going?"

Darien grinned at Kelly and back at Anna, warmly and distantly in that Darien way.

They had one day off a week, sometimes two, on top of the evenings. One Friday night when it wasn't raining, the four of them left the uncles and headed for the beach. Tucked out of sight in a cave among the cliffs, Jackie rummaged in her backpack and pulled out a bottle of Malibu.

"We're underage," said Darien, waving it away from himself and Anna. "We shouldn't have any."

"Stiff ass," Kelly slapped him playfully.

"Hey!" His protest took the same light tone.

"I don't care about you," Jackie shot Darien a look, "but we're playing truth or dare. And if you won't take the dare, you have to take a drink."

Cliff shadows cut various angles across the group's faces. A pair of seagulls squalled by, one in pursuit of the other.

"You first," Kelly pointed to Darien. "Truth or dare?"

"Truth."

"OK—have you ever questioned your sexuality?"

Darien paused for a moment. "Yeah."

"And?"

"Well, I wondered when Uncle Matt came out of the closet. I scared myself trying to look for any crushes I might secretly have on boys and wondering if that's why the thought of sex was so awful when I was 12 or something, but I guess I was just too young to be interested in it. I can't think of any times I've really been interested in a guy, even though I've looked for those times." He tried a weak laugh.

Kelly took a swig of Malibu. "What about the rest of you guys? Anyone questioned?"

"Yeah. Pretty damn straight," said Jackie.

"Not me," said Kelly. "I like girls sometimes. Actually—swear not to tell anyone, OK? But I made out with one of my female cousins before."

Anna caught Darien staring goggle-eyed. Kelly grinned at him. She seemed to be enjoying this a bit too much. "I've made out with a girl," Anna said. "I used to have a sort of thing with one. We didn't go that far—we were young and all."

"You never told me that!" said Darien.

Jackie and Kelly looked at her with a new respect. "How was it?" Kelly asked.

She shrugged. She felt that familiar guilt engulf her. Inhaled.

"Do you like girls?" asked Darien.

"I guess I do, sometimes. Yeah."

The seagulls kept flapping past. The waves continued their placid wash inward. Kelly grinned, and Jackie and Darien looked on with friendly neutrality. It was the first time she'd said it out loud.

"But don't expect a threesome anytime soon, *Darien*." She kept her voice teasing and winked clumsily as her hand latched onto his wrist; winking wasn't something she did very often.

"OK, your turn for a truth or dare," said Jackie. "Darien, give her the question."

"Truth."

"What's the most scandalous thing you ever did?"

Anna wasn't going to mention the broken violin or making out shirtless to her mother's porn, and she couldn't think of anything else terribly scandalous. "Um, I shoplifted some bracelets from the dollar store once." She didn't mention that Sarah had egged her on, and she'd felt bad about it for a week.

"Somebody needs to loosen up," Kelly nudged her. "Make out with some more girls. OK, my turn! Can I get a double dare?"

"Double dare," said Jackie, "um. Go skinny dipping."

"Ooh, good one!"

The girls peeled off their clothes and arced towards the water, their bodies smooth as dolphins, their hair quickly darkening as they submerged and reappeared. Anna remembered her long-ago conversation with Liss about stripping in the schoolyard, and both their reluctance. Another Anna, a freer Anna, would have joined them if she'd been dared to and laughed as she splashed back and forth, maybe kissed Kelly unsuspectingly, but Anna wasn't sure if she could. There were some boats not so far in the distance, but the girls didn't seem to care. If anything, the element of exhibitionism egged them on. Back in the cave they made a display of their bodies, shaking shining droplets from their skin with each infinitesimal pose.

A while into the game, Kelly invited Anna and Darien to a friend's party that night.

"I'll go tell my uncles," said Darien.

"Your uncles won't care." That seemed true enough.

Anna followed Darien to the party and found herself half wishing she'd stayed home. The room was dim and crowded with shadow puppets, raucous human shapes she could only partly see. Techno dance music blasted from a speaker somewhere, and a string of lights shaped like chili peppers surrounded the room. The carpet smelled of spilled beer. She was introduced to people whose names promptly sieved through her brain, crammed between crowds who squashed past on either side, and soon everyone she'd come with was out of sight. A guy named Michael or Mitchell, tall with tattoos on his arms, was asking where she was from and how she liked Tofino and pressing a glass of sangria into her hand. She wanted to say she was too young to drink, but thought of Jackie and Kelly naked in the water. Why not? Why the hell not?

Some of the red drink spilled on her shirt. She found herself too conscious of the stain, of her t-shirt's black plainness amid a sea of sequins, of her tiny tripping steps next to Michael-or-Mitchell's big confident ones. Voices jostled, and it was harder to notice people. Michael-or-Mitchell encouraged her to drink faster, grabbed another drink when she finished the first, and gulp after gulp poured down her throat. She felt dazed, dizzy, sleepy, but her eyes were too numb to close. They moved towards the dance floor where singles and couples swayed, their bodies dripping before her eyes like paint. A hand grabbed her forearm, tightened wrench-like. She found herself being spun. Michael-or-Mitchell's breath came at her, rank with beer. She reeled away.

"You OK?" his face was further off again, at a safe distance.

"I have a boyfriend."

"I'm sorry. I had no idea. Wait, how old are you anyway?"

"Sixteen."

"What are you doing at a party like this?"

The speakers crackled some electronic noise. The chili pepper lights were blurry. "I don't know!"

She bolted past more people dancing, and in the next room, couples sprawled on couches. Time got swallowed somehow, and she opened her eyes on the floor.

"Hey kid, you wanna join the game?" It was Jackie. "We're playing Sociables."

She didn't really want to. Thoughts of going home to her house in the P.E.I. woods, of crashing in her familiar bed, beckoned her. Then she realized that she wasn't even on P.E.I. anymore.

She sat up with a drink between two guys who looked much older than her. Jackie was the only one she recognized in the circle around the deck of cards. There were too many people, and the rules were confusing. Girls take a drink. Pour some alcohol into the King's Cup in the middle of the circle. Make up a rule—no names, no pointing, take a little man off the rim of your cup every time you take a drink, give each drink you get to the player beside you. Everyone but her seemed to be laughing.

At last they were done. The smell of beer was getting to her. She needed some fresh air. To the door, into the sweet-smelling outside, past more groups and couples huddled around the porch, smoking cigarettes, smoking weed, entwined. There was Kelly, and in her arms—

No. Yes. No. No!

She and Darien, arms moving like snakes. Their faces pressed together.

I'm sitting on the ferry, about to make the crossing to the Island. A lot has built up to this. It's the first time I have been on such a boat, and I have never been on the water for as long as I will have once we're over. There are two decks, a small restaurant with sandwiches and other take-out items except of course there is nowhere to take them out to, and a video arcade where you can play some game with grainy blue polar bears. I don't like the way this thing tips around. Most of our belongings have been sent already and are waiting in the house.

I had a dream in which the baby was a raw skinless blob and another in which it was a genius and yet another in which it was a frog. I know I shouldn't be worried, realistically, except that my stomach has inflated into a sloshing cast-iron blimp with something kicking in it, and nausea has taken over my morning routine. My body has morphed itself into the container for another being. How could I not be worried?

If the child is a boy, Hank wants to name him Robert after his father. I suppose that would be a fine name, like Robbie Burns. If it's a girl, I wanted Carmen but he hates it, so we settled on Anna. Whoever it is, it's thumping on my belly as the boat is thumping on the waves. I hope to avoid getting sick. Hank arranged to have his sister's piano transported to the house. I'm grateful to her. When we get there I will play it every day, and make Hank sing along with me. He has a better

voice than he realizes, a lovely rich tenor. Now if only he could paint!
Then he would be truly perfect.

Accusations. Apologies. In the cafe, Kelly laughing and Darien brightening at her approach. Anna's suspicions had been right all along. How could she have done nothing? How could she have done anything?

"What do you like about her?" she dared to ask. And Darien, as always, was honest.

"She's so laid back. I can relax around her."

"She makes you relax, you mean."

"That's not a bad thing."

She forgot entirely about practicing. The piano was a despicable black box blaming her whenever she looked, so she didn't. The bed was difficult to sleep in.

Technically they were still together, so it hurt when Kelly bounced in with some anecdote about her friend escaping the police and swung an arm around Darien's shoulder.

"Leave him alone," shot Anna.

"Oh, he doesn't mind. Do you?"

Darien said nothing.

This is it! Our house is cramped with every kind of box imaginable.
We spent hours figuring out how to set up the bookshelves. As for the
island itself, the spaces are wide and you can breathe. Hank showed me
all the varieties of trees in the woods behind our yard. There are poplars,
red maples, sugar maples, spruce, white pines, white birches, lindens,
and I don't remember what else, but the variety is astonishing as is their
smell. The yard is overgrown with clover, thistle, and dandelions that have
gone to seed. Hank pointed out some chamomile plants growing in the

driveway.

I met Hank's sister Bet. She is a darling little creature with the same hair as his and bones like a swallow's. Her husband Theo is large and friendly, if a little childish, and they have a kid of their own. He makes so much noise! I wonder how I'll manage this. Hank's brother Jeffrey also dropped by with some firewood.

The piano is beautiful, with foliage carved into the wood, albeit a little out of tune. Well, I will find a tuner.

My mother called today. "What are you doing, Carrie? Come back home!" I don't let anyone call me Carrie anymore. If they can't manage Caroline, then Carol will do.

She worked sullenly, talking to no one. She was an excellent waitress, industrious and precise. And within a month she typed up a resume and spent her days off walking it around to other cafes. She found a hostel and looked into the rate to stay there—reasonable. She had enough saved up. She got a call back from a little yuppie place by the water called Cafe Omega. She wore her best to the interview—a sleek black dress and a red silk scarf she'd nabbed from her mother's room. There was a piano in this cafe, and they were interested in her as a musical entertainer as well as a waitress.

"How long can you stay on for?" asked the manager at the end of the interview.

She thought of school, of Laine, of her failed concert and how little she really wanted to go back to trying, of home and expectations and the revulsion of spending another year at school with the Boy Who'd Cheated! On! Her! It was an especially nice day in an especially nice town, with enormous trees and a walkable center and actual things to do. Ay-a's voice sang *Freedom! Possibility!* You can be anyone here. She found herself answering, "As long as you want."

Chapter 17: *Convergence*

Ages Fourteen to Twenty

Anna wasn't around to see Liss cry, although she must have done so. Maybe she didn't realize the damage until she got home and, much later, opened the case to practice and found splinters. Maybe she knew right away, from the change in heft. Maybe her parents were there when she opened the case and shrieked, or stood quiet and heavy as marble. Maybe they weren't.

Anna made up her mind to step lightly around Liss the next day, to mention nothing, to put on her best unaffected face. But Liss caught her shoulder in the locker room, and Anna spun around to face a set of narrowed eyes.

"What were you thinking, breaking my violin like that?"

"I—"

"If you don't love me, you should've just told me so!"

Anna's mouth moved in dumb flapping gestures.

"My mom's going to have to pay thousands of dollars to replace it. You have no idea. And the memories, and the sound quality, and everything, I worked with it for years, it was mine. You know what, I think you're crazy."

"Look, I don't know what happened to me, I'm—"

"Sorry? No, you're not. You hate me."

"I don't!"

Did she?

"You know what, Anna, you fucking genius who thinks she can get away with everything? I don't want anything to do with you anymore."

Her gesture of dismissal was tentative—the first syllable hurled, the second trembling into a question mark. It stung that much harder because the weakness, too, went into Anna's blood. She deserved it. She deserved much worse, she told herself as she trudged to class with her head down, passing Ed and Louise with their fingers entwined. Just because Liss had—

Chen was the only one Anna told. Anna had always been closer to Chen than Liss had. In confession, she guilted herself over and over again, laying it on so thickly that all Chen could do was tell her to ease off, that Liss would be fine, that no, she wasn't a monster, that everyone goes crazy when they're upset sometimes.

Anna waited a few days before trying to talk to Liss again, but Liss wouldn't answer. "I'm sorry," she tried many times, her voice minuscule. Liss kept her eyes on her desk, and Anna watched dust motes float in front of her face. She often caught the smaller girl looking towards her in class, then turning her head when she realized Anna was watching. Liss was as loyal an enemy as she had been a friend.

They spoke, finally, the day Liss told her she was moving away. "I'm going to find them, too." Anna knew she meant her birth parents, the ones she thought of as her real family.

"I'll miss you."

"You have other friends."

At night, a tongue disturbing hers. The crack of wood

underfoot.

᛭

My mother took me to my first opera when I was only five. Louise was nine, and I got jealous whenever she got taken to a performance and I had to stay home with the babysitter. Mom remembers it being Tosca. I do remember her explaining that day that the lead singer was acting the part of a made-up singer. The stage was impossibly glamourous— churchyards entwined with ivy, castles with golden pillars, men in capes and the woman with a long red dress and jewels nested in her hair! Louise remembers me saying they must have cost billions of dollars. And the music! I'd heard these sorts of sounds only on the record player. Mom and Dad sometimes hummed around the house, Louise sang little ditties, but until that day I didn't know real people could sing like that.

In the car ride back I sang all the arias I could remember, inventing nonsense words. I knew nothing about operatic ranges yet, and my baby soubrette voice tried its best at the baritone parts. As I'm told, Louise wanted me to shut up but Mom told her to let me keep on going. I must have heard "Shut up" a lot in the following months.

I would never have been a Maria Callas anyway. My voice was too weak, and even at McGill I had trouble with the deeper chest tones. Professor Roslin would say, "Pretend your gut is a big balloon. Suck in breaths until it expands." No doubt it has never occurred to Professor Roslin that it's impolite to compare young women to balloons.

There is no opera company on P.E.I. The best I can do is listen to tapes on repeat, plunk at the piano with my swollen belly, and sing to the ceiling. I do it all the time.

Seventeen. Eighteen. Nineteen. Twenty. The years

trudged by in 4/4 time, and stasis was easy. It started in mid-July to August at Cafe Omega, a move into the hostel with Jackie's help, a refusal to answer any of Darien's messages. She called Mom from her new number, and Mom worried but there was nothing she could do, said Anna, now was there?

"If you want to drop out of school, I can't legally stop you," Mom agreed, "but I won't have you living under my roof. And if you've got your heart set on staying out West, for whatever reason, there's that music academy in Vancouver—"

But the desire to go back to school never did return. She drifted from Cafe Omega to Cafe Sunlight, playing piano and sometimes clarinet to audiences as discriminating as the one at Kelly's, waiting tables when she wasn't entertaining. The routine wasn't so different from music school. There was one main difference—no one expected her to be extraordinary. No concert audiences, no critics, no Laine. No grand pianos or church organs, only small uprights that needed tuning.

She felt her skills slipping. The talent that had first buoyed her could only sustain itself with practice, hours each day running scales and polishing the tricky bits of pieces, hours of listening that her ears could no longer endure. There were a few times she sat herself back down and tried to focus hard, but her mind blanked or her fingers fumbled. The garden of moments was finite. There was freedom in spending those hours, in defiance of Darien, sitting on some stupid beach.

There were scholarships, Mom reminded her. Laine missed her. She was letting her potential stagnate. Did she not at least want to finish high school, for god's sake? Did she have any dreams? Any regrets? Ever? She could do a GED, and it wasn't too late to take up music seriously again.

When Anna let her guard down, hearing those things stung, but she didn't let on that she cared. No one would know that Ay-a showed up in dreams sometimes, a ludic figure in too many coats, scolding in an icy variation of Laine's voice. Or Another Anna sat in front of a baby grand with inspiration pouring tide-like from her fingers, her rapt face stony, impossible to connect with. Anna's ideal was present somewhere in the realm of mind, but she couldn't live under its weight.

She told none of this to Gary, a young chef at Cafe Sunlight who asked her out dancing a few weeks in and spent the night correcting her steps. Gary was six years older and an inch shorter than Anna, woodchuck-shaped with a beautiful thatch of black hair, charming, decisive, and unimpressed. He seemed to know everyone in town, and he wasn't even from there. He liked Anna's playing but they'd gotten that out of the way before the dating even started, and he clearly preferred her in bed to onstage. Anna wasn't sure how she felt about that, and when she started writing little pieces for herself, she refrained from sharing them. His room was full of unfolded laundry, and he complimented Anna on the shape of her lips, the way waves of hair fell over her collarbone, the slow way she laughed. He waterskiied, grew bamboo and avocados and sweet potatoes and a few spindly sprigs of marijuana, and read people's tarot cards and tea leaves although he wasn't sure if he believed in them. He was everything Darien wasn't.

After a year of dating, they moved to Vancouver where they got hired, then fired from The Red Geranium Cafe two weeks in. "The manager's a nutcase," shrugged Gary, and he proceeded to get them jobs at a daycare some of his friends had started. Anna found herself diapering and undiapering squalling infants, spontaneously singing as she shuttled kids around the room in an attempt to keep attention, eating child-sized portions of the same mushy lunch she spooned into some little one's mouth, and retelling Dad troll stories to kids who were supposed to be napping on their mats. Gary was the charismatic one the kids all loved, but she was the first to cuddle whenever someone cried.

During nap time little Kendra sobbed regularly for her parents. Anna sat her on her lap and stroked her forehead and sang all the lullabies she knew, until one day Kendra crawled onto Anna's lap of her own accord. Caught in an unaccustomed tenderness, Anna found herself wondering how she'd do as a mom, what it would be like to pack Kendra's lunch and send her off to school each day, to tuck her in and drive her to soccer practice. To live with Gary in a little house on the outskirts of town, to adopt a cat and a younger sibling for Kendra. To keep the house gleaming and well-stocked, the yard landscaped with tangles of hollyhock and nasturtium and a little herb garden and a fish pond. To cook meals that everyone would eat. Another Anna would never have entertained such thoughts, her fingers lighting into a flawless Debussy. That might-have-been Anna was lithe and elegant and lived in a studio loft with leather couches. Maybe she even had a chandelier. She didn't care as much for space, since songs were her garden. Instead of children, she birthed compositions. Anna faced this woman and wondered.

Gary left her after a year and a half to go back to university in Guelph. She found a job at the Blue Spot Cafe and moved in with roommates who filled the rooms with smoke fumes and kept neglecting to put the garbage out, then another set who held anarchist meetings in the living room, before deciding that she'd rather live alone.

By twenty, Mom and Tom had gotten married, Dad and Gwen had gotten married, and Anna was working at the Green Staircase, a small Vancouver restaurant that served organic foods and held live concerts three nights a week. As manager and concert coordinator her own artistry went unwitnessed, but her taste was quickly respected. She took to listening to a local indie radio station and finding acts that the cafe-goers and staff all loved. She emceed the shows and watched from a seat near the stage as bands filled the spotlight and audiences applauded.

"You're lucky," said Dad, "to have a job. And in your field, even." Anna knew he told the truth. The news was full of articles on the recession. Her old friends, who she kept in touch with only sporadically, were hiding out in university or working jobs even odder than hers. She was lucky to have resources, safety nets, things not everyone got. Even if she'd done everything right, it would have been hard for her to move right into music. All these hopes and dreams, for what? Potential, in this economy, meant nothing.

Dad said other things too. At first Anna's shoulders stiffened whenever he called, but he talked about starting a little sustainable farm with Gwen, seeing a therapist, getting treatment, working on his anger issues. "I'm sorry," he said, and Anna exhaled the breath that had been waiting on those words for years.

Now it was her mother she edged around. "Does it ever bother you," Mom asked, "to invite all these professional musicians in and hear what they're doing and not be involved in any of it?"

The "No" caught in her throat, too much of a lie to surface.

After that conversation, she took to tuning and playing the piano at the community center after work and on weekends. It wasn't the same thing, but it was an outlet and a pressure-free performance venue. Sometimes the kids playing pool or arcade games meandered over to sit and listen. Word got around of her Sunday afternoon concerts, and a small crowd of youngsters would gather from time to time.

It was on one such occasion that a small boy's mom came along and laid a hand on Anna's shoulder after the show. "You could be a concert pianist, you know."

Anna tried to hide her surging emotions. "I've thought of that."

Thought of that, before Liss had left and Darien had left and Gary had left. It had been too long since she'd been full, so she'd left too. There was no longer room for her in the pictures her imagination used to conjure.

Anna, you quitter, you loser.

She took to dressing with studied elegance, maybe because she knew she'd never be one of the pointy-hooded, dreadlocked strangers who navigated the few parties she attended with vexing relaxation, and maybe because Mom and Tom weren't there, Dad and Gwen weren't there, and Chen and Michelle, Irena and Sarah weren't there. There was no one to set any standard she cared about, to live up to or to rebelliously let down.

One day she returned from Goodwill with a silver jacket

that cinched around her waist and a pink-tinted cameo brooch that she stuck through the collar. She turned on the radio and rummaged through her closet to see what would match the jacket.

The music caught her while she was pulling on a pink blouse and dark gray pencil skirt. The guitar chords were harsh and raw, the percussion thunderous, the backup vocalist's voice a husky rasp, yet the lead vocalist's notes were glass. It wasn't often that Anna heard such contrast. She felt stones spill down her back and ice water pour through her.

I lay under the morning and I said it was a gift
The sun was all full-frontal and the grain fields all were lit
The mysteries were there and almost earthbound, almost snow
Say, what are those mysteries? I'd really like to know.

Pretend it's something regular like Coca-Cola and Alka-seltzer
Love's a shorter word than fucking but it takes a longer while
Poke on some lip gloss. Try to feign a smile.
Can't you see I'm not a real-world runner?
(Maybe I am)
Gonna play that hurt like thunder
(Maybe I shouldn't give a damn)

In a dream I took the ferry to an island by the coast
It was press'n'sealed for tourists, a retirement home for ghosts
And I found another lover but I had to catch the plane
And as I ran I saw you sitting on a stone, your face like grain.

There was something uncanny about that mix of harsh

and fragile, especially the lead vocalist's breaking-crystal sound, but Anna couldn't place her déja vu. She listened for a name.

"That was 'Grain Field' by Felicity and Grace. Next up, we have the lovely Isabelle Peters with 'Forgot is Not a Word.'"

Felicity and Grace. Anna wrote it down to look up later. They'd be great to bring to the restaurant.

Today the sun was low over the garden, the beans ready with another crop to pick, the zucchinis and tomatoes nearly ripe, and I discovered I could hit low B. Yes, my voice fell with ease, the chest tones resonant, almost as if I were a mezzo-soprano. No more struggle. No more cringing at my choked attempts to reach. I tried the low end of the scale a second time, then a third, to check if it was a fluke or if I'd heard wrong. But my sense of pitch is not known to fail, and today was no exception. I have that note now. It's real.

As soon as Hank got home from work, I called him over to listen. He nodded. "Very nice."

"But don't you get it?"

"Yeah. Your singing's great."

An unreasonable anger swept through me. I didn't want to have to explain. I wanted him to get it. I'd complained about my vocal range before, so he should guess what I was on about, right? But of course I couldn't assume that of someone. How was he to know one note had changed if I didn't tell him? Yet I felt so tightly wound in response to his apathy that I could have hit him.

"I can hit low B now!"

One note. It sounded pathetic, his enthusiasm insincere. "Yeah, I heard you singing. You're great."

Felicity and *Grace* announced the website banner above the group's latest CD cover—a globe engulfed by an ouroboros, a glossy serpent biting its own tail. In the pallor of the globe, two women's faces in profile, regarding each other. It was difficult to make out much apart from their beauty.

About Felicity "Liss" MacKinnon
About Grace Bear
Discography
Tour Dates
Photos
Blog
Contact

No way.

⸙

Dear Liss,

This is Anna from school. Remember me? I heard your song 'Grain Field' on the radio and loved it without realizing it was you. Congrats on your awesome band and your CD! When I say I'm stunned by your music, I mean it entirely.

I'm working as concert coordinator at a restaurant in Vancouver called The Green Staircase that has live shows three nights a week. I'm wondering if you and Grace would have any interest in coming up and doing a show. We have a stipend we could offer. It would be amazing to see you again after all these years. Let me know if you're interested or want to talk it over further, and even if you don't, it would be great to hear from you and hear what you're up to.

She paused. Love? Xoxo? Sincerely?

All the best,
Anna Stern

ANNA!!!! God, I've wondered so many times what happened to you, gone looking for you online, everything, but you just disappeared. It sounds like you've got a cool job. How ever did you end up in Vancouver? It's a brilliant city, but everything you do is brilliant. As for me, I ended up in Ottawa, and Grace and I started making music together. We're kind of a thing but not a thing—it's complicated. You might say I went rogue after I left school. Finished high school at a stupid public school, but did my music on the side. There's so much to tell you, but we should save that for in person! We'd love to come up—in a month? Would that work?

xoxo
Liss

Grace was statuesque with a sweep of black hair, a cape-like coat and a painted-doll face. Anna saw her before Liss. *Click, click* went her heels on the airport floor. Then Liss caught up with the luggage, a suitcase and a hockey bag, and twined her arm through Grace's. She wasn't quite the elfin creature Anna remembered. Her face had filled out a little, grown womanly, and her dark berry lipstick matched her girlfriend's. She'd toned her style down but maintained some rough edges—she walked in clunky platforms, and her denim jacket was artfully frayed with buttons and zippers in odd places. She strode briskly and purposeful as always. Her hair was still the fox-faced first grader's.

Anna had little time to observe this picture. Liss had already broken away, dropped suitcases, and ran forth with hair flaming. Arms wrapped around Anna and breath warmed her neck.

"Anna!"

"Liss!"

She smelled the faint tang of citrus perfume.

"My god, I've missed you so much. You have no idea."

An unexpected clutch in her throat prevented her from answering.

"Tell me everything about your restaurant."

Next to this bold woman, a real singer now, Anna felt a little stupid. "Well, there isn't much to tell, really. It's a little organic place downtown, decent food, we grow our own herbs, and we have concerts three times a week. I think I already told you that. We've had some good groups come up, like Sahara Soundscape, CrossWiseEyes, Lily Alvarez—"

"I love Lily Alvarez!" said Liss. Grace stepped next to her and stared pointedly. It took Liss a minute to react.

"Anna, this is Grace. Grace, Anna." She turned to Anna. "I've told her all about you."

Anna wasn't sure she liked that. Coolly, they shook hands.

"Nice to meet you," said Anna.

"Likewise."

What kind of person said "Likewise?"

"So tell me about your music." Anna tried to address them both at once.

"It's an amalgamation," said Grace. "Folksy lyrics, sound influenced by punk and metal as well as some classical, vocal mix inspired by some strands of Gothic opera—"

"Basically anything we find interesting," said Liss.

"Liss is the lyricist," Grace interrupted, her voice like the cinnamon spread Anna slathered on toast. "I do guitar and bass, and work with synth effects."

"Great," said Anna. "Should we take a cab to my place?"

"Actually, we have a friend in the city we're going to be staying with," said Grace.

"We?" said Liss. "You can stay with Julian if you want. I'm staying with Anna."

Grace sniffed. "Take the hockey bag, then."

Liss had them wait until Julian arrived with his glossy shades and sparkling blue car, leaned in to kiss Grace on the cheek (Liss bristled), and let Grace and Liss mash lips together while he watched, smirking. Then they drove off, man and woman looking like a movie still.

"My place is small," said Anna. "I hope you don't mind."

"Of course I won't. It's not like we live in a castle or anything."

They piled into the backseat, the hockey bag shared between their laps, and ignored the cabbie. Their bare knees met easily, but the space of years sat dust-like between them.

"Grace didn't use to be like this," said Liss.

Anna looked out the window and wondered what to say.

"It's like the music's gone to her head. The popularity's gotten to her, and she thinks she can get away with anything now. You were never like that."

"I was, actually."

"No way."

"I *did* use to think I could get away with anything," said Anna, her chest clenching. Next to Liss, she and her life felt small. "Then I learned I couldn't, and gave up, I guess. I'm not one of those people with the will to be good."

"That's bullshit."

"You have to care more. You have to want it more than anything."

"Of course not! You only have to want it enough." Liss looked toward the window where a beach bloomed at the feet of skyscrapers. "God, Vancouver's beautiful."

"Look at you, Liss. You didn't give up. That's because you have it. I just don't."

"If you keep talking like that, I'll kick you."

So Anna changed the subject. "Tell me about everything you've been up to."

"Just music, basically." Liss drummed her fingers against the seat. Suddenly her face brightened. "Oh, I didn't tell you—I found my birth parents."

In Stanley Park the trees engulf her. They are nothing like the spindly maples and modest spruces of the woods behind her P.E.I. home, although the gold dust of wonder falls on them like it fell on the small trees of her childhood. Elephantine—she rolls the word on her tongue. Canada geese and their tenderly awkward goslings, babies grown nearly parent-size, waddle away as she crosses the little bridge. A couple looks to the water where a swan flexes muscular wings. The man has a camera out, and they're too intent to notice Anna, to wave. That suits her fine. Closer, she sees they've propped a tiny rubber duck on a stone and are snapping its picture in front of the swan. Anna wants to laugh, but they seem very solemn.

Through a marsh forest, where leaves rustle all around the ancient trees' feet. Then higher, drier woods. The Atlantic woods had once been sacred, but now their trees are dwarves. Real trees have furry masses of needle spreading from reddened trunks. Real trees are marked by height as sentinels of the skyline.

She wants to find a place to sleep out here. There are rotted stumps she can fit inside, and the ground is hallowed with red needles. She almost yields, thinking she'll wake up to some nosy morning kid—*Mommy, Mommy, there's a lady in the woods!*

"I don't know what I was looking for," said Liss, her feet dangling over the arm of Anna's secondhand turquoise couch. "But whatever youthful ideals I had about my family. . ." her voice trailed off.

"Did you go on a road trip or what?" Anna wondered which version of the story Liss had lived.

"No, I found out through the adoption agency once I was eighteen. We sent some letters back and forth, and I met my mom and dad at different times. They were never married. I was born because of an affair."

A love child, Anna thought.

"What are they like?" she asked. "Do you have any good stories?"

Liss told her.

Groceries. Supper. Anna to bed on time. Mop floors. Clean

bathroom. Mow the lawn, or make Hank do it. Ten more documents to translate (I hate this job). Why am I wasting time writing in here? I must remember that it's not a waste of time, but an investment.

There may have been other opportunities for love, had I waited, or other circumstances in which Hank and I could have lived happily ever after and both pursued some measure of our dreams. Caroline Stern, lyric soprano, singing Juliette or Carmen before a sold-out crowd. My sister cheering from the front row, my father, and even my mother. Sometimes I wonder what could have happened if I'd remained in Montreal. Maria Callas used to practice five or six hours a day. I hardly have the energy to practice one.

Luckily Anna seems to like my singing, although she's not much of a singer herself. Her pitch is good, as far as I can tell from a kid, but she mostly hums and claps. She bangs out fancy rhythms with pot lids and that toy zebra of hers, and she wants me to have a tape on all the time.

I'm not committed for life, necessarily. Things change. Who knows how long Hank will even have this job? And the idea of packing up a suitcase and Anna with it and jumping aboard the ferry never to return, while laughable, seems not inconceivable. When it comes to doing right by your dreams, a life is a long time.

Blackberries grow along every stretch of path, wicker shapes offering fruit the color of bruises. Anna must eat four dozen. She reaches for the highbush blueberries, just as tall, and plucks their tiny globes. Then more blackberries, those omnipresent plants that always have something to offer.

Her mom had called her last weekend and asked if she was happy. "I love you," she'd said. "You know that, right?"

Liss's mother was Mi'kmaq and worked at a grocery store

on the reserve. Her father, an immigrant from Mumbai, had worked his way up from waiting tables to selling TVs. They met at a party; he was ten years older and married.

"They were Indians of two different kinds," said Liss. "That's the joke my mom made."

They passed the bowl of chips back and forth, each scooping a handful.

"Each has their own little life," said Liss. "He has his Indian wife and kids, all very nice and polite, and she has her Mi'kmaq husband and a couple boys who wanted me to play video games with them. It was fun, but strange. I asked them all if they were into music, but none of them are hugely into it." She crunched some chips.

"That must be weird," said Anna. "Meeting all those new families."

"I look like my birth father," said Liss. "But I talk like my birth mother. She invited me to a drum circle over on the reservation. You'd love the rhythms!" She stilled for a moment, pensive. "Someone like Grace has had her whole life to know her culture. She does Anishinaabe beadwork. Used to go out and harvest maple syrup in the woods with her dad. Even my sisters know all that Scottish stuff. I feel like a baby just learning to walk. I've got a lot of catching up to do."

"Was that some of the drumming you were talking about, on your radio song?"

Liss gave her small smile—the shy one, not the bold one. "Yes."

"Then I think you're walking just fine."

Liss stretched out her arms and seized Anna, squeezing. "You have no idea how great it is to see you."

One of the buildings in the park has been rented for a private party. On the porch, couples in tails and tulle canoodle to twenties dance tunes, until the speakers begin an incongruous rush of pop. A week ago Joel White, the lead singer of Surrender, died of a drug overdose, and Anna has been hearing this song all over town.

I'll be standing here where the beaten paths unwind
I'll be standing here when remembrance stains your mind
I'll be standing here grown half dumb and almost blind
I'll be standing here and I won't be hard to find

And I promise, this I promise, I will never
Never move since I'll be standing here forever

A gesture of honor, but this version is a bad remix by someone she can't identify.

At the outdoor theater, singers stomp and screech. They chant what sounds like the same few lines, stridently over and over again.

❧

Liss has gotten onto Anna's computer and found the songs she's written. Liss has told her they're good, but Anna doesn't believe her. She's set up one of them on a loop, the chime-like melody enough to drive Anna crazy. She should really simplify it, tone down the trills in that middle section.

"Things aren't going so well with Grace," said Liss over

her fifth glass of wine, her hair sprawled across the couch.

She stirred, and her foot knocked against Anna's. They giggled. Anna thought of pulling away, but Liss's foot came on top to pin hers down. Liss's face looked soft, and Anna felt the urge to cup it, to trace the outline she had often wished her own to have.

"Sometimes I wonder—" Liss began. "You remember how we used to cuddle and such?"

"Yeah."

"Ever wished we could take back what we had then, and take it further? Ever wondered what it might've been like?"

A heat and fear she hadn't felt in years seeped through her. *I wonder what would've happened if—*

"What about Grace?"

"Grace doesn't matter. We haven't fucked in months, and who knows what else she's been up to?"

Anna wondered how she could be so laissez-faire about this. "I've never really . . . done anything with a woman before."

"Good." Liss's typical ferocity. Possessive? Anna fumbled uselessly with her wine glass.

Abruptly, she set it down and lunged. She swept an arm around Liss and pressed her lips against her cheek, kept them there shaking, then pressed them to her lips. Felt Liss's breast against her breast, raw skin under shirts. Liss's tongue broke into her mouth and did not surprise her.

The sky lingers pale at night, through the rose garden with its tidy rows, around the forest-bound Beaver Lake which has been so invaded by water lilies Anna doubts any beavers could fit. She laughs at the mallard ducks and ducklings which paddle, just barely, between lily pads. Her MP3 player has been on since she got—not lost, but temporarily misplaced. Wagner speeds her stride. *I am marching towards a purpose, towards a clearing in the sky...*

Liss was trapped beneath her, a small animal breathing out animal noises. Her hips jolted upwards as Anna tried to keep to the same spot. Her rhythm was erratic, Liss's frantic. Her hands reached clumsily to stroke Liss's sides, trace her ribs. She wanted to meld to the figure on the bed, to possess her, and this was as close as she'd ever been. Liss's transport frightened her just as it aroused. She wished all those articles on sex had had something useful to contribute to this situation. There was no way she was any good, she thought. As Liss shivered and she felt the smaller girl's skin against her warm and trembling, a sympathetic tremor passed through her. She suspended thought.

Supposedly it was difficult to satisfy a woman. That wasn't the case with Liss, tremulous as a sound wave, who then went at Anna fiercely. She'd been waiting years.

Anna alternated between closing her eyes and opening them to look down at Liss's envied hair, at the sharp little fox face she'd seen sobbing on the swing all those years ago.

Anna presses herself against the rubber of a swing in the playground, hands to chains, and arcs skyward.

Liss's smile was fresh and slightly timid. Anna tried to grin back, but her mouth stretched into a yawn.

"Tired?"

"Exhausted."

"Where should I sleep?"

"Isn't that obvious? Unless you want your own space— the couch folds out."

"I just thought you might not want me in the same bed. You know." After so many years, Liss was deferential and uncertain around her. The initial excitement had run its course, the hormonal highs had faded, and neither knew quite what rhythm to adopt around the other.

"I don't mind. I mean—I don't mind at all!"

Liss got up and walked over to the African violets on the windowsill. "Nice plants." They both snickered; the words were ridiculous. "Do you think we could sleep in the same bed and manage to keep our hands off each other?"

"Why do we need to?" Anna was hit by another surge of heat. She tested her reactions. She didn't regret this, yet.

She was woken that night by a quiet whine: "Anna?"

Anna looked over. "Liss?" she whispered. The smaller woman's eyes were closed, her body still, and she seemed quite asleep.

A gaunt man stands at a garbage can with bags, long-haired in an old vest and jeans. She calls out a hello, and he reciprocates brightly—"Hello, how you doing?"

"Great," says Anna. "It's a nice night to take a walk."

"Yeah, we're lucky to have this park. It's quiet. I get away here as much as I can, even when I'm not doing this—" he waves the bags—"just to get away from the noise of the city. We're really lucky."

"Yeah, we really are." She nods dumbly.

Anna moved from her emcee perch in front of the microphone to a wooden chair in the front row, between a middle-aged man whose dreadlocks coiled to his waist and two generously bosomed teenagers in tank tops. Onstage, Felicity and Grace faced each other. They had an autoharp and mouth organ and all kinds of cool instruments propped between them. The sound began with a long throbbing note from Grace's throat. Liss put the violin to chin and stroked out a tremulous hum. Her vocals joined with Grace's, and the taller woman's electric guitar riffed after. Liss's gaze toward Grace blazed in that familiar, unexpected way, and Anna tried to decide which was more astonishing—Liss when coming, or Liss when caught in the song. She had to conclude they were equal. Grace returned the gaze with what seemed even from a distance to be parallel heat. Layer upon layer, they built.

I found a little daisy tucked among the morning dew
It was looking white and perky and a little bit like you
And I pulled the petals singly as I sang an old-time song
Loves me, loves me not, until the petals all were gone.

An interplay of complex sensations and desires, storming the audience, concentrated in a single ever-changing point. Whatever the strife in their relationship, Liss and Grace's musical harmony was perfect. Growing ever more intent, they reached convergence. Seared. Soared.

The audience bloomed into clapping. A multitude of hands moved in all directions and Anna fell between them, the floor dissolving beneath with no one and nothing there to catch her.

⸙

Today I was a witness to the most extraordinary thing.

Anna's growing up fast, and she wanted to help stack wood. I let her for a while, then told her to go inside because the poor thing looked exhausted. When I went to check on her after a few minutes, she'd somehow hoisted her little body onto the piano bench and she was plunking out the notes of Bach's Flute Sonata in E. She tried once, sounding things out, then played the song a second time from pure memory. The melody was nearly faultless, with rhythm and dynamic shifts in place. I'd heard of this happening with others before, but I've never seen the like, and not even my dreams had dared imagine this from Anna.

She didn't want to leave the piano after that. It was Sonata, Sonata, Sonata, in tunnel focus. I wonder how long that will last! Hank had the nerve to say she looked like a piano robot. I admit her fervor didn't seem quite human, but that's probably just because it came as a shock. He joked (was he even joking?) that I'll get sick of it soon. I dragged her to supper and out to the garden—the child needs breaks—but she's at the piano again as I write this. I don't think her aptitude is even the most amazing part. Watching her fingers fly (I'll have to teach her proper technique, she's all over the place), music erupts for the sheer joy of it. Her playing is not just technically perceptive, but lush and fiery. Her body bends into the music. I can see she's smiling.

Dark descends abruptly. The sea below the street, sheer turquoise in the lights, makes a violent lapping sound. On P.E.I. the trees are narrow and beaches vast; in Vancouver the two are reversed. Here there are only waves, interrupted by stone steps and a slim branch of sand. She climbs down, shucks off socks and shoes, rolls up jeans, and runs. With each footfall the soft gray sand absorbs her soles. She stops to scrawl a message in it between countless others blown half inscrutable, *Stars in my body, stars in my soul,* and watches the waves lap until the letters are smoothed over. They might as well never have been.

"What are you going to tell her?"

"Grace? She never has to know."

"Do you even love her?"

"I do, or at least I did. But I loved you first," she hissed across the coffee table. "And I still love you!" Liss's face twisted in a mask-like grimace and she was fourteen and closing in on Anna, lust-eyed and frightening. "Do you hate me for saying that?"

Water closes over her ankles. The chill shocks just as the lapping soothes. For no reason, Ay-a springs to mind. The very concept of the goddess seems trite. Another Anna stretches in her plush armchair, takes a sip of Daiquiri, writes a countermelody for her sonata. Ay-a stands apart on an arm of sand, cloth-covered—Anna has never seen nor imagined the body underneath—and small as a jellyfish. Anna presses a hand to her own face because nothing else feels real enough to touch.

"Just come with us! We can have three people in the band."

"I can't just up and leave."

"Why not?"

"And Grace would be furious."

"She'll get used to it. Or we can leave her and have our own band. We'll be better anyway."

"How would that even work?"

"How does any band work?" Liss leaned forward with sudden violence and clutched at Anna's wrist. "Look, Anna, it's been forever since I've wanted to be with you! Last night was so amazing I can't even explain it. I saw you, Anna, and I saw that I'll never be able to let you go. You've got to agree that there was something not normal going on. I mean, come on, you felt it. It wasn't just sex or anything like that. It was like our old concert, is what it was. The—the—"

"Convergence?"

"Yeah, exactly! A convergence at last of something that had been building up for all those years. And that's how I know I can't leave you. We have to stay together. If it's so true and real it can't possibly be wrong."

Part of Anna wanted nothing more than to close the very small distance between them, to clutch Liss against her, ravage her mouth, and refuse to ever let her move. Part of her wanted nothing more than to take up music again, to feel the delirious joy of the spotlight again, to live and collaborate with this woman who still made some of the most striking sounds she'd heard from a human being. To make something of herself. To claim the heated, warped, fierce loves, artistic and human, that had trailed her since childhood.

Had she run from Liss for the same reason that Darien had left her? It was so much easier not to be tied to someone whose talent made her marvel—the weight of that, of love and hate and envy and desire distilled, was too much to hold.

So she'd left Liss and the music, both, and was leaving them again. Much as she loved it, music belonged to Another Anna, a human prism refracting centuries of sound. Those who worshipped it couldn't see her through it.

Could she go back?

"Anna, say something!"

Her memories came like shadows cast by the trees at night, or the ephemeral play of light between those shadows. The time when music had been everything existed somewhere in its own small capsule, irretrievable, so distant from the present it might never have happened at all.

Another capsule held Felicity and Grace, their gazes blazing in perfect convergence, their music complete between the two of them. Such chilling and delicate chemistry. Anna knew good music when she heard it, and she knew her own truth as surely as Liss knew hers—it was a thing she could never bring herself to destroy.

"I can't," she said.

"Or if you have any songs to send us…"

There's a highway right above the beach, but the railing hides Anna if she stays close to it. A shape on a tiny rock island in the water looks suspiciously like a person, but it must not be, since it hasn't moved since she got there.

She watched Liss and Grace, Felicity and Grace, climb aboard the plane. She stood on the asphalt and waved. The plane took off and she kept waving until it was a speck in the clouds, then invisible, and her arms ached. Her eyes would ache often afterwards.

She waited a week, then made an appointment at the clinic. She went to the forest, climbed to the end of a half-fallen trunk that reminded her of the cat tree, and prayed in gratitude when all the STI tests came back negative. The light there was leaf-sieved, mixed with the scent of sap and pine needles. She lowered her head and heard Valkyries in the distance, though her MP3 player was off.

She whispered everything into the bark, and wondered not if, but why, she'd made the right choice.

What if someone catches you?

Muscle follows intent, stunningly instant. Stripped, she arcs above the water and she's in, dog paddling, back floating, tasting salt, the cold no shock. The blood in her body warms as turquoise envelopes her and towers glint their lights from the opposite shore and suddenly there's sound she's never heard. It washes over her with the current, piano chords shimmering. Fountains, raindrops, tiny flowers falling from their domes. She catches them. Naked beneath the road and spinning and possibly watched, she catches every bit, to remember.

Scores of drops shake loose from her skin. She pulls underwear and her dress over sand-scraped limbs. The important thing is this piece's existence, truly hers. Fragile but insistent, if she gives it her attention, she has something to preserve.

Climbing the stone steps, she plans. She will buy some new music books, learn new pieces to practice, see if this town has a place for another musician. She will look into programs to get her GED, and maybe then into scholarships. She will take out her purple notebook and do her best to jot down the melody, harmonies, call and response. Liss can't be the only one looking for a freelance composer. Another Anna bends over the music, writing busily.

A blue heron flaps dripping through her path. She walks along the night road wearing unseen salt and sand stigmata. She has been walking for five hours straight.

Melanie Bell is a Canadian multi-genre writer living in the UK. Her books include a short story collection, *Dream Signs*, a nonfiction title, *The Modern Enneagram*, and the YA novel *Chasing Harmony*. She has written for several publications including *Contrary*, *Cicada*, *The Fiddlehead*, and *Huffington Post*. She loves music, art, and nature, and aspires to see as much of the world as she can.

Thank you to the faculty of Concordia University's Creative Writing program, especially Mary di Michele, who supervised the first iteration of this novel, and Josip Novakovich and Andre Furlani, its first readers. Thank you to my fellow Master's students for journeying with me. Finally, a big thank you to Read Furiously's publishing team for bringing this book into the world with such care.

A Note to our Furious Readers

From all of us at Read Furiously, we hope you enjoyed our latest title, *Chasing Harmony*.

There are countless narratives in this world and we would like to share as many of them as possible with our Furious Readers.

It is with this in mind that we pledge to donate a portion of these book sales to causes that are special to Read Furiously. These causes are chosen with the intent to better the lives of others who are struggling to tell their own stories.

Reading is more than a passive activity – it is the opportunity to play an active role within our world. At Read Furiously, we wish to add an active voice to the world we all share because we believe any growth within the company is aimless if we can't also nurture positive change in our local and global communities. The causes we support are culturally and socially conscious to encourage a sense of civic responsibility associated with the act of reading. Each cause has been researched thoroughly, discussed openly, and voted upon carefully by our team of Read Furiously editors.

To find out more about who, what, why, and where Read Furiously lends its support, please visit our website at readfuriously.com/charity

Happy reading and giving, Furious Readers!

Read Often, Read Well,
Read Furiously!

Look for these other great titles from

The One 'n Done Series
What About Tuesday
Girls, They'll Never Take Us Alive
Brethren Hollow
Helium
The Legend of Dave Bradley

Fiction
Working Through This
Chasing Harmony

Anthologies
The World Takes: Life in the Garden State
Stay Salty: Life in the Garden State

Poetry
Until the roof lifted off
Whatever You Thought, Think Again
Dear Terror
Elk City Sparrow
All These Little Stars

Graphic Novels
The MOTHER Principle
Brian & Bobbi
In the Fallout
Pursuit: A Collection of Artwork
Northwood Meadows: Lifestyle
First

Non-Fiction
Putting Out: Essays on Otherness
Furious Lit: Tell Me A Story
We don't do "just okay" anymore
Nerd Traveler
I Feel Love: Notes on Queer Joy

Children's Books
The Little Gray Witch
The Little Boy Who Wasn't A Witch